THE RUIN OF DELICATE THINGS

THE
RUIN OF
DELICATE
THINGS

BEVERLEY LEE

Published by Ink Raven Press
Copyright © 2020 Beverley Lee

ISBN-13 978-0-9935490-4-5

Cover design by
Design for Writers

For my father,
who loved to read,
and who I hope would have been proud
of the writer his daughter became

PART ONE

WITHIN
the woods

ONE

As the sign for the village flashed by, Dan Morgan knew he would rather be anywhere else but here.

In this car, with the rain beating down on the windscreen. On this road, which led to his childhood, with all of its muted meandering memories. Back when days had gone on forever. After thirty years he was racing back towards it, searching for its enchantment, fruitlessly hoping it could cast its rose-tinted spell upon the agonising hellscape of his life.

He glanced in his rear-view mirror, watched as the sign disappeared in the distance, the whoosh of the tyres on the wet road a constant background noise. Faye stared out of the rear passenger window, one finger tracing a line of mingled raindrops. A typical British summer.

She'd said she wanted to sleep, but Dan knew the real reason she had moved from beside him was because she couldn't stand the wall of silence that had descended on the long journey down. He could see her profile etched against the thin light, almost as if she was trying to disappear into it. Dark curls mussed around her face, her nose a slight aquiline, which gave strength to her otherwise fragile features.

Sometimes he caught her watching him as if he had turned into a creature she didn't understand.

A sharp pain jabbed Dan—*Dan to his friends. Daniel to*

his colleagues. But never Danny, not since that summer—in the ribs.

The rot had set in on the night Toby had been sliced from their lives. Dan's fingers clenched on the steering wheel.

How can a child go out one day and never return?

It had been a brutal year. And the weight that hung in the air between them was like the blade of a pendulum, gradually severing the fraying connection to which they were both clinging.

Faye's ears were covered by her ever-present headphones, plugged into the world of audio books. It was much easier to immerse herself in other people's stories; her own hurt too much.

An image of Toby, laying cold and still on the hospital gurney, covered in a white sheet, invaded his thoughts. Dan had watched from the safety of the small room, that clinical sheet of glass separating him from his son, watched as the young doctor with the dark circles under his eyes pulled back the sheet. Dan wanted to scream that it wasn't Toby—this shell of a boy with the pale blue lips couldn't possibly be his son. His boy had been loud and kind and lovable. His son had yelled, 'See you later, Dad!' as he swept past the study, hopping on one leg as he stuffed his foot into a trainer.

Dan hadn't turned his head, just raised his hand in reply. He'd been too busy, too focussed on the marketing plan in front of him, the ever-approaching deadline looming like a hand grenade with a loose pin.

Dan bit his bottom lip, closing his eyes for a moment to stop the images. Stop the guilt.

A loud, dull thud, the weight of an impact hitting the front of the car. Dan's eyes flew open. He braked hard, water splashing onto the bonnet, the wipers sweeping back and forth in a pattern that set his teeth on edge. *Please God, don't let it be a person…*

He glanced in the mirror again, found Faye's questioning eyes.

He swung the door open, rain instantly soaking his shirt. His heart hammered in his chest as he came around the front of the car. Blood streaked the white paintwork, shreds of fur hanging from the front grille. On the road lay a young roe deer, its legs bent underneath it at impossible angles, the side of its face split open. *Toby's skull was crushed, that side of his head sensitively turned away on the gurney.* Dan gagged and the taste of vomit filled his mouth. He wiped his fingers over his lips.

Then the relief of realising he hadn't killed anyone turned his knees to a jellified mass. He steadied himself, one hand on the bonnet. A shudder ran across the deer's pelt. It tried to stand on legs that would never stand again, one soft, brown eye focussed on his. A small bleat came from its throat.

'Fuck. Fuck. Fuck.' Dan stepped back, the remains of his service-station meal rose again in his gullet. He couldn't stomach dead things. Couldn't even sweep a dried spider off a windowsill without gloves. And he definitely didn't like things that were nearly dead. That awful realm in between, where decay is only a few breaths away.

The back door opened and Faye stepped out. Dan swore again as his own inadequacies sang a sibilant song in his head. Now he had to tell her he had just about killed Bambi.

'I didn't see it.' An apology tore out of his mouth. 'With the rain. It just ran out in front of me.' Of course, if he hadn't been deep inside his own thoughts…

Faye looked at the deer, her eyes rising slowly to his, headphones slung around her neck. 'You can't leave it like this, Dan. It's cruel.'

He'd expected tears, or, at the very least, a lip tremor. But that was the old Faye. This one only sighed, her arms crossed over her chest, hands hugging her elbows. All cried out. She waited for his answer as the beating rain plastered her hair to her pale face.

'Right. Okay.' Dan produced a firm and confident tone from his stash of business acumen. 'Get back in the car, love. I'll deal with it.'

She looked as though she wanted to say something else, but, to Dan's relief, she did as he asked, glancing back only once. Through the windscreen, as the wipers continued their infernal arc, he saw her pull her headphones over her ears.

Dan crouched down, sweat prickling his soaking scalp. He reached out and grasped the deer's neck in both hands. One quick wrench. How hard could it be?

The fur was silky soft and warm. And matted with sticky blood. A white patch of skull glistened through the crimson.

He lost the battle with his meal, heaving it onto the wet road, bile burning his throat. The musky scent of the animal forced its way into his nose, poisoning his airway. A high-pitched buzzing sounded in his ears and he slunk back to rest against the front of the car, concentrating on the grounded feel of the bumper against his spine as his heart galloped off into a thousand different directions.

His muscles tensed into hard knots of disgust. He banged the heel of his hand against his forehead, hating himself for turning into a weak, pitiful creature when all he had to do was put the deer out of its misery. Hating himself for not being the kind of husband his wife needed. For not being the kind of father to kiss his son for the last time.

And then he laughed, a crazy, strangled sound, turning his face to the rain as though it might wash away his sins. A car passed by on the other side of the road. A glimpse of a woman's face behind the anonymity of glass, her eyes surveying the scene. Dan thought he saw pity in those eyes. He prayed she wouldn't stop. Her car disappeared around the bend, the red glow of her brake lights sharp against the rain.

Dan exhaled.

It had been a momentary weakness. His attentiveness broken. Now death hovered at his feet. Is this what it had been like for the driver who hit Toby?

But Dan couldn't equate what he had done to the events of that afternoon. Anger rolled slowly through his veins like molten lava. He concentrated on the rivulets of rain running across the road, trying to calm the embers before they ignited.

What use was it to go over old wounds? To pick away at something he was trying desperately to heal?

Stress knotted itself between the fibres of his muscles, dug its claws into the raw flesh of his nerves. His decision to come back here for a visit had seemed like a good idea. He wanted to spend quality time with Faye, showing her the places he had explored as a boy. He wanted to reconnect, to make her smile again, to show her they both could rise from this terrible loss as long as they had each other.

But another part of him hadn't really wanted to return. In fact, at one point he had sworn he never would. But sometimes you have to do things you don't want to. It was called taking responsibility. And maybe this was exactly what they both needed.

He wiped his bloody hands down the front of his shirt, grateful for the fact that it was black, and climbed back inside the car, flashing a quick and sympathetic smile over his shoulder. Faye met his gaze, her eyes wide and questioning. A small part of him wondered if she knew.

Soaked to the skin, Dan pressed his left foot to the clutch, and his finger to the ignition, turning up the air con to clear the fogged up screen. The engine burst into life. Reversing smoothly, he checked his mirror and swung out, avoiding the small bundle on the wet road. He gunned the accelerator, quickly moving up the gears.

One last look back in the mirror, before the road curved.

The deer lay there, its head arched in quivering agony.

TWO

By the time they reached the track that led to their destination, it had finally stopped raining. Dan reached across and flicked off the air con, then slid his finger over the button that lowered the windows. He swung right, the car leaving the smooth tarmac of the road, for the bumpy, dust-covered track. Birdsong filtered down through the trees, the late-summer sun a fireball through the dense, green canopies.

It was like stepping into a different world.

They passed a sun-bleached wooden bench, its legs swallowed by long grass. Behind it stood the old stile, gateway to the forest. Dan's lips tightened. Over the single-track stone bridge with the camel hump, the evening sunlight dancing across the burbling stream.

The troll bridge. Dan could almost feel the chill of the stone as he hid underneath it, ankle deep in the water, minnows flitting around his toes. How old had he been then? Twelve? Thirteen? So naïve compared to today's kids. But that innocence had given him freedom, riding out after breakfast with lunch stuffed into his saddlebags, returning with the sunset, filthy and triumphant.

'Who's that?'

Faye's voice cut into his thoughts. She had unfastened her seatbelt, her head poking through the gap between the front seats, one hand on each head rest.

'What?'

'You said a name.'

Dan hadn't realised he'd said anything at all, and the memories were already fading like the raindrops on the windows.

'Just reminiscing.' He tried to keep his voice light. 'It's weird being back.'

'Did you spend *every* summer here?' Faye's eyes flicked towards the forest.

'Pretty much. My parents had to work all through the holidays, so they packed me off here.' A cloud of tiny midges hovered outside the window, and Dan let his eyes follow the frenetic flight, glad he was safe behind glass. 'I didn't mind though. Aunt Lucinda wasn't much for rules, only that I had to be home before dark.'

Through the rear view mirror Dan saw Faye's eyes widen. He could feel her warm breath on the back of his neck.

A sudden heat had unfurled, taking the scent of the forest and turning it into a pungent soup. The years rolled away as the perfume of memory plunged him back. Into that place, where all was silent. Where the shadow from the house seemed to engulf everything. He could taste the fear on the back of his tongue, feel the weight of his insides pressing against his skin. Tightening his fingers on the steering wheel, he drew in a couple of sharp breaths.

Sometimes glimmers of childhood surfaced through the mist of his everyday life, vivid sparks of colour in the grey. *Eating sandwiches under the old willow tree by the lake, the cheese sweaty and warm. Tying string around the top of lemonade bottles to cool them in the water. Playing hide-and-*

seek in the forest, trying to scare each other stupid, the sun beating down on their backs. Lying in bed, telling each other ghost stories and watching the moon rise through the trees.

And then, suddenly, it is gone.

Dan hadn't been back here since. But right now it felt as though he had never left.

Through the trees, the side of the cottage came into view. A stone-built structure with a wooden porch and a weathered thatched roof, patched with moss. Tiny windows with lead lights, and the wooden door that swelled in the heat in the summer. To the side of the door the small oval window, its stained glass aflame in the last of the sun's rays.

He stopped outside, the garden an untamed and abandoned mass of wildflowers and grasses. A winding creeper had fastened its trails around the gate. Huge purple flowers bloomed through the rails. Nature reclaiming what was hers.

Dan climbed out of the car, stretching his shoulders back. The rich sweetness of roses hung on the still summer air. He tapped on the glass of the rear door and Faye looked up, her eyes roving over the cottage.

If Dan was being truthful it looked a bit shabby. He wondered if it always had, if the magic of childhood had made it beautiful.

He opened the tailgate and pulled out his bag, waiting as Faye joined him. Yellow pollen stained his fingers as he untangled the creeper from the gate, the weathered plaque bearing the cottage name hiding underneath. The gate creaked in protest as he went through, sunflowers standing sentinel along the path, bright gold in the settling dusk.

He paused. Faye stood before the gate, her bag slung over her shoulder

She glanced up at him, the tip of her tongue protruding through her lips.

It was a strange name for a cottage. Dan remembered Aunt Lucinda saying the postman could always find her with just two names. The cottage and the village. Even when postcodes were introduced, she refused to use them.

Dan slid the key from his pocket, ducking under a mass of overgrown wisteria, which trailed from the front of the house. Faye was silent and he was trying to work out if it was a good silent or a bad one.

He turned the key in the lock and pushed against the door with his shoulder. It opened reluctantly, as though it had been sleeping.

'Welcome to Fairies' End, Faye.'

She arched an eyebrow and edged past him as he struggled to get the key out of the unforgiving lock.

For better or for worse, they were here, in his place of childhood, which now belonged to him.

THREE

The hallway seemed smaller than he remembered, but Dan guessed that was just his adult perception doing battle with his childhood memories. Two doors led from it, the one to the right shut tight.

It was the door to this room Faye pushed open. A musty scent rushed out to greet them and Dan wrinkled his nose. An old rocking chair sat by the red-brick fireplace, a basket of logs on the hearth. Rows of china dogs and horses peered down from a high shelf that ran all the way around the top of the room.

'What are those?' Faye's tone carried a note of disgust. At the far side of the fireplace, set into an alcove, was a glass case filled with taxidermy.

His brow creased. How had he forgotten all about these? It was one of the reasons why he hadn't minded being banned from this room; he always had the feeling those still, glass eyes could look right through him.

'Why would anyone want them?' She shivered, crossing her arms across her chest. He wanted to reassure her with a touch but she was so unpredictable now, he feared what her reaction would be.

'Aunt Lucinda was a bit odd really. The other kids used to say she was a witch, living all by herself in the woods.'

Faye's solemn eyes flicked to his, searching his face. He'd meant the comment to be flippant, to try and lighten the mood, but it had come out wrong.

Faye moved across to the case, her fingers hovering close to the glass. The curls in the nape of her neck were still damp. 'Did she, you know, do these herself?'

'Oh God, no!' Dan answered, visions of Aunt Lucinda pulling bloody innards out of rabbits and birds flashing through his mind. 'She got them from…' He paused, searching his memory for the name. 'Robert McCallum. His family have been gamekeepers here for years, even going back to when the old house was built. This place was one of the tied cottages.'

Dan didn't know why he'd dredged this little snippet up. Memory was a funny thing. Sometimes all it took was a seed and the whole damn flower decided to tag along. And sometimes that seed withered in the ground.

Faye didn't look like this little piece of local history was of any interest, but then Dan couldn't blame her. It had seemed like such a good idea to bring her to the wild, open spaces of his childhood, but now he was starting to second guess his decision. She didn't belong here.

The phone call had come at the end of May. He'd been stuck in a traffic jam on the M4, late home, as per usual, and his frustration factor had just amped up a thousand degrees when a motorbike squeezed past his car and knocked his wing mirror. He leaned out of the window to shout abuse, but the bike had already cut through another three cars in a haze of exhaust fumes.

His phone rang. An unknown number. Normally, he never answered these, but right then he didn't have anything else to do, so he pressed accept on the call screen on his dash.

'Mr. Morgan?' The male voice was crisp, polished.

'Speaking.'

'My name is Albert Jenkins. I'm afraid I have some bad news for you.'

Dan cleared his throat; his fingers white-knuckled on the steering wheel.

'Lucinda Latimer died at home this morning at 10 a.m. In her hand was a note, requesting that I ring you.'

'Fuck.' The expletive slipped like oil from his lips. 'Sorry…it's a shock…'

'I understand, Mr. Morgan, and may I extend my heartfelt condolences on your loss.'

Dan had an extremely weird reality check as he sat amongst the traffic with his window down, the setting sun pouring onto his arm, which was propped on the door. Music blared out from the convertible next to him, a young, blonde girl applying lipstick in her rear view mirror.

At his other side, a fraught woman turned to two kids in the back seat, her face contorted in annoyance. The motorway signs proclaimed an accident up ahead. In the bright blue sky a plane circled on its way down to Heathrow.

And now some guy he had never heard of was telling him the woman he hadn't seen since the summer of his fourteenth year was dead.

'I'm sorry,' Dan found his voice again. 'Did you say she had a note for me?'

'Indeed. I believe you were the last of your family to visit her.'

The news sliced through Dan like a particularly nasty paper cut. He was forty-four. Guilt bloomed in his gut. He was as bad as the rest of his fucked-up family. He didn't even bother sending birthday or Christmas cards.

'What are the arrangements?' Dan was mentally checking his diary for the next two weeks, which was, as usual, back-to-back with conference calls and other meetings.

'Lucinda was very insistent on one thing, I'm afraid. She doesn't want anyone to attend the funeral. Which will actually be a cremation. And she wishes her ashes to be scattered in the lake.' Albert cleared his throat at the other end of the line.

'How do you know all this if she just died?' Dan's voice carried a hint of accusation.

'Your Aunt and I were friends outside of my business duties, Mr. Morgan. She often told me things.'

Part of Dan wanted to ask what kind of things.

'Again, please accept my sympathies. I will be in touch soon regarding the estate.'

'The estate' had consisted of this one cottage, with the caveat that he never sell it, and a modest amount of cash which Dan had immediately donated to charity. For some reason the money felt tainted.

'Dan, what's that in the corner, under the blackbird?'

Dan dragged himself out of his own thoughts and forced himself to focus. Faye's finger pointed to something barely visible amongst the dark mounds of dried moss and logs at the bottom of the case.

He pressed his palm to the glass. Goosebumps raised the hair on his arms and his scalp tightened.

'It's nothing. I told you, just fucked-up country stuff.' His reply came out far too irritated and Faye bit the edge of her lip.

The familiar wall of silence fell between them, and all Dan could think, as the ticking of the clock on the mantle grated against his nerves, was that trying to fix the present with one foot in the past might be the thing to break them both.

FOUR

'I can't get any signal.' Faye's agitated voice followed Dan up the narrow staircase that led from the hallway. This was how Faye operated now, swinging from frozen silence to intense frustration. He wasn't sure which mood he hated the most.

He ducked his head as he neared the top, remembering how the ceiling sloped down. The stairs had originally been white but had dulled to a dirty yellowish-grey. Dan had always tried to creep up them without being heard, but Aunt Lucinda had a sixth sense when it came to his wanderings and would poke her head out of her room, her keen eyes pinning him to the spot.

He dumped both bags on the tiny, windowless landing, the bathroom door facing him, and the two bedrooms at either side. Sweat trickled down his spine but his fingertips were frozen. His mouth felt as dry as sandpaper.

He closed his eyes for a moment and bit back a sharp retort. 'We're in the middle of nowhere, Faye. I doubt there's a phone mast closer than Meadowford Bridge.'

The sigh behind him spoke louder than words, but he let it ride. They'd had a long journey and he wasn't in the mood to argue about an inadequate phone signal. What he didn't tell his wife was that this place had always seemed to live in the past, as though it had carved a nice little niche out of time for itself, and was content for the rest of civilisation to go hurtling headlong into a blazing future without it.

'Which room do you want?' Dan pushed open both bedroom doors. Stale air filtered out.

That was another thing that had died with Toby. Intimacy. They had both tried back at the beginning, after the first few weeks when they had clung to each other, weighted down with the anchor of grief. But Faye only went through the motions. It was like making love to a diluted copy of the person she once was.

Faye examined the one to his right, the largest room, which had been Aunt Lucinda's, overlooking the cottage garden. It still smelled faintly of her perfume, a mixture of crushed roses and the green of the forest. But then the whole house had that smell. The trees weren't content to live only outside. He wiped his hand over his brow and his fingers came away wet.

'I'll have this one.'

Faye stood in the other bedroom. Evening sunlight glinted through the leaded pane window behind her, dappling her dark hair with gold. For an instant, all of the heartache fell away.

Resolve snapped inside Dan's chest. He would find a way back to her. He had to. Because if he didn't, she would drift away like a sea mist. Beautiful and otherworldly and worth far more than what he constantly strived for—the newest car, the expensive holidays and meals at overpriced restaurants. He wondered why the trinkets of modern life were never truly attainable. There was always something else, something he needed that bonus for, something if he just closed this deal, he could get. But money couldn't buy everything.

17

An image of his son danced across his vision.

He brought his thoughts back into focus and leant against the doorway, watching her pull clothes from her bag, throwing them onto the bed. The last items were a sketch pad and a small oblong tin. The contents rattled as she tossed it on top of the bedspread. Dan smiled to himself. He'd asked her if she was bringing those, a shrug being his answer. And he was glad she had, because he loved her artwork, simple pencil lines that came to life on the page. The way she could convey feeling and movement with only a few effortless strokes. She always used to have a pencil in her hand. Before.

He let his eyes flit over the room. The single bed with the faded patchwork bedspread, the matching curtains and lampshade. The rose-covered wallpaper. All with their own tired quaintness. Painted floorboards covered by a circular rug in front of the bed, a hefty wooden wardrobe in one corner. This had been his room, and a small wavering shadow of himself had never left.

'Don't leave the window open.' The words tumbled out of his mouth, the same ones Lucinda had uttered every night.

Faye paused and turned to him, her brow creased. 'It's boiling here. And it's not as if there'd be any burglars. Not in a place like this.'

Dan contemplated telling his wife what Lucinda had told him when he was younger. That if he did, the forest creatures would call his soul away into the night. He never slept with it open after that, even in the height of summer. Dan wasn't sure whether it was because he believed her, or that he was terrified of her finding out if he disobeyed.

'There'll be moths here. Big ones,' he began, aware of how lame it sounded, 'if you leave the light on and the window open.'

'Moths?' Faye frowned. 'I'm not seven, Dan. I'll just squish them.' She banged her sketch pad on the bedhead for emphasis.

The noise echoed around the small room, both of their eyes drawn to the wooden headboard. In dark wood, it was at odds with the rest of the faded prettiness. Solid and imposing and covered with intricate carvings from the forest. Soaring trees and meandering pathways. Faye leant across and ran her fingers over the patterns, her head slightly inclined.

Dan wanted to shield her from it, to protect her from the things hidden within, so she wouldn't feel the fear he had in the small hours, tracing the lines with the thin light from a torch. But that was only his childhood imagination, running amok. There were no high-pitched shrieks in the light of day, no lips sewn shut or darkened doorways. Other things, too, there only when the light fell a certain way.

In the quiet of the forest evening, the sun dipped below the tree line and the room darkened.

The light in the hallway flickered.

'Don't worry,' Dan whispered, and he wondered if that was for Faye's benefit, or his own. 'There's no mains electricity here and the generator struggles sometimes.'

Faye flashed a point of white light in his face. 'Might as well use this as a torch then.' Her eyes behind the beam from her phone were as dark as pitch.

'I'll see you in the morning.' Dan hovered, wanting to hug her, to feel her arms around him, the scent of her hair rising like a song. 'Sleep well.'

She half smiled, but it was more gesture than emotion, her dark curls hanging over her face as she rummaged through a washbag on her knee.

Dan slipped from the room, remembering the nights when they couldn't wait to tumble into bed, feverish lips and roving hands and whispered sweet nothings that tripped both of their switches.

Now they didn't even say goodnight.

FIVE

Faye waited until she heard the door close to Dan's bedroom. It was only then she let the tension slide from her muscles, allowed herself the luxury of leaving herself open. It was safe to do it now, in the dark, with no one to see. Safe to fall apart.

In truth, she didn't know how she held it together most days. That's what the headphones were for. People left you alone if you wore those. It was as good as holding up a sign saying 'keep out'. Half the time she didn't even have any audio playing. That's what had happened today in the car. She had seen Dan glance in the rear view mirror, had seen the way his eyes flicked to the passing countryside, his tongue wetting his lips. This was where he had spent a lot of his childhood, but it didn't look to Faye like the memories were all good ones. That was the other thing about the headphones; people acted like you couldn't see them watching. Faye had learned a lot about people since her world had shattered into tiny pieces.

The weight of her sketch pad and pencils lay at the bottom of the bed. She kicked off the bedspread, which smelled like old ladies and rooms that had been shut up for too long, and padded to the window, easing the stubborn latch and shoving the glass with her other hand. The window creaked as old wood rubbed against old wood, her husband's words filtering back through her thoughts. Don't leave the window open.

Well, she wasn't scared of moths, and she had to do something to get rid of the smell. It had already worked its way up to her temples, leaving an ache that throbbed in time with her heartbeat.

She pushed the window fully open, resting her elbows on the wide sill, letting the cool night air wash over her face. The scent of the forest seemed stronger now. All of the green amplified by a darkness that had fallen quickly. Tree tops rustled as the night breeze brushed through their canopies. The city girl in her was more used to the hum of traffic or the constant noise of people. Even in the small, dark hours of morning there was always someone on the streets. On the nights when she couldn't sleep, she imagined a line of wandering, exhausted insomniacs searching for elusive sheep.

She'd expected perfect quiet but it was the blackness that surprised her. Here, far away from artificial light, the dark had a weight to it, a solidity.

Faye closed her eyes. She felt strangely vulnerable here amongst all this space. It was easy to hide in the city. In a workplace where everyone ran through their own clockwork routines. Easy to go through the motions and return home. To lock herself in her room after they'd eaten, cover her existence with her headphones, take out her sketch pad from under the bed, and just let her hand run free. It was only in those simple lines and the flow of charcoal that she felt the barbed tethers of her pain lessening.

She created her art in secret now, her fingers moving quickly over the paper, lost in their own rhythm, sometimes not even glancing as the images unfolded.

Something brushed against her cheek and her eyes flew

open. A smile broke out on her face. Only a moth. Dan had been right about that.

Below her window the soft yellow of the sunflowers glowed in the moonlight, the hard shape of their car parked outside the fence. As Faye continued to study the darkness her eyes became accustomed to the gloom. Just beyond the dirt road they'd driven in on stood the first line of trees leading to the woodland.

Goosebumps raised on her bare arms, the instinctive human reflex causing her eyes to narrow on the spot where the trees became one with the darkness. A shape moved in between the trunks of the oaks, a slow, measured motion.

Faye's mouth ran dry. Her fingers fumbled for her phone on the bedside table. She sent the harsh light of the torch into the blackness. It didn't reach far, but it was enough to startle the shape in the trees. For a split second she caught the outline of a stag, its antlers a glorious crown upon its head. She met its wide-eyed gaze as its nostrils flared, and she tried to hold on to this fleeting connection. But in an instant, it was gone, back into the heart of the wild.

Her throat constricted. Connections were like that, however long they lasted.

A floorboard creaked in Dan's room. Some small part of her wanted to knock on his door, to ask him why they were here. Why he had taken away her only sense of security, the place where their son had breathed and laughed and lived, and brought her to this.

Faye grabbed her sketch pad from the bed, her fingers finding a stub of charcoal in the tin. The coolness of the blank page seeped into her palm as she rested the book on the sill, half kneeling in the dark, wanting to keep the image of the stag alive before sleep stole him away.

Moonlight pierced her window, and, in the pearl glow, Faye began to sketch.

The sunflowers dozed and the trees whispered. In the heart of the forest, the stag came to the edge of the lake. But he did not drink. Because he knew.

Daniel Morgan lay half-awake in his bed, his mind caught in the snare of the past, unaware of his wife in the next room capturing moments before they were torn away. Unaware that resting against the sun-warmed brickwork of the old cottage, the tiny hairs on their legs and feelers clinging to the surface, their wings glistening wetly, were the creatures who had stolen his memory of that long-ago night.

SIX

The boy's feet flew over the forest track. He could hear them at his heels, their wings humming in the dark, willing him to lose his focus for one brief moment.

But he was wise to their cunning now, knew to look for the disturbed patches of ground, the scant cover of dead twigs hiding a hole large enough to send him sprawling to the forest floor. He had learned one thing in his years of being the rabbit to their hounds. The thrill of the chase was almost as important to them as the moment they pounced.

He reached the remains of the lightning tree, leaped its stunted body, and veered off to the left, away from his usual track.

It was a risk. He didn't know the terrain and wasn't sure how long it would take him to double back. He crashed through a copse of brambles, his arms crossed over his face, the jagged thorns slicing across his limbs.

A shriek sounded from the lightning tree, and a grim smile of satisfaction settled on his lips. If they caught him tonight, he would pay dearly. Pain throbbed in his fingers. The ones that weren't there anymore. He shivered, stumbling slightly as a tangle of ivy snagged his ankle.

Eyes on the prize. He repeated the mantra over and over as he raced through the woodland. The sound of gurgling water drew him on, the small brook that wound through the forest, a faint silver line in the shafts of moonlight streaming through the trees. He had long since developed the vision of a creature that lives in the dark.

He slid down the soft embankment, caught a glimpse of a patterned, coiled shape by a rock. Momentum carried him forwards but he threw his body to the side as the snake struck, its soulless eyes glinting in the dark.

His pursuers could twist the minds of anything that lived in these woods.

His feet hit the cold water. A burst of panic jarred his senses and he lost valuable seconds, but he was up in an instant, clambering up the opposite bank on all fours. He crested the top, the trees thinning as the dirt track came into view.

He fought the burning pain in his muscles, forcing his feet forwards, glancing behind as he veered back into the forest.

But then he paused, his heart thundering in his chest, as a scent wafted through the dark. A scent he thought he recognised.

A flurry of translucent wings blurred his vision. He threw up his hand, wincing as the edge of a needle-sharp mandible pierced his wrist, the poison sliding quickly into his veins. He crashed to the floor, crawling on his hands and knees, fighting the toxic flood, feeling the pull on his heart's rhythm.

The boy collapsed, his cheek resting on a patch of dead leaves. His fingers curled into the dirt, fighting to the last ounce of his strength, even though he knew it was useless.

He could hear the soft beating of their wings, their gleeful chitter echoing through the forest. They squirmed under his loose-fitting shirt, tiny legs making his skin shudder. But the boy knew what came next. He closed his eyes for a few seconds, prepared himself for the pain.

The largest one settled a few inches from his face, two small eyes as vicious as knives, gleaming in the darkness. Corrigan.

'This is a bad place for you to be, boy.' That whisper, that sounded like the breeze brushing through the canopy of the trees.

He knew what she meant. It was too close to the edge of the forest. Too close to the place that weakened his limbs. A sticky feeler reached out and stroked his cheek.

'Do it.' He clicked his tongue against the roof of his mouth, using her language, hoping it sounded like he didn't care.

Corrigan inclined her head at an impossible angle.

The creature drew closer, so close the boy could see the hinged joints in her praying-mantis-type forelegs, the plump, hair-covered round of her belly, her lower jaw as it slid side to side, the furled proboscis as it quivered.

A single click rattled into the darkness.

As the stings pierced his skin, he tried to stop the scream rising in his throat, but it grew its own wings, fled out into the night, echoing through the ancient trees.

Corrigan stayed, licking the tears from his face.

Because Corrigan fed on despair.

SEVEN

You watch as they drag his body back into the house. He will have no recollection of this, no recollection of anything unless you deem it so.

Maybe once upon a time, as the old stories go, you would have felt some wave of emotion, something humans call sympathy. But then, not all humans have it so you might as well treat them with contempt: creatures with the understanding to do so much, but who squander away the best parts of who they are. They are the only species to do this. The only species who kill without hunger.

They lost something of themselves as the years passed, and you can see the date of their extinction glowing. They can see it too. But they don't do anything about it.

You stretch your wings, turn your head to see the faint red veins lining them, a patchwork quilt of wonder to your eyes, even after all of these years.

You are tired but you will not show this weakness to the ones who call you queen. They crowd around you, mill at your feet, desperate for your instruction, feeding off the hate you exude. It has been your armour for so long, and you needed it in the beginning. Back when the atrocities destroyed the world you had always known.

You don't remember what it felt like to be pure. To fly

through the forest, marvelling at its glorious bounties, to feed from the gifts they left you. Because those humans knew how important you were, to the forest and to everything that dwelt within, and to their livelihood. It was an unspoken pact that had gone back generations. They provided for you in the warmth of the spring and the summer, the time where all your energy was drained flitting from flower to bush, pollinating and enriching, making sure that nature gave up a plentiful harvest for them as the year grew old.

They taught their children about you, about the importance of respect, and you, in turn, let your children play amongst them. If you listen really hard, you can still hear that laughter as it lilts on the wind. Or maybe it's just the ringing of bluebells. Respect is such a simple word.

You never dreamt your world could be so catastrophically changed.

The house had been the start of it. You had watched, day after day, as wagons trailed the huge dark stones through the forest, leaving deep ruts along the pathways, crushing the fragile wildflowers. You tried not to weep when the first trees started to fall.

But your fears had been soothed when William Kidd brought his family here. Despite being a man who lived in a place where brick and stone sucked the life from the air, he was an intelligent and gentle man. He may not have believed in the stories about you, but he understood how important you were to the village folk. The ones who worked the forest.

His children gambolled in the woodland, together with the children from the village. No parent ever worried, because if a child were lost, a faery would bring them home. That's what they called you then, back when your form was much like theirs.

Things change.

You change.

You try not to think about the first time you saw what the monster had done.

EIGHT

Dan awoke to the sun streaming through the thin, cotton curtains, birdsong chasing the sunlight as it played on the white-washed floorboards. The years fell away, and for a moment, he was a boy again, a boy who couldn't wait to run outside, to taste the freedom of the summer heat, back when seven weeks away from school seemed to last forever. Only with age did the years speed by, and although Dan wasn't on the fast track to senility, the months raced past. And what did he do with those months? He made money. He spent money. The eternal hamster wheel of modern life.

He pushed the sheets away and stepped out of bed, his fingers rising to the small white scar on his throat.

His stomach rumbled, and suddenly he was starving, yesterday's service-station meal a distant memory he'd left in a pile on the road. Why hadn't he put the deer out of its misery? The thought flipped through his head, suffocating his hunger.

It wouldn't have been a pleasant task, but it was what a responsible, caring person would have done. Yet when it came to dead things, Dan was the extreme opposite. Necrophobia, they called it. He had spent hours surfing through dozens of websites, a little bit relieved what he felt was normal, in the strangest sense of the word. He could have gone for therapy, but then he would have actually had to deal with it. It was so much easier to bury it, to sidestep anything that might bring those awful feelings of dread and trepidation hurtling back into his life, like a comet with a barbed tail.

Until things like the deer happened.

It was why he hadn't been able to give his son one last kiss.

Dan shook his head angrily, lifting the latch on the bedroom door. Faye's room stood open. He peeked inside. His eyes found the crumpled bedsheets. And the open window.

His heart jumped into his throat. Please say she didn't sleep with it like that. But even as this internal voice pleaded, the common-sense part of him squashed the plea. His fear was a memory, and being here had brought it back into play. It was only superstition drilled into his young, impressionable mind by an old woman.

Faye's sketch pad lay open on the sill, sunlight pouring onto the white page, bleaching the charcoal away. If she was drawing again, surely that was a good sign? He glanced over his shoulder, desperate to look, but fearful of her reaction if she caught him.

The page showed an open window, the perspective slightly angled. Smudges and lines became the night forest beyond, the canopies of the trees etched in perfect detail. Dan exhaled softly. This was incredibly good, more so than what she used to draw. Or maybe he had never really looked before. There was something caught in between the trees, and he squinted in the glare, trying to make out the shape.

Footsteps sounded on the bare boards of the stairs, and Dan crept away, arriving at the doorway just as Faye appeared.

The bloom of shame rose to his cheeks and he hoped she wouldn't notice.

'Someone left eggs and bread in the fridge.'

Dan had no idea who their guardian angel had been, but his hunger resurfaced with a passion.

─┼─

The knock on the door came as they finished breakfast. Faye was stacking their dishes by the white Belfast sink, early morning sunlight winking from the copper saucepans hung over the range.

An elderly man stood on the threshold, dressed in a black suit. A man who wouldn't have looked out of place a hundred years ago. Dan tried not to stare at the impressive tangle of bushy sideburns and the wisps of silver hair sticking out at odd angles from his head. Clutched in his hands was a small, earthenware jar with a lid.

'Mr. Morgan?' Dan blinked, his eyebrows raising. 'Albert Jenkins. Your Aunt's solicitor.'

When did solicitors start making house calls?

'I hope you don't mind the intrusion. But telephones don't always work around here, and the matter is very important.'

Dan stepped aside. Faye had disappeared, her usual default against strangers.

'Your Aunt's final wishes were very specific. You understand from the will the cottage is now yours, and that you must never sell it?'

Albert Jenkins had unruly white eyebrows, like pale, hairy caterpillars, and Dan found his gaze lingering there before he snapped his focus back into place. A sliver of annoyance burned its way under his skin. He knew all this and had signed the numerous papers saying as such. The word death vibrated along his senses, the familiar tightening of his scalp as his heartbeat quickened.

Albert Jenkins placed the small jar on the breakfast table, amidst a pile of toast crumbs and empty egg shells.

'The remains of Lucinda Latimer, Mr. Morgan. Her last request was to have her ashes scattered in the lake.'

Dan recoiled from the jar— the urn— as though it were poison. He fought to keep the revulsion from showing on his face.

'There is one other thing.' Albert cleared his throat, one hand reaching into his pocket, tugging out a handkerchief. 'She wished for this to be done in the dark.'

Dan struggled to find his voice. His throat felt like it had been filled with glue. 'Any particular night?'

Albert wiped his brow. 'She named no preference. I believe she thought that you would know.'

Dan stood with the morning sun warm against his back, but the first stirrings of panic had begun to swirl around his gut.

'I will leave you in peace, Mr. Morgan. My job here is done now.' His eyes fell on the egg shells. 'I took the liberty of leaving a few items in your fridge. But if you're going to put these in the compost, I'd advise you to break them first. As a deterrent against any unwelcome visitors.'

Dan forced his eyes away from the heavy presence of the urn and ushered the solicitor out into the sun. The man walked down the path, ducking under the sunflowers, the creak of the gate signifying his departure. There was no car parked next to Dan's and no car visible along the track.

'He was a bit weird.' Faye appeared at his shoulder, headphones slung around her neck.

How much had she heard?

But the real problem was that urn on the table, an inconspicuous brown jar containing the powdered remains of Lucinda Latimer.

NINE

Dan stacked the last of the breakfast dishes on the wooden drying board, watching as the soapy water swirled down the drain. Faye was taking a shower and the pipes in the walls whined and clunked, a sound that set Dan's teeth on edge. But maybe that was just the presence of the jar behind him.

The morning was bright and cheerful. Golden sunlight poured in through the windows at the front of the house, casting diamond-shaped patterns on the floor. The soporific drone of a bee as it flitted through the lavender patch at the side of the door.

It was all so damn peaceful, the kind of peace most people didn't think existed anymore, caught up in their world of constant background noise, glued to each ping from their phones.

Dan's lips twisted into a grimace. Wasn't he describing himself?

But there was something rumbling underneath that peace, an unease he couldn't put a name to, something just a little bit spoiled, like sour milk. He ran his tongue over his front teeth, his distorted expression reflecting back from the vintage brass tap.

Drying his hands on a tea towel, he crossed the small hallway. Slowly, he opened the door to the room with the glass case, half expecting to hear Lucinda's sharp reprimand in his ear.

The leafy smell rose to greet him as though it had been simply slumbering, awaiting his return. If he was keeping this place he'd really need to rip everything out and modernise it. But there was no if. He had signed a legal document saying he would never sell it.

He had brought Faye here because he remembered the summers of long ago, wanted her to experience the joy and the freedom. Wanted to claw back what they once had. But maybe he was seeing his past with rose-tinted glasses.

What happened in the past is important, Danny. The mistakes we made we have to live with, no matter the consequences. Lucinda's voice, as clearly as if she stood right behind him. He wheeled and found Faye standing in the doorway, her hair still damp from the shower.

He suddenly needed to be free of these four walls with their ghosts and their judgements.

'Shall we go out? I'll see if I can remember the paths through the forest.'

Faye's gaze flicked to the glass case in the corner. Dan shook his head, confused as to why he'd come in here in the first place. Stubble bristled against his fingers as he ran his hand over his jaw.

'Leave it, Dan. It suits you.'

She retreated to the bottom step, thrusting her feet into trainers that were still tied, her curls springing up as they dried. She raised her head, caught in a slanting sunbeam as it sliced across the hallway.

Dan captured the moment and basked in the rare compliment.

He crossed to the kitchen and grabbed two water bottles from the fridge. A smile curled on his lips.

The front door creaked as she went outside, the chittering of birds suddenly filling the house. Dan tossed the bottles into his rucksack and slung it over his shoulder. He closed the door to Lucinda's room, the soft click of the latch falling into place the last thing he heard as they headed out into the day.

+

They had walked around in a complete circle. Dan had been positive he knew where he was going, his steps sure and confident, glad to be out in the open. Glad to be free of the whisper of four stone walls.

The tracks near the cottage were wide enough for them to walk side by side. Dan recognised landmarks. The stunted skeleton of a tree struck by lightning, the oak with a red and blue kite wrapped around its trunk, the decayed remains of a huge beech stump dressed in a mantle of green moss and fronded lichen.

Snapshots from his past, a little more scarred by time.

But they had pushed deeper into the heart of the forest and veered away from the broad track, now wandering those slithering into the tangled undergrowth. A stiff breeze rustled through the trees, sending a shower of old leaves skittering across their path. Faye stood in a brave shaft of sunlight as Dan tried to find his bearings. They were well and truly lost, but at least she had the good grace not to remind him of it.

Dan unzipped his rucksack, handing Faye a bottle of water. Her eyes swept past him and Dan turned to see two people walking towards them. One was Albert Jenkins, the other a middle-aged woman wearing a pale blue jacket and jeans, her hair swept up into a severe bun. Albert held a large plastic bottle, the woman a long-spouted watering can, the type people used for houseplants.

Dan stared at the watering can with the fascination of a toddler.

'Mr. Morgan.' Albert's voice greeted Dan with the same self-assured confidence from only a few hours earlier. The man raised his hand towards his head, and Dan had the strangest feeling he was looking for a hat that was no longer there, wanting to tip it as a mark of respect towards Faye.

The woman said nothing but her eyes were fixed on Faye. Quiet eyes, but the kind that didn't miss a thing.

'Are you a little lost?'

Colour rose to Dan's cheeks. He was more than a little lost. He was a great fucked-up-and-ceaselessly-wandering lost.

'Don't worry, these woods have a habit of never looking the same on any given day. But you are a little off the pathways strangers tread.'

Something about the weight of these words sent a shiver across Dan's skin.

'Come, I'll take you to the track you should be on.'

Albert didn't wait for an answer; he turned and pushed his way through a deep tangle of undergrowth, the woman following in his wake.

Dan looked across at Faye and she shrugged, her finger twirling in the air by her head.

Albert Jenkins was definitely an enigma, but Dan didn't think his mind wasn't anything but crystal sharp.

He jogged a few paces to catch up before the pair disappeared from view. Faye muttered something under her breath.

Through the mass of brambles and waist-high ferns Dan

could see the pale blue of the woman's jacket. He paused and felt Faye at his shoulder. Dan pushed aside the green sea of ferns and stopped dead, feeling like a voyeur at the scene unfolding before him.

Albert was filling the watering can in the woman's hands from the bottle, his actions slow and deliberate. He placed the bottle on the ground and reached up, and for a moment, his hands were lost from view.

Dan's breath stalled in his throat as Albert's fingers appeared, clutching what looked like a small glass lantern with a curved metal dish at its base. The woman carefully poured the contents of the watering can into this base, before Albert hoisted the lantern up out of view.

Dan let out his breath in a shuddering exhale. There was something eerily familiar about what they were doing.

Albert turned towards them, summer sunlight haloing around his head. He had known all along that Dan was watching. Guilty frustration made the sweat on Dan's skin prickle and he straightened, pushing his way through into the small clearing.

'If you take the right turn at the old beech, you'll find the pathway will lead you into the village.'

The fact Albert hadn't mentioned anything about what he was doing both intrigued and concerned Dan. It was as if the old man knew that somewhere in Dan's memory a fuse had been lit.

With a nod of his head towards Faye, Albert and his companion set off in the other direction.

Dan glanced up at the glass lantern as the gleam of sunlight encased it in gold. On the breeze came the faint sound of a wind chime.

'It's all well and good telling us we need to turn right at the beech tree,' Faye's voice, edged with agitation, interrupted his thoughts. 'But how do we know which one that is?'

Dan studied the clearing in front of them. The surrounding trees seemed to touch the fabric of the summer sky.

He knew exactly which one was the beech. Not because he was any kind of expert on trees, but because it was the one that bore his initials on its trunk.

TEN

Albert's directions were faultless, and the pathway from the woods soon led them to the short cut across the fields to the village. Cotton wool clouds floated in the sky. Cotton wool sheep grazed by a hedgerow. In the distance they could see the pointed spire of the village church piercing the skyline.

The only pub in the village looked as if the 1970s had wandered in and never left. Faded flock wallpaper, mirrors behind the bar with slogans etched into their surfaces. It smelled of old beer and even older nicotine, but the fish and chips Dan and Faye both chose were home cooked and delicious. Or maybe it was because they were starving by the time they got there.

It was a beautiful afternoon, so when Faye suggested spending it in the park by the river, Dan didn't object. In fact, he was overjoyed. He couldn't remember the last time she had suggested anything. It felt strange to have this amount of time with her, though, and he was almost glad when she flopped down in the shade of a willow tree and pulled her headphones out of her bag.

He glanced across, watched as the wavering shadows of the willow moved like a dappled ocean across her skin. Her face was propped up in her hands, her bare feet crossed on the grass. Occasionally, she would move to flick away a bug that had strayed too close, but she was lost in her own little world.

Dan read a few work emails he'd received on the journey down, but soon his eyelids began to droop, mottled sunlight and the soft hush of the breeze in the trees teasing his consciousness away.

Be home by dark. Be home by dark. *The words go around and around in his head as he runs, brambles ripping at his skin and clothes. Terror is a beast that is alive in his throat, its tentacles sucking all the air from his lungs as he crashes through the trees.*

A single, long shriek splits the night in two.

But he doesn't pause, doesn't turn.

Be home by dark, she said. And now he knows why....

Someone touched his arm and Dan turned towards them, instantly awake, but still caught in the cobwebs of sleep.

'Hey.' Faye's pale face looked down on him, blocking out the sun, her headphones slung around her neck. 'Wake up. You were dreaming, muttering really weird things.'

A flush of heat rose to Dan's cheeks.

He could still feel the hot breath of the dream licking at his throat.

'Sorry,' he mumbled. The word felt like sawdust on his tongue. 'Blame it on the heat and that cider I had at lunchtime.' He dredged up what he hoped was a reassuring smile. And wondered what he'd been saying.

Dan couldn't remember the last time he had fallen asleep during the day, but he'd tossed and turned last night, and the long drive here had been anything but restful.

The sun had arced across the sky, a few grey clouds flitting through the blue. The park was emptying, save for a man walking an old Jack Russell on a long leash and a young family eating ice cream by the wooden bridge spanning the river. A duck ushered her brood of fluffy, grey ducklings back into the water, the splash of tiny bodies somehow setting Dan's nerves on edge.

'Are you sure you're okay?' Faye asked again, shoving her headphones into her bag. He didn't miss the way her eyes lingered on the family, especially the little boy, half asleep in his mother's arms.

He nodded in reply, but the hairs stood up on his arms as the dream left its shadow on his skin.

+

The grey clouds of late afternoon were smeared across the sky, their edges licked away by the first breaths of twilight. Dan had wanted to be back at the cottage before dark, but after a quick snack at the pub, they had called in at the local shop and bought a few necessities, and somehow a bruised dusk had fallen.

The light from a torch—purchased at the shop—bounced on the forest track, but the beam was a scant offering in the gloom.

Dan was confident he knew where he was going. He had mapped out the route in his mind as they'd walked to the village. But it all looked so different in the dark, and sounds were amplified. Long shadows bled from the trees and their canopies blotted out the little light left in the sky. He concentrated on the crunch of their feet on the track, his eyes searching for familiar landmarks ahead.

An owl hooted deep in the forest and Faye glanced up, her eyes widening. The creak of a branch overhead.

The night pressed in around them, sticky and warm.

And suddenly, all was silent. No chittering of crickets,

not even the wind in the trees. Dan held his breath, moving closer to Faye.

A sensation shivered down his spine. The age-old human instinct of being watched.

'What did you mean in the park, Dan?' Faye's voice was too loud in the silence. 'You said 'be back by dark'…'

Dan's hand came to rest on her shoulder. Tentatively. 'It was nothing. I can't even remember it now. You know what dreams are like.'

Lies. All lies.

High above them, the clouds bathed the rising moon in a soft, grey wash. From the heart of the forest came the high-pitched shriek of something that sounded like laughter.

Faye flinched, and Dan pulled her close, wrapping his arm around her shoulder. 'It's only a bird, love. The forest distorts the sounds, especially at night. Used to scare the crap out of me. You'll get used to it. By the time we leave you won't even notice it anymore. Come on.' A trickle of sweat glued his t-shirt to his back.

He let his arm fall, not wanting to push his luck. Dan hoped his explanation had been the truth, because right now all he truly wanted to do was run. And that was not the way to reconnect with his wife.

There was nothing to be afraid of. They were safer here than wandering along a city street.

But he made sure the torch beam stayed on the track. Away from the cavernous dark of the trees.

After a few minutes, his light picked out the charred body of the lightning stump. Relief flooded through his limbs, making his fingers tingle.

'See, easy as pie.' He grinned, relishing the way Faye had

walked close by his side most of the way home. There hadn't been a lot of conversation, but it was a start.

The cottage gate welcomed them with a soft creak, the moon still partly hidden by the ghostlike fingers of cloud. As Dan turned the key in the old lock, the torch tucked under his arm, Faye pulled the yellow crown of one of the sunflowers towards her, her fingers touching the seeds.

'We grew one of these for Toby. Do you remember? And then that summer storm snapped the stem, and I had to rush round to a neighbours and beg one of theirs, before he got back from nursery.'

Dan swallowed the lump in his throat at the sight of her smile, born from melancholy and the wistful warmth of memory.

He pushed open the door and flicked on the hall light, his eye caught by the pale forms of a few letters left by the postman on the small bench in the porch.

Faye's scream split the night in two as the light flooded out into the darkness.

Dan's head jerked around, panic rising, filling his lungs with its frenzied dance.

The threshold of the cottage was a seething mass of shiny, black beetles.

ELEVEN

Faye lay awake, staring at the shadows from the trees, moonlight dappling the wall.

She replayed the scenes from the day, trying to find the logic in some downright illogical situations. The first had been the appearance of Albert Jenkins right after breakfast.

The urn still sat on the kitchen table. Dan hadn't mentioned it at all, although she hadn't missed his gaze flicking to it every now and then. And she had listened in from the hallway as they talked. A lake? Scattering ashes in the dark? Her brow furrowed as she tried to find a cool place on her pillow.

Then Albert's second appearance, with the strange woman whose gaze had been filled with suspicion. Faye had no idea what they had been doing. It was just another oddity to add to the list amassing in her thoughts.

Lunch had been strained. Dan had tried too hard to get her to talk, injecting interest in her one-word answers, talking too quickly to fill in the silences. She knew she should be grateful for his attention, and she knew she was hell to live with, but all she wanted to do was to be left alone. Since Toby's death, alone was a place that felt safe. And being with Dan somehow brought the memory of Toby back. Her son had had his father's eyes.

At least she'd had some quiet time as they sat by the river. She was relieved when Dan began to doze and she could remove the headphones that were making her ears itch. He looked younger as he slept. The lines disappeared from his brow as his face relaxed, his jaw slackening slightly, the new wash of stubble highlighted in the sun.

But it hadn't taken him long to begin muttering, and then the lines had deepened and the tension had strung its way into his neck.

Be home by dark, he'd said, over and over again, the words turning to an incantation on his lips.

She turned to lie on her side, facing the window. A welcome breeze fanned in with that deep scent of green. Of course she'd opened it again; it was hot enough to boil a lobster with it closed.

The beetles. Faye shivered as she thought about how they'd crawled all over each other, black and glistening, their pincers opening and closing in unison. Dan had said it was because the cottage had people in it again, that they were looking for food, but his face had turned to the colour of milk as she retreated upstairs. When she came down, they were gone.

She blew out a breath through her lips and picked up her phone. No service. The light from the screen illuminated the small space, reflecting from the carved, dark wood headboard. Faye sat up and moved to her knees, studying the detail in the wood. She ran her fingers over the surface, the etching so beautifully done she could see more and more the longer she looked at it.

There were tiny things that looked like dragonflies in the trees. She recognised the burnt-out remains of the lightning tree. And just visible at the rear of the carving was something she had never noticed before. What looked like the roof of an old house, tall chimneys reaching to the sky.

She tossed her phone onto the bedside table and threw herself back onto the pillow with a sigh, wondering how she was ever going to survive the next few weeks. The mottled shadows on the wall fluttered and danced, and she raised her arms, pressing her wrists together and opening her hands, making a shadow bird for the shadow trees. A smile crossed her lips, just before the sudden small thud of something landing on the roof.

Faye held her breath, her hands frozen in place, a statue in the dark, the only movement the galloping of her heart against her ribcage.

Then something slid down the thatch, the rustle of straw and reeds sending a whispering echo through the ceiling. The sound stopped above her bedroom window.

An owl. It must be an owl. Her reasoning rattled inside her head. Her eyes flew to the open pane, the old glass distorting the moonlight.

She let out a strangled gasp and slid out of bed, the bare floorboards rough under her feet, acutely aware of the dark space between the floor and the mattress. Her ears strained against the silence but the noise had stopped.

The city girl within scoffed at her fear.

The soft night breeze played against her skin as she reached the window, her eyes scanning the treeline for any signs of movement. Faye hopped up onto the wide sill, shuffling so her back rested against the inside of the window, her knees drawn into her chest. There was such beauty in the stillness, something magnetic about the way the moonlight skimmed the tops of the trees. She reached for her sketch pad and flipped to a fresh page, her fingers stroking the blank sheet with swirls of charcoal. Her eyes flicked from scene to page, the fear from a few minutes ago chased into the soft hum of focus and creativity. The sketch was much the same as the one she had done the previous night, but the lines were deeper, more assured, the image a crisper twin of its earlier interpretation. Her eyes stopped for a moment, searching for the stag, and there, in a patch between the outer edges of the trees she caught a glimpse of movement.

Faye leaned forwards, the stub of the charcoal poised above the page, her brain already constructing the curved lines of antlers.

But whatever was in the forest wasn't the stag.

On the night breeze came the sound of a tiny bell.

A bank of cloud scuttled over the face of the moon, plunging the shadows into a playground of darkness. Irritation forced a noise from her throat. Faye watched the veil over the moon slowly fade, some small part of her willing it to quicken.

And as the pale light once again illuminated her view, a blurred figure shifted between the trees.

She fought to make sense of the shape, goosebumps rising on her bare arms. Instinct told her whoever it was, was watching her.

Some part of her wanted to jump down from the sill, to go hammer on Dan's door to tell him there was a stalker in the woods, but another part, fuelled by curiosity, told her to stay put.

The figure didn't move. Nor did she.

Her breath misted the window pane.

And then, as quickly as it had appeared, it was gone.

Faye opened the window as wide as it would go. She leant out and peered into the deep dark of the forest. All was still.

But right above her window, on the edge of the sloping thatch, the creature with the praying mantis limbs rocked gently to and fro.

TWELVE

'Does anyone else live near here?'

Dan stopped chewing his mouthful of toast, surprised by the question. Faye had been quiet all through breakfast, stirring her cereal around and around with her spoon. He leapt on the first sign of interest from her.

'Depends on what you call close. Robert McCallum, the gamekeeper I told you about, used to live at the other side of the forest by the lake, but I've no idea if he's still around.' *Or still alive.* Dan poured milk into his mug of tea, pushing away the trails of thought in his mind. 'Apart from that, the nearest row of houses is on the main road, by the old sawmill.' *Right where I smashed into Bambi.*

He'd had another profoundly restless night's sleep, brought on by having to sweep the mass of beetles away with an old broom he'd found in the scullery. Some had caught on the pointed bristles of the brush, tiny legs rotating as if they were clockwork, their underbellies ripped open.

Faye pursed her lips, her eyes flicking to the window. Her elbow was on the table, her chin propped up in her cupped palm.

'What makes you ask?' He curled his fingers around his mug.

'I thought I saw someone last night, on the edge of the

wood…a boy.' Her voice tailed off.

Dan's jaw tightened. Toby. She just couldn't let him go. Part of him wanted to take her by the shoulders, make her look into his eyes and see the harsh reality of what existed now.

'It was probably Albert Jenkins.' Dan forced a lightness into his voice he didn't feel, trying to thaw the sudden ice between them. 'He does seem to wander about here an awful lot.' But he was acutely aware that the ghost of their son's memory had followed them here.

The prospect of a day where this hung over them raised its awkward head. 'How about a swim? There used to be a lake by the old house—we can wander over and take a look.'

Her face brightened, chasing away the shadows in her eyes. Faye had always loved to swim, had, in fact, been on a county team in her younger days.

A recollection tapped him on the shoulder. He'd swum at the lake before, many times in those long-ago summers, jumping off the long, rickety wooden jetty and landing with a whoop, the shock of the cold water mingling with the exhilaration of being alive.

Back when health and safety was only uttered on building sites. Not in school playgrounds when kids wanted to play conkers. And hadn't he come here to show Faye a slice of his own childhood?

Keeping her busy, he decided, was a much better option than letting her dwell on some crazy notion from last night.

But part of him really didn't want to go to the lake. Or to the old house that watched over it.

+

The water glittered through the trees, ribbons of silver leading them on as they walked, pushing their way through the sea of bright green ferns carpeting the forest floor.

No one had been this way in a very long time.

Faye paused, plucking a dried leaf from her hair. 'Didn't anyone worry about you when you were wandering about on your own?'

It took Dan a moment or two to realise she was talking about his childhood. He pulled a bottle of water from his rucksack and handed it to her.

'It was different then.' He wiped his hand over his sweating brow. 'And I was never on my own.'

Faces swam in his mind, kids he had run with and fought with throughout long summer days. Kids who been terribly important to him at that particular moment in time, in a way that only children understand.

There had been one who was special but he couldn't remember what had happened to him. Had he moved away or had they simply drifted apart?

'Freedom.' Faye whispered the word, her tongue licking her bottom lip, as though she was trying to taste it. A shadow crossed her face.

'Come on then.' He shouldered the rucksack, eager to shift her melancholy. 'The water awaits. I'm going to show you I can still swim across it without stopping.'

Dan hoped that part was true, three decades, and more than a few pounds, later.

They set off and soon the trees began to thin as the ground sloped downhill. A patch of overgrown land greeted them as they stepped out of the forest, the wind rippling the long grass. The lake was a glistening coin beyond, a single, battered jetty jutting out into its centre.

Dan paused, scanning the surface. His gaze swept through

a line of trees standing at its eastern edge. A shiver danced across his skin.

Barrington Hall.

The black stones of its frontage brooded in the late morning sunlight, sucking the warmth from the day.

The lake. The house. Nothing had changed. It was as if it was existing in its own slice of time.

The shiver became a cold chill, tightening his scalp as though it suddenly was one size too small.

They crawl in through a broken window, soaked to the skin, forked lightning turning the surface of the lake to molten silver, the wind whipping through the trees like an uncaged beast. Two young boys caught between the storm-cloud dark of the summer sky and the whispering gloom of a long-abandoned house.

Scent engulfs them, the green of the forest washing over their skin, the smell of ozone pulsing on the air as thunder rolls over the roof of the house.

And then the sound that makes them both wheel in terror, filtering down from the top of the staircase, a flash of lightning highlighting the cobwebs strung from the old chandelier like dusty garlands.

'Dan?' Faye's voice seeped through the shrouds of those long-ago thoughts. Dan fought to shake the memory away, but the ghost of it lingered like a second skin.

She was standing at the edge of the lake, dressed in a polka dot bikini, long limbs pale against the grey of the water.

The need to protect her flooded through Dan, the kind of need that wanted to wrap her up and take away all the pain, all the grief.

She dipped a toe into the water. The soft breeze ruffled

her dark curls.

Dan quickly stripped off his jeans and t-shirt. A blast of cool air wrapped itself around him, as though the breeze had developed teeth.

He didn't want to go in. In fact, he wanted to take Faye's hand and pull her away from the water. He hesitated, wondering how he could find the right words. Words that didn't make him sound like a complete idiot.

Faye strode out into the lake until the water reached her thighs. She dived, as graceful as a ballerina. Ripples spread out across the water and Dan held his breath until she surfaced, his own fear tip-tapping along, an echo of his heartbeat.

Sunlight wicked from the surface of the lake, turning her into a shimmering mirage, something that was both there, and very lost.

Dan forced his feet forwards, resisting the urge to swear as the cold water lapped at his ankles.

Gritting his teeth, he strode out until the water was up to his waist. The swaying moment of unbalance caught him unawares and he lifted his feet, letting his body submerge. He gasped at the chill. At the pressure against his ears. He could see Faye's legs treading water, the reeds at the bottom of the lake wafting in the current.

Beyond, lay the deep darkness of the jetty's underbelly.

He rose through the water and broke the surface, slicking his hair back as the sunlight bleached away his vision. Dan rubbed his eyes with the back of one hand and waited for his sight to readjust. But the first thing he saw wasn't the rippling water; it was the two windows at the top of the house, reflecting that same sunlight. Two windows burning brightly in a face of cold stone.

'They know us now,' the boy says, the colour draining from his face.

And Dan laughs, punching his best friend on the shoulder as they run home through the tail of the thunderstorm, the scent of wet earth, like a freshly dug grave, crawling in their footsteps.

THIRTEEN

Faye struck out for the centre of the lake. She was a strong swimmer and the chill of the water didn't seem so bad now. She concentrated on the movement of her limbs, on the rhythmic repetition of her breath. Tried to find a calmness she wasn't sure existed anymore.

She wanted to ask Dan about the ashes on the table, about why Albert Jenkins had been in the wood. About the deer. Which she knew he had left to die miserably on the road.

And that wasn't like him. He wasn't a cruel man. Toby had once owned a hamster that had got itself stuck behind the skirting boards, and Dan had ripped them off the wall to rescue it.

But something had definitely got to him since arriving here. She knew, without turning, that he'd still be gazing towards the old house, lost in his own thoughts.

The outline of the jetty came into view. Its centre was sunken, the wooden planks skimming the lake, the boards bleached by weather and time.

She paused, treading water for a few moments. Ripples lapped at her outstretched fingertips. The sun was almost directly overhead.

Faye glanced across to the house. It wasn't one of those beautiful old places, more like an aging relative that nobody liked, as old as dirt but still hanging on, refusing to be forgotten. The artist in her sketched lines in her mind, her brain already exploring perspective and depth. It wasn't a place to create in the light though. It needed brooding skies and the approach of night. It needed—she pursed her lips, trying to find the right word.

But finding any words was hard now.

Faye blew out a breath and let the buoyancy of the water take her onto her back. She floated there, arms and legs apart, like a little fallen star.

All she could hear was the gentle sound of the water and the wind whispering in the trees.

No traffic. No background hum of people talking. No rush of life as it sped onwards.

She didn't even really miss the fact that her phone didn't work. It would only be full of people talking about themselves. And she found that tiring, especially as she was the woman who wanted to disappear. To be left amongst the comfort—and the prison—of her own thoughts.

Most of her friends didn't know how to talk to her anymore. And she didn't really mind. Talking was simply too painful. She didn't want to rehash the feelings again and again, pinning her grief on the wall for them all to share, like it was some kind of art exhibit.

Something brushed lightly against her fingertips.

They tingled as she looked through the first few inches of water for fish, but there was nothing there. And then, from the corner of her eye, something flashed. Something lightning quick. Two quick bursts before it disappeared under the shadow at the end of the jetty. Faye struck out again, curiosity overriding any apprehension.

Dan called her name and she stuck an arm out of the water, pointing to where she was going.

The shadow of the jetty enfolded her as she swam into its shade. The temperature dropped and she shivered, pushing wet hair out of her eyes. Pondweed floated under the weathered boards, the water thick and dark. The scent of green, the same one she had smelled in the cottage. The same one that seemed to surround them in the dark.

But this time it had a bitter edge.

A sudden flash of bright blue light amidst the mass of weeds.

Faye ducked under the jetty and pushed the feathery pondweed apart, her legs brushing through submerged vegetation.

Sunlight glinted at the other side. It was only an arm's length away. But underneath the bleached, battered slats it was cold. The type of cold you get when you open a fridge door.

The light skittered just under the surface of the lake, and she reached in, wet fronds clinging to her skin.

Something was floating a few feet down in the water.

She took a deep breath and submerged, her eyes searching the gloom of the jetty's underbelly.

Disturbed dirt swirled in the water, blocking her sight as air bubbles rose from her nose.

Something cold and heavy brushed against her leg.

The dirt settled. Something pale inches away from her calf.

The scream that was rising through her throat burst out. Water gushed into her mouth. A shooting pain rocketed into her sinuses. She kicked out but the weeds had wrapped themselves around her ankle, holding her down. Horror tore through her veins as she thrashed in the murky water.

Sunlight glinted down from another world above, a reminder things could be so normal. And so wrong.

She heard the ring of the doorbell, the policewoman standing outside, hazy through the frosted glass in the door. The sound rapped against her skull as she fought against the weeds, her lungs on fire. She heard the thud of earth as it fell upon her son's coffin.

And then a hand reached down through the water, clasping her wrist in its strong grip. The weeds eased their hold and Faye kicked against the pull, gasping and spluttering as she broke through the surface, Dan's arm sliding around her body. She let him pull her back to the shore, tried to calm her heartbeat as it thundered against her ribcage, telling herself that what had just happened wasn't real.

But the terror of what had touched her refused to slip away. And maybe she had even glimpsed a pale, pale hand, its fingers outstretched towards her.

FOURTEEN

'There's nothing there, Faye.'

Dan emerged from his third dive, breathing hard. He'd explored every inch under the jetty but all he found was slimy vegetation and the trailing remains of some cloth wrapped around one of the jetty's piles.

Faye was sat on the bank, a towel around her shoulders, her eyes too large in her pale face.

Dan swam towards her and climbed out onto the shingled lake shore, shaking the water from his face. The sun had gone behind a bank of ominous grey clouds.

She looked up at him. Pulled the towel a little tighter. 'Are you sure?' Her voice trembled slightly.

He nodded. 'Positive. But let me have a look at that leg.'

He knelt and the sharp stones bit into his knees. An angry red welt encircled Faye's ankle, the skin raised and inflamed.

'I don't know what you got caught up in, love.' He tried to keep his tone light and matter of fact, but he wouldn't meet her gaze.

A cool wind skittered over the surface of the lake, ripping the grey into irritated ruffles. Faye's eyes were still focused on the jetty, her lips slightly parted.

'Do you want to head home?' The last word jarred against Dan's senses, as if someone had brushed against an exposed nerve. It wasn't home, but Lucinda had made damn sure he couldn't get rid of it. Right at that moment, he desperately wanted to know why.

'No, it's okay. We'll stay.' Faye dredged up a smile.

They ate in silence, the slightly uncomfortable kind. Dan found the apples and cheese they'd bought at the village store hard to swallow. Whatever taste they had was doused by the bitter tang of the lake on his tongue. He hadn't really wanted to come here, and his common sense warred with his gut feeling over whether he had known something would happen.

The sun still hid behind the bank of grey cloud and Dan shivered, goosebumps raising the hair on his arms. He glanced down at Faye's ankle. Didn't want to think about the outcome if she'd been alone.

They were sitting with their backs to the house and Dan had to fight the overwhelming desire to glance over his shoulder. Faye was spooked enough without seeing that part of him still felt like he was fourteen again.

He had wanted to take her away from the place that still held onto Toby's memory. And he had ended up bringing her here, where his ghosts were nibbling at his senses, picking away at the scars of childhood.

There was one person he could ask, who might remember what had happened long ago, and that person was Albert Jenkins. The man might be ancient but his mind was as sharp as a tack.

All of his apprehension might be absolutely nothing, simply his imagination playing tricks on a stressed out, wound-up-tighter-than-a-fucking-spring brain.

But as Dan packed away the remains of their meagre picnic, pulling his clothes onto damp, chilled skin, he wondered whether unearthing memories that should stay dead was asking for trouble.

$$\dagger$$

Faye went straight to her room when they arrived back at the cottage, leaving Dan alone in the kitchen. Or not quite alone if you counted the remains of Aunt Lucinda on the scrubbed pine table.

The urn sat there, its silence judging Dan more than words ever could.

Dan emptied the rubbish from his rucksack into the bin. The afternoon sun drifted through the window, a hazy, golden summer light. A bee droned close by and Dan felt his eyelids drooping. A little nap would suit him just fine.

The garden gate slammed against its post and Dan was forced from his thoughts of slumbering.

'God damn you, dog, come here!'

Dan glanced out of the window to see a spaniel darting up the pathway to the cottage. The door was slightly ajar and in a few seconds a pointed nose had pushed its way into his rucksack slung on the floor.

'Tilly!' A man's voice boomed across the hallway. Dan walked through to greet it.

The man filled the doorway, a broad-shouldered, full-girthed figure with a shock of red hair, a ruddy complexion and an impressive beard. Two hazel eyes shone through the mass of red.

Tilly slunk apologetically out of the kitchen and settled down at the visitor's feet.

Dan found himself under scrutiny. He wiped his hands down the back of his jeans and held out his right hand. 'No harm done.' He found a smile and pasted it on his face. 'Dan

Morgan. My aunt used to live here….' He trailed off as those hazel eyes glinted.

'I didn't think I'd see you in these parts again, Danny.'

The soft Scottish brogue settled over him, and Dan knew instantly who this man was.

Robert McCallum. Thirty years older but still as large as life.

'I didn't think I'd be back either. But Lucinda—'

'Left this place to you in her will,' Robert interrupted, nodding.

Dan nodded back, because nods were like yawns, highly contagious.

Tilly grew bored and sniffed her way along the floor. She pushed her nose against the bottom of the door to Lucinda's room. It opened.

A wag of a liver and white coloured tail as she disappeared inside.

Robert McCallum made a noise that sounded very much like a growl. 'I just picked her up the other day, and she's as flighty as they come. Beats me why folks get dogs and then leave them to their own devices.'

Before Dan could answer, Robert followed Tilly into the room.

Dan had forgotten to open the curtains, but the light filtered in through the faded cotton, a few stray beams picking out the layers of dust on the dark-wood coffee table. Tilly had found the remains of something edible under the couch and was hunting around for more.

'The place looks the same. Half expected to see your Aunt sitting in that chair.' Robert nodded towards the rocking chair by the hearth, Lucinda's knitting bag resting against the arm.

Then the old gamekeeper's eyes fell on the glass case on the left hand side of the chimney breast. He strode towards it, if strode was the right word, because the room was tiny. 'Haven't seen these for a long time.' He tapped on the glass, like you might at a fish tank, if you wanted to alert the inhabitants.

'I believe you made them, Robert,' Dan said, feeling as if he were the visitor here. A little voice in his head told him that he was.

'Aye, I did. All apart from one.'

Dan walked across and peered around Robert's large frame. 'Which one didn't you do?'

'The one that's different.' His words made the hair on Dan's nape prickle. 'If you ever want to get rid of them, call me up. Don't go giving them away, or selling them. That would be a really bad idea.'

Robert inhaled deeply through his nose, then drew his finger down over the dusty glass. The man's eyes flicked to the corner of the case.

'I don't know what I'm going to do with the old place yet—' Dan began, and was interrupted again, this time by Faye's voice calling his name from upstairs.

'Someone else with you, Danny?'

Robert snapped his head around and Dan took a step backwards.

'My wife, Faye.'

'If I was you I'd take her home. This place is wild, and wild has its own ways.' Robert called Tilly to his side, ducking his head under the doorway as he walked through to the hall.

'We'll be staying for a few weeks, but thank you for your

concern.' Dan followed Robert out. He watched the big man and his dog walk quickly down the path.

The gate slammed again, announcing their departure.

Dan rubbed his nose with his fingers and replayed the weirdest of conversations. Why had he thanked a man who had barged in and more or less told him that Faye was in danger? Something else bothered him about their conversation too and he couldn't fully grasp it. He went back to the glass case, Robert's finger trail clearly marked on the front.

Dan peered into the corner, where Robert's attention had been, even though the gamekeeper had tried to be subtle. Under the blackbird with the harsh yellow-ringed glass eye, was the thing Faye had noticed on their first night here.

Something almost obscured by a moss-covered log. Something pinned there with open wings. Dan's lip curled in disgust.

And then what was bothering him poked Dan in a tender place. He had introduced himself with his name, but Robert had insisted on calling him Danny, *whom he was once, but never again.*

He had shed the skin of that name but the withered husk of it still lived on.

This place is wild, and wild has its own ways.

He could stay put and let the niggling doubts nibble away at what should be a time of healing, or he could talk to Albert. The old man would probably think Dan needed certifying, but it wasn't as if their paths would cross much, now that the funeral stuff had been sorted.

At the back of his mind, another justification flared. He didn't want Faye to know if anything bad had happened all those summers ago. To have any other reason to think that her husband was losing the plot.

Dan glanced at his watch. 4 p.m. He could talk to Albert and be back here before dusk fell. Faye would be fine. It wasn't as if strangers ever found their way to the cottage.

But what she had said about seeing someone in the forest pinged against his radar.

He closed the door to Lucinda's room. The satisfying click of the latch pierced the golden light filtering through the windows.

Faye sat at the top of the stairs, her sketch pad open on her knees, a pencil poised between her fingers. He wondered why she had yelled for him.

'I'm going into the village.' She raised her head slowly. 'I'll take the car so I won't be long. You don't have to come if you don't want to. I need to finalise some stuff with Albert, but I'll be back by supper time.'

'Okay. You go. I don't want to come.' She pushed her hair out of her eyes. The pencil twitched in her fingers.

'Will you be all right by yourself?'

It seemed a ridiculous thing to say to a grown woman, and she graced him with the kind of look that told him so. Maybe it was because voicing it would let him off the hook if anything crawled out of the woodwork. Dan quashed the thought quickly, annoyed his own insecurities were having far too much of a good time in his head.

He sucked his bottom lip into his mouth, torn between a need to go to ease his own uncertainty and leaving her alone. He scooped the car keys from the old console table in the hallway, glancing at a dusty black and white photo of his aunt in her younger days.

'Dan.' He turned as he made his way to the door. A slant

of sunlight from the bedroom carved his wife's features into two, one half of her face in complete darkness. 'Bring me ice cream.'

Dan smiled. 'Strawberry ripple.' He raised his hand, his thumb out, and closed the door behind him.

The sunflowers arched their golden crowns over his head as he walked down the path to the gate. The scent of rose and lavender wafted across from the overgrown flower beds. The thatched roof of the cottage brushed against a picture perfect blue sky and the air was filled with the chittering of finches.

All of his doubts settled, laid to rest by the beauty of the moment, this slice of country heaven that belonged to him.

FIFTEEN

Faye waited until she heard the car crunching down the track, the noise of its engine finally disappearing into the distance. She slumped over her sketch pad. The tension left her shoulders as though someone had snapped a string holding it there. She knew Dan was trying really hard, but she wasn't sure if she was ready to accept that peace offering. There'd been so many times when she'd needed his touch. Needed the simple comfort of his presence. And he hadn't been there. So she'd found her own comfort, and within those blank pages, when the charcoal or pencil took on a life of its own, she felt safe.

But there was one thing she wanted to do now she was alone. Something she'd wanted to do all day.

Faye dashed into her room, grabbing a canvas tote. She slid her sketch pad inside along with a few different pencil grades in a suede case and a tin of charcoal stubs. Her eye caught her phone lying on her pillow. About as useful as a brick for what it was meant for, but the camera was pretty decent, and if she didn't finish her sketch, she could work from photos. It wasn't ideal but it was something.

She ran down the stairs and thought about leaving a note. But decided against it. She'd be back long before Dan returned. She pulled open the fridge then grabbed a bottle of water and slung it into the bag.

The door to the other room was closed. Faye's fingers hovered over the handle. No. Her hand dropped to her side.

What she needed wasn't here. It was in the middle of the forest. The indescribable craving to capture it on paper was like an itch she couldn't scratch.

Faye closed the front door behind her, the wood warm against her back as she leant against it to tuck a loose lace into her trainer.

The forest beckoned her just over the track, a sea of assorted greens. Sunlight danced through the leaves and the summer breeze was soft against her skin. She set off, striding along the pathway, using trees as markers when the pathway forked, following the trail they had been on earlier. She pushed away the images from the lake, the strange light and the weeds under the jetty, the thing in the water—that wasn't a thing. Dan had swum out to check, had dived under the shadow of the jetty more than once. Only a trick of the sunlight through the water, her reasoning whispered, coupled with her anxiety at being away from home.

Faye paused at the blackened hulk of the lightning tree and took a few sips from her water bottle. But she could see the narrow track from their earlier trip, leading her on like breadcrumbs, just like the carving on the headboard.

Sweat trickled down her spine as she set off again, her t-shirt sticking to her skin. She couldn't remember the last time she'd been this alone. If she didn't count alone inside her head. But that wasn't really true, because Toby was always there.

In the city, alone was a bad word. A word that had you glancing over your shoulder as you walked in the dark or checking the locks for the hundredth time. Alone was a place to fear.

A dragonfly landed on her arm and she shivered, the shimmering flash of its wings caught in her peripheral vision.

She passed a copse of thin-limbed trees on her right, the ground beneath them covered in dead needles. In the middle of the copse someone had made a kind of wigwam, broken branches stacked together coming to a point at the top. Kids playing in the woods like Dan had. But there was something unsettling about the long, intertwined finger-like branches, something that made her skin tingle.

It was eerily quiet here. No birdsong. No wind. Just a forlorn silence.

Faye turned in a slow circle, her heartbeat thudding in her ears.

Go home, a little voice whispered.

This isn't home, she whispered back.

Hoisting the bag more firmly onto her shoulder, she strode away from the copse, glad to be back in direct sunlight. She was hyper aware of each sound, each scent, as they drifted through the trees, her senses more alive than they had been in months.

Maybe I live in a cocoon. The thought flitted across her mind and she shook her head. 'Maybe you're a little bit crazy,' she muttered, and deep in the woods, a bird cawed. A wry smile touched her lips.

A few wispy clouds hung in the sky as a cooler breeze brushed across her face. That scent of green came with it, washing over her senses, chilling the sweat on her skin.

The trees thinned as the glittering surface of the lake came into view, watched by the whispering grasses that grew on its bank. At the other side of the jetty, the long feathered fingers of an old willow tree dipped their tips languidly into the water.

As Faye stared out at the lake, the presence of Barrington Hall glowered at her through the thin line of trees. The weight of it was as imposing as a mountain, as though it had always been here, and it always would.

She remembered the way Dan had looked at it that morning, the way his throat had rippled as he stared. The way he didn't look like Dan anymore. She wanted to ask him about the summers he'd spent here, but that would mean letting him in. And she wasn't really sure if he'd want to talk about it anyway. It wasn't anything she could put a finger on, only a feeling. Whatever she'd expected coming here, it wasn't this. This feral forest and this brooding lake. This house.

Her eyes roamed over it. The severe lines of its stones, the way it cut into the skyline without so much as an apology. The way its windows both reflected the light and held a darkness so deep rooted it was as if it had erupted from its own grave. A shiver ran over her skin.

Faye glanced up at the sky. Weak sunlight speared through a bank of moody cloud.

A dingy yellow light tarnished the surface of the lake.

She tucked a curl behind one ear and settled herself down, dragging the contents of her tote bag out onto a patch of tufted grass. If she drew the house from here she would have the perspective of the trees in the foreground. A satisfied noise left her throat and a startled bird took flight close by.

Pencil or charcoal? Faye mused as her artist's eye wandered over the house. Pencil would give more detail—but she picked up a stubby piece of charcoal. More severe, but it suited the heavy presence of the building.

Unfolding her pad to a clean page, she caught a glimpse

of the sketch she had done of the figure at the edge of the forest. It was barely more than a few scribbles, but he had a wildness about him, as though he wasn't just in the forest but part of it. The way his limbs looked as pale as silver birch bark, the way his eyes were wary as the stag's the night before. She wondered why she was so convinced these few faint lines were a flesh-and-blood boy.

It was possible that she had made him up out of heart wrenching hope—even here, her thoughts still turned to the son she had lost. And she could still see the way Dan had looked at her when she mentioned the figure. The pity in his eyes.

A brisk wind snatched the page from her hand, flipping it away. The yellow in the sky had deepened to the colour of a healing bruise.

Faye found a clean page again and leaning over her pad, began to draw. Quick, sure lines, a scribble of shade, a curve in the foreground where the trees stood. She worked quickly, aware of the fading light and the onset of a fractious summer storm. Far to the east, thunder rolled through the sky.

The house took her by the hand. It spurred her on, demanded every ounce of her focus. Occasionally, she would glance up, the edge of her bottom lip caught between her teeth as she committed the structure to memory in case the rain came down and made her stop.

Faster and faster she worked, her fingers flying over the page, creating something that might be an indescribable mess, but it didn't matter because this was where she felt alive, in the creation of something that had never existed before.

A petulant wind ripped at the edges of the pad, and she pressed her arm against it as the yellow light seeped into the page, leaving a sullen tinge.

The surface of the lake quivered, the willow fronds dancing to the storm's song. The first few inflated drops of rain fell.

Faye swore under her breath. She scooped everything into her bag and darted towards the house, clasping the sketch pad against her chest, needing to protect what she had just created.

The rain bounced off the ground as she ran, coming down so heavily she could see the vertical hard lines. Heat came with it, the day's warmth spat out in anger. In a few short seconds she was soaked to the skin, the outside of her sketch pad sodden too.

With a cry of frustration she hurtled across the sparsely pebbled ground in front of the house, tufts of long grass brushing against her legs. She was travelling so fast that she slipped on the wet stone steps, landing with a hard thud against the stately double doors. An echo sounded deep within the house. A latch clicked.

One of the doors opened a few inches. Faye raised herself to her feet, rubbing her knee where the edge of a step had grazed it.

She pushed the door with her fingertips, caught in that space between curiosity and the awareness she was trespassing. Beyond the door stood a vast hallway cloaked in shadow, any light eaten by the filth on the windows. She peered inside, the sketch pad still clutched to her chest. The rain changed direction, driving against her back.

Faye made a split-second decision, slipping inside as thunder boomed over the roof of the house. She felt the vibrations deep in her chest, the hair on her arms standing to attention.

Placing her sketch pad and bag on a dust-covered chair between the door and a window, she took a few hesitant steps forward. No one lived here, that was obvious. It wouldn't hurt to stay a little while.

A grand staircase rose from the hallway, sweeping up in a palatial curve, dried leaves scattered on its lower stairs. A huge chandelier hung to the right side of the staircase, the remains of tapered candles festooned in shreds of thick cobwebs. The wall on the same side housed a tall, stone fireplace, its hearth empty of all but memories.

A shadow-heavy gloom filled the hallway, as though any light present had been sucked into the darkness. A bright fork of overhead lightning interrupted that gloom, but even though the brilliance illuminated the blackness, it failed to penetrate it.

Another boom of thunder. It echoed down the chimney, rolling through the house.

The door clicked shut behind her in a sudden squall of wind that rattled the glass in the windows. And as she turned, she caught a glimmer of light reflected in that glass.

The same light she had seen in the lake.

Faye's soaked clothes stuck to her skin and she shivered. She didn't like it in here, but it didn't make sense to go out in the storm.

From somewhere up above, a floorboard creaked. She held her breath. *Old places do this* she told herself, taking a few tentative steps. Now that her eyes had become accustomed to the lack of light, she could see the curve of the staircase as it looped back on itself, the upper gallery enticingly visible through the balustrade rails.

Slowly, Faye edged towards the bottom of the staircase.

Hard wax puddles smeared the lower steps. Her wet feet left damp imprints in the dust. She scrubbed her toe along the floor, clearing a small arc. Black and white squares, like a chessboard, appeared through the grime.

She craned her neck to see a little bit further, her gaze rising to what hung on the wall at the top of the stairs. An ornate gilt-edged mirror.

Faye hesitated. Was she brave enough to creep upstairs? It would only take a minute. There was nothing to stop her. Only that scatter of pinpricks on her skin raised either by the cold or fear of the unknown.

A blast of rain battered against the door and Faye jumped, her heart leaping into her throat.

Run to the first landing, an inner voice challenged her, just like it had done when she was little and was scared of the dark. Even though then it had been more of *close the wardrobe door and be back in bed by the time you count to three.*

Wetting her bottom lip with her tongue, she took a deep breath and sprinted up the first flight of steps. She paused on the landing and turned to look at the door, at the pale shape of her sketch pad on the chair. Her eyes found her damp footprints. And then they found the dry ghosts of more.

But where hers were close together, these were far apart. She slowly turned her head to the next flight of stairs, curving past the huge mirror. Footmarks on those steps, but not on every one.

Someone else had been here. Someone had been running.

Another blinding flash of lightning, followed by a clap of thunder so loud it made Faye's eardrums ring. The staircase stood out in stark relief as the shadows retreated, and for one brief moment the upstairs gallery was filled with white light.

And there, reflected in the old mirror, was the face she had seen in the forest.

SIXTEEN

The boy watched the woman creeping up the stairs, her image cast back to where he stood, shrouded in shadow in the doorway of what had once been a guest bedroom. Behind him in the gloom, a four-poster bed canopied in moth-eaten, pale blue silk, a filthy blue-and-gold rug in front of the hearth. Ruined, like everything else in Barrington Hall.

He knew her scent already, and it was ripe here, rounded with fear.

The woman paused at the curve of the stairs. Her eyes darted to the mirror. He froze, halting his breath as if that might make him invisible. Part of him wanted her to continue, but a bigger part wanted her to run like hell.

He knew what it meant when you crept inside this house. The terrible line that you crossed. He knew that to his own cost.

He saw her gaze fall to the stairs, wet hair curling against the pale column of her throat. The line of her collar bones stood out under the thin fabric of her t-shirt. *Little girl lost,* came a whisper against his ear. A glimmer of blue in the corner of his vision.

A flash of lightning arced across the windows and he flinched, sinking into a crouch with his hands over his ears. *One, two, three, four,* he counted in his head, stealing himself for the crack of thunder as it resounded through the roof. The rain hammered down onto the slate tiles. Insistent. Merciless.

The boy opened his mouth, inhaling great gulps of air, riding the fear as it coursed through his blood.

Because it doesn't matter if you know a thing can't hurt you; if it lives in your head, it has teeth.

Then he heard the sound of her feet on the stairs. Running.

He was happy that she was. But scared of what would leave with her. Because one thing was for certain. If you entered Barrington Hall, you never left alone.

The great door slammed behind her, the noise echoing through the empty house. But it wasn't truly empty. He could feel them, stirring.

He wanted to go to the window, to watch her as she ran, but the rain was a wild beast pummelling against the glass, driven by the ruthless wind. They wouldn't let him out tonight. Because the hunt would provide no amusement when he wouldn't run.

The boy crept along the hallway. Strips of mouldering wallpaper hung like flayed skin from the walls. He looked over the stair rail, saw her wet footprints in the dust. And something else.

He padded down the wide stairs as thunder rolled across the valley. Rain lashed against the doors and he closed his eyes, willing his fear to settle for just a few seconds. A gust of wind rattled down the chimney, scattering sooty dust and ancient cobweb fragments along the entrance-hall floor.

And then, as storms sometimes do, it took a deep breath.

He sprinted forward, snatched hold of the tote bag on the chair, his hand closing over the edge of the sketch pad. The scent of rain crawled into his throat and he whimpered, skidding back the way he had come, his prizes clutched in his hands.

At the top of the staircase, by the old mirror, he sat and opened the bag, withdrew the contents slowly. He ran his fingers over the label on the water bottle, carefully unscrewed the lid, inhaled the wet, fresh smell of the water within. But this was good water. He took a deep draft, the chill running down his throat.

He opened the small oblong tin, a nest of charcoal stubs inside. He unzipped the suede case, let his fingers run over the soft fabric, removing the pencils one by one. He did this all slowly, reverently, savouring each moment, these little treasures that had fallen into his hands. The boy in the mirror did the same, although he did not see the look of wonder on that face.

At the bottom of the bag was something he didn't recognise. It was small, with a glass screen. He shook it but it didn't rattle. Raised rubber buttons sat along its long edges and at the bottom three different-shaped holes. He had no idea what it was but it must have been important to the woman if she had brought it with her.

The sketch pad he left to the end, on purpose. He had seen it on her knee the night he had stood on the edge of the forest, her slight frame curled up on the window sill. She had no idea what watched her from the roof, but the creature knew he was there. Its displeasure was palpable.

Slowly, he opened the pad and leafed through the pages. The sketches were all in black and white, some done in faint pencil, the detail within them taking his breath away. Here was a cat, lying in the sun, patches of light striping its fur. Here was a dying flower, its head drooped, a single leaf still clinging to its stem.

Others were done in the charcoal stubs from the tin. These were heavier, the lines more sure of themselves, but angry, as though whatever she held inside was escaping through her fingers. But the heaviness wasn't clumsy. Each line had a purpose, a part of the whole. And that whole was beautiful.

He found the page from the night he had first seen her. Knew she'd only caught a glimpse of him before he was pulled away. Strong vertical lines, created swiftly, smudges of charcoal as she'd crafted the tops of the trees impatiently, all the time her eyes searching for the tiniest hint of movement. And there he was in the gloom, his face gazing up, pale against the darkness. Hollow eyes and dishevelled hair, his clothes hanging on a gaunt frame. Only a few lines of charcoal on a blank piece of paper. But she had caught him there, as surely as if she had laid out her own snare.

He shivered. But he was strangely touched.

He turned over the next sheet of paper, the one still damp from her dash into the house.

Whilst the sketch before had been a simple affair, this one was blunt and dark and brooding. The charcoal was heavy, the lines sharp and unforgiving. And from out of this temper rose the black hulk of Barrington Hall. Thunder clouds rolled over its roof, the windows not quite dark, like half closed eyelids.

The boy's heart began to race as he stared at the detail. At the house that was both his prison and the only place that held the tattered shreds of his safety.

His fingers hovered over the sketch, one part in particular making the hairs rise across his skin.

One of the great doors was open, and if he looked closely, he could see the noose hanging from the chandelier.

SEVENTEEN

The late-afternoon sun warmed Dan's arm through his rolled-down window. He passed the place where the deer had been, all that remained a few scraps of fur in a dark red smudge. A flush of heat bloomed on his cheeks.

The drive into the village took longer than he expected, as a road was closed due to resurfacing and he had to follow a diversion. But shortly after five, he left his car by the post office, pulling out one of the letters he had received from Albert. He walked for a few minutes, looking down side streets for the address on the letterhead. Eventually, Dan pulled out his phone and brought up his map app, but the page refused to load.

'Those things don't work too well here.' A voice came from behind him and he turned to see a small woman with wispy grey hair, her lips covered in the brightest red lipstick Dan had ever seen. A tiny dog at her feet looked up at him through a fringe of hair.

'I'm sorry?' Dan went into typical British mode, apologising for something he was clueless about.

'Mobile telephones.' The woman nodded at his hand. 'It's because of the hills,' she added, her voice softening as though Dan were a small boy.

'Ah, I see.' Some part of him wanted to say his phone

worked well enough in other hilly places, but she was only trying to be friendly. 'You could help me actually.'

The woman scooped the tiny dog up. It shivered in her arms. *Rat on a lead,* he thought unkindly.

'Do you know where Hillview Avenue is?'

The woman's eyes flicked to the letterhead. 'They won't be open now, it's Wednesday.' She sighed, as though she was stating the obvious.

'I was looking for Albert Jenkins,' Dan said, his tone faltering under her shrewd scrutiny.

'Were you now?' She stroked the dog's head and it licked her hand. A long pause followed. 'You'll probably find him up by the old cottage. That's where he wanders now.'

'I own the old cottage.' Dan suddenly felt like he was missing more than a working phone. 'Lucinda Latimer was my aunt.'

Something passed over the woman's face. Pity?

'Lucy was a dear friend, and what happened to her broke my heart.' She glanced away, her fingers trembling slightly.

Dan waited, hoping she wouldn't burst into tears.

The woman sniffed and kissed the top of the dog's head. 'Just you be careful up there, young man. That cottage knows things, and you'd better be prepared to listen.'

Without another word she set off down the street, and Dan found himself rooted to the spot. He watched until she had disappeared around the corner.

That's where he wanders now. It was a strange statement. But maybe she meant Albert had a cottage somewhere in the woods? It would explain why Dan kept bumping into him there. The forest covered a huge swathe of land and Dan had only really explored a tiny part of it.

A grin tugged at the corners of his mouth as he headed off towards the small grocery store at the end of the high street.

✝

Dan approached his car, the tub of ice cream tucked under his arm, and found two people standing beside it with their backs to him. He smiled to himself. In the city his car was nothing special, but out here it was probably an impressive sight.

'You shouldn't have left it here.' A thin man, wearing a white shirt with a grimy collar, turned to him. He pointed to the road beside Dan's car. Faded painted letters by the kerb.

'Fuck it,' Dan swore. But it wasn't at the word, which he could now make out said *Private*, it was at the bright yellow wheel clamp smugly attached to his near-side front tyre.

Dan hadn't noticed the faded letters, but he was parked in front of a battered wooden gate that led to the rear of the post office.

'This is bloody ridiculous!'

The woman accompanying the man tutted at Dan. 'Now, now, young man, that's not going to get you anywhere.'

Which was true. But if there's anything more annoying than seeing your car clamped, it was someone rubbing your nose in it. And it was the second time Dan had been addressed as 'young man.' Both times he could almost hear the word *outsider* behind it.

'You'll need to ring Porter's, and Jem will come out. After you pay up, of course.' This from the man who was grinning from ear to ear as though Dan's predicament was the funniest thing he'd seen all month.

Dan took a deep breath and fixed his gaze on a crack in the pavement. He concentrated on the chill of the ice cream against his skin, willing it to diffuse his anger.

'It's Wednesday. Jem only works half day on a Wednesday.' The woman inclined her head like a blackbird looking at a worm. 'You'll have to leave it here, and come back tomorrow.'

'I'm sure that's not legal.' Dan forced his voice through gritted teeth. Wednesday was becoming a word that was rapidly pissing him off.

'Legal or not, that's what goes here. If you break the rules, you pay.'

Dan raised his eyes and met her resolute gaze. For a brief moment it didn't sound like she was talking about the car.

The couple walked off without another word, leaving Dan speechless and seething on the pavement. He crouched and took a photo of the offending clamp, then rang the number painted on it. He wasn't surprised when the call failed to connect.

Okay, Dan, you can do this. It's not the end of the world. In the scheme of things it was only an irritation, but he had promised Faye ice cream and by the time he walked back through the woods it would be pink sludge.

The oddness of the day grated against his skull as he made his way down the high street, past the war memorial and the iron bike racks, past the pub with the odd name The Wet Whistle, past the little houses with only the narrow pavement separating them from the road.

He crossed the old brewery yard, now deserted apart from the tufts of grass pushing through the dirt, the weathered barrels still stacked by one of the huge doors. He climbed over the fence at the other side, remembering how he used to vault it with ease.

From here, the edge of the forest beckoned him in, early evening light slanting through the trees, bird song alive in the branches.

The sun was warm on the back of his neck, his feet quiet on the dusty ground. As he got further in, the track narrowed as the undergrowth spilled out hungrily to claim it.

Not many people came this way.

And that one fact alone had Dan glancing over his shoulder. Which was absolutely crazy. This wasn't the middle of the night with the wind howling. But still Dan had the strangest feeling he was being watched. That there were eyes in the trees, in the bushes—sly eyes with a knowing glint.

Eyes that had been waiting for him to come home.

EIGHTEEN

Faye fled from the house, fear flying like a cloak in her wake. She heard the door slam against the wall but she didn't dare look back. Every childhood nightmare she'd ever had danced in her head, the images all running together in a coagulated, hellish mess. Squalls of rain splattered against her skin, but the storm had cried itself out now and the sky was beginning to lighten.

A sharp pain creased her side as she sprinted along the side of the lake and she had to stop for a moment, the sound of her own heartbeat thundering in her ears. The earthy scent of petrichor hung in the air.

'Crap!' The word flew from her mouth in a wail as she realised what she had forgotten.

Diluted sunlight seeped through a bank of melancholy cloud, washing across the windows of the house.

Faye knew she would have to return at some point. But that point wasn't today. She was too jittery and too angry for too many things. Forgetting her bag and sketch pad. Going into the house in the first place. Losing Toby. A scream tore out of her throat. It echoed over the water, a startled bird fleeing through the reeds.

She couldn't shake off the face she had seen in the mirror. Those haunted, hollow eyes. Her heart ached. No one should have to live in a place like that.

The early evening sun warmed her back as she made her way through the forest, drying the damp clothes clinging to her skin. Her curls sprang into coils against her cheek as she followed the path. Thirst lay heavy on her tongue.

The copse of trees with the wigwam came into view. Again, that eerie, silent heaviness she had felt before. The angle of the sun didn't pierce the gloom here. A shiver tripped across her skin and she quickened her pace.

But the path ended abruptly in a tangle of thorns and bracken. She paused, her mouth twisting. She didn't remember coming this way, but yet she had because the wigwam was there. Unless there was more than one.

Faye glanced around and found a small windfall branch with a pointed end. She picked it up and stabbed at the undergrowth. A fly buzzed against her ear and she swatted it aside impatiently. She took a few steps forwards; thorns snagged in her hair as she stamped on the trailing brambles. The needle-pointed ends left red scratches that itched like crazy.

The fly returned. And this time it had brought friends.

But Faye had come too far to go back, and she was running on the remnants of panic and the need to get home before Dan returned from the village. She couldn't face explaining where she'd been or why she'd wanted to do it.

The flies buzzed against her ears and eyes and she swore at their persistence. Part of her wanted to sit down and cry. A simple walk through the woods to draw a picture. And she had managed to turn it into something from a disaster movie.

Curses spilled from her lips as she pushed on through the mass of creeping, razor-edged brambles. Her hair stuck to her face, other strands caught in the claws of the thorns as she fought, making painfully slow progress through the dense undergrowth. A smell arose beyond the tangle, sour and rich. It made her want to recoil but there was no way she was stopping now.

With a cry of triumph, Faye burst into a clearing of mottled sunlight.

What she could smell lay before her under the shelter of a solid oak. A rabbit caught in a snare, its eye eaten away. And then she saw why the flies were there. The snare had caught the rabbit by its hind leg, the wire ripping through fur and muscle, exposing wet, pink tissue. And the flies were feasting.

Faye froze in horror, her hand clasped over her mouth. She had never seen anything so wild. So cruel.

She forced her eyes away, even though part of her was caught up in the morbid curiosity of studying death up close.

In her peripheral vision a small flap of paper wafted in the breeze. There was something pinned to the tree bark.

Faye stepped over the rabbit, gingerly. The cloud of flies rose from its ravaged body in an angry mass. Her hand trembled as she reached to flatten the note.

A gift. It's not much. Hope you find it.

The words were scrawled in a spidery hand as though they'd been written quickly. Or in the dark.

Disgust curled her lips into a grimace.

Dan's idyllic childhood home was a place where people stuffed dead animals and put them behind glass, and left mangled rabbits as gifts.

She stepped back, carefully, and tried to find her bearings in the trees. A fly landed on her arm and she glanced down to see it lapping at the blood from a deep scratch.

Revulsion rose in her throat and she wafted it away. A deep-seated anger followed as it came back for a second course.

Her heel caught on something solid half-buried in the grass and she stumbled. At first she thought it was just an odd-shaped moss-covered rock. But as she knelt down beside it, and ran her fingers over the worn stone surface, the realisation of what it was chased away all thoughts about the fly.

It was a small grave.

But it was a weird place for a gravestone, out in the middle of the woods, away from everything.

The name was completely masked by green fur, and Faye felt a sudden pang of grief. *Forgotten.* The word scraped along her heart.

She wondered who would look after Toby's grave when she and Dan were dead, and the thought he could become one of the lost made tears prick at the back of her eyes.

Dry twigs cracked under her shins as she smoothed her hand over the stone, the moss soothing against her fingertips. The sun dipped further behind the trees.

She bowed her head and closed her eyes, tried to find some peace from the bewilderment of her thoughts.

A bird chattered in a nearby tree, the harsh call of danger, and she opened her eyes to find a blackbird watching her from above, its bill sunflower gold amidst the green.

A wave of weariness settled in her limbs. Between her fingers were little lines of scratched-off moss, her nails coated in the same colour. She glanced up at the gravestone. To the name she had uncovered. But where it had once been was only crumbled stone, the knowledge of it dust on her fingers.

Underneath where the name would have been were more letters. She leaned in and squinted, focussed her eyes on the worn inscription, letting one finger trail across them.

Mons...

That's all it said, the rest wiped away by time and unmerciful seasons.

Dusting off her hands, she stood. Remorse uncurled itself like a sleeping snake in her stomach. She felt like she had almost desecrated this lonely stone, had scraped away what it had gathered over the decades, destroying its protection.

On a whim she looked around, avoiding the mangled remains of the fly-coated rabbit. A patch of wildflowers nestled under a sprawl of feathery ferns. She plucked a few and gathered them together with a strand of long grass, laying the posy at the foot of the stone as a kind of peace offering.

A breeze swept across her skin and she shivered. The approach of twilight hovered just beyond the trees.

As Faye walked away, she paused, glancing over her shoulder. 'I hope I helped,' she whispered. 'You're not forgotten.'

She set off in what she hoped was the right direction, finding a narrow track that wound its way to a wider one. The unsettling events of the past few hours churned in her gut as she walked.

A strange, confused elation flooded through her as she came across the charred shell of the lightning tree. It seemed to be too close, as though the forest had done what it needed to do and was now letting her leave. Which was a frankly ridiculous thought. Faye chastised herself verbally.

Ten minutes later the thatch of the cottage came into view, and Faye had never been so glad to see a sign of civilisation

There was no car parked by the gate as she stepped out

of the wood. Dan wasn't back yet, which was probably a good thing. She didn't want to have to explain.

Faye pushed open the gate, ducking under the line of sunflowers. She stopped for a moment to glance back into the trees. A glint of blue in the darkness. Or maybe it was a trick of the setting sun as it speared through the leaves.

She lifted the latch on the door, realising she'd never locked it when she left. A page from an old picture book flooded her thoughts, one of Toby's favourites. A family of mice gambolling outside a cottage much like this one, silver bells jingling on their tails. *Country folk don't lock their doors.*

As she entered the hallway, the awful thought loomed: maybe the reason why, was because whatever was out there, would always find a way in.

✠

Silence hummed against Faye's ears in the shady coolness of the hallway. She wasn't used to how loud it sounded. There was no TV here. Not even an old radio. How had Lucinda passed the time all by herself in the middle of nowhere, with only those awful creatures in the case for company?

The door to her room stood slightly open. A crease formed on the bridge of Faye's nose. Hadn't it been shut when she left?

She pushed it fully open and that same scent of bitter green wafted across to greet her.

A knitting bag sat on the seat of the rocking chair. A ball of white wool poked out of the top. Faye eased the handles of the bag apart and the ball tumbled onto the floor.

Faye froze. She half expected to see some kind of ghost filled with disapproval, but there was nothing but the evening sunlight raising dust motes in the air.

She scooped the wool from the floor and started to wind the loose thread back onto the ball. Her brow furrowed. Intricate knots had been tied along the length of the wool at even intervals. She pulled out more balls. Her fingers skimmed the threads. They were exactly the same.

Faye didn't know much about knitting but she was sure knots weren't involved.

She sat on the chair with the bag on her lap and delved down into its contents. Embroidery thread, a few thimbles, a scattering of mismatched buttons.

Something sharp bit deep and she yelped. A droplet of blood welled from her thumb. She sucked it off, grimaced at the copper tang on her tongue.

Faye tipped the bag upside down and a rain of needles tumbled out. The one that had pricked her was easy to find. It was very thin, one end honed to a dagger-like tip.

Her eyes snapped up to stare at the glass case in the corner. All of the shiny eyes stared back.

The needle was the same as the one piercing whatever was hidden in the moss and logs at the bottom of the case.

Faye stood and walked slowly across, the taste of her own blood alive in her mouth. Dust smeared the glass, making the creatures inside look like they were shrouded in mist. She stood on tiptoe and ran her fingers along the top of the case, looking for the edge of a lid.

She dragged a hard-backed chair from the corner, climbing onto its seat. Now she could see much more clearly. The case was sealed completely. Like a tomb. Whatever was in there was in there for keeps. She rubbed the bottom of her t-shirt across the dust, clearing a wide arc, and peered down onto the stage of dead animals and birds.

From here she could see the tip of the small knitting needle poking out from the moss in the corner of the case, and as Faye's eyes became accustomed to the shade, she thought she could make out the edge of a translucent wing. But it was too big for an insect.

A final shaft of sunlight pierced the leaded panes of the window as the sun found a valley through the trees, illuminating the case in a sudden golden glow. The creatures inside became sharper. The inside of a mouse ear as pink as a conch shell. The pale fluff under the tail of the rabbit as white as snow.

But under the needle, amidst the moss, another colour sparked into life. A tiny blur of kingfisher blue.

What she kept seeing gnawed away at the edges of her mind. At the lake. In the house. And now here. Far too much for coincidence.

Fairies. The logic of adulthood laughed in her face.

She leaned across the top of the glass case, tried to see if there was any way in through the back. After all, someone had put these things in here. Her fingertips grazed what she thought might be a tiny hinge. She stood on tiptoe, stretched for a few more millimetres. And felt the chair moving backwards.

Fear lurched in the pit of her stomach as she tried to grab hold of anything to stop her from sliding. That moment of freeze frame as everything slowed around her.

The front door slammed shut and Dan's voice called out, just as the chair toppled over and sent her crashing to the floor.

NINETEEN

It had taken Dan nearly two hours to walk through the forest to the cottage. He'd walked around and around in circles, each time sure the path he was on would lead him back home.

Home. The word stuck in his throat. The cottage no longer felt like it had done when he was a boy. It felt suffocating, as though it wanted to pull him in and crush all the air from his lungs. Which was bloody ridiculous. But still the feeling hovered.

He was so thirsty he'd tried to drink the strawberry pink sludge that used to be ice cream. But all that had done was thicken his thirst. He'd tossed the container into the undergrowth, and in his mind's eye Aunt Lucinda shook her head at his littering.

Dan had actually thrust his fist into the air as the cottage came into view. He'd had a fucked-up and miserable day and all he wanted was a couple of pints of water and to forget any of this had happened.

He pushed open the door, called Faye's name. And was met by a deafening crash.

Dan flew into the room, his eyes taking in the scene before him. Faye was sprawled on the floor, blood pouring from her nose, a chair on its side against the wall. It didn't take a genius to know what she'd been doing, and inside his head he screamed.

'Jesus, Faye!' He rushed towards her, his heartbeat cartwheeling in his chest. Her hands were over her face. Blood oozed between her fingers. Dan forced down the vomit rising in his throat. 'Hold on, I'll get ice. Pinch the bridge of your nose and tip your head back.' Christ, that wasn't right. 'No, pinch the soft part of your nose and lean forwards.' Faye's eyes met his, filled with exasperation. That was a good thing. He didn't care if she thought he was an idiot.

He sprinted into the kitchen and tore open the yellowed door of the old fridge. There were no ice cubes in the tiny ice box, just a built-up deep coating inside it. He yanked open a kitchen drawer, fishing for a knife, then used it to prise a small pile of ice shavings from the box.

Grabbing a tea towel, he scooped the shavings into it and sped back to Faye.

She was on her feet, leaning against the glass case. Her face was ashen. Dan eased his arm around her shoulders and pressed the makeshift ice pack to her face.

'What the hell were you doing?'

She mumbled something incoherently through the mass of tea towel jammed up against her nose.

Dan's eyes swept over the case. Everything looked the same. He didn't understand his own train of thought. It was filled with stuffed long-dead creatures, why the hell wouldn't it look the same?

With a final backward glance, he led his wife into the kitchen and pulled out a chair. The urn with Lucinda's ashes stared up at him reproachfully.

Faye lowered the tea towel from her face, the bloodied cloth held in her hand. Dan tried hard not to look.

'I think it's stopped now.' Her voice was thick and congested. A pink lump marred the pale skin of her temple.

Dan's mouth had dried to the texture of sandpaper. 'Do you feel sick? Or dizzy?'

She shook her head, then winced. 'I feel stupid.'

Dan sat on the chair opposite, his hand resting on her arm. His eyes fell on the green tinge around her nails. He asked the question again, tried to keep his voice level. 'What were you doing?'

Her eyes met his and there was something there he couldn't read.

Tell me a lie, he thought. *Just don't tell me you were trying to get inside that case.*

A flush of anger prickled across his skin. But it wasn't anger at her silence; it was anger at himself for not being here to protect her.

A pounding ache began a war dance in his head.

Dan pushed his chair away. He rifled through a kitchen drawer in the vain hope there might be headache tablets lurking, and then remembered that Lucinda had only ever used herbal remedies. Of course, he did have tablets, but they were back in his car. His clamped car. He groaned, resting his brow against a cupboard door.

'Did you ever go inside Barrington Hall?' Faye's sudden question made him wheel. The throbbing in his skull screamed at the sudden motion.

Her hands rested in her lap as she waited for an answer. Dan had longed for this moment, longed for her to show some interest in life again. But dear God, not about that house.

He leaned back against the worktop, folded his arms, tried to be nonchalant. 'I did once. We were swimming in the lake and it started to rain, right out of nowhere. A real sudden thunderstorm.' He laughed, and to his ears, there was a touch of madness there. 'I don't know why we even went in—we were wet already.' There was something he was missing, curled inside the mist of his memories.

Faye sat forward, clasping the bloodied cloth in her hands, her lips slightly parted, hanging on to his every word.

Dan paused and a heavy silence ticked away between them.

'My car was clamped in the village.' Dan steered the conversation in a different direction. 'I swear this place has it in for me.'

'Did anything funny happen?' She traced a knot in the wood on the table top with her finger, his last comment ignored. 'I mean, when you were in the house.'

The sound he'd heard arose from his memory, leeching all the warmth from his body.

'Why do you ask?' His eyes locked to hers. And she glanced away. And then he knew exactly what she had been doing.

Robert McCallum's words echoed in his head.

'I think I'll go lie down.' She pushed back her chair, dropping the bloodied tea towel into the sink.

Just for one moment there had been a connection, the chasm between them narrowing to something Dan felt they could negotiate without losing any more of themselves in the process. But the irony of it was the thing that might bring them closer, was the thing Dan wanted to protect her from.

TWENTY

The boy lay sprawled on the filthy library floor. His fingers flicked through an aging nature book. The edges of the pages were mottled with brown, damp to the touch, the watercolours a pale imitation of their former glory. He paused at an illustration showing three plump sparrows in a honeysuckle bush, the pale yellow a beautiful contrast to their mouse-brown plumage. Someone had once told him these little birds carried the souls of the recently deceased to heaven.

Now he often wondered if they carried souls to hell too, and that's why he could hear them calling from the jagged rooftop.

He closed the book and jabbed the paltry fire he had managed to light in the hearth with the end of an iron poker. It wouldn't last long; Corrigan would make him douse it. But he did it anyway.

He stood, watching the small flames as they licked at the kindling he had salvaged from the forest. The image of the woman on the stairs danced across his mind, along with the sketch she had drawn. She had somehow seen the deranged history of Barrington Hall, had peeled back its rotted layers and exposed its ungodly bones.

He had smelled her despair, her loneliness. She was looking for something to hold onto. And maybe that's why

Barrington Hall had opened itself to her, spinning its web until she was hopelessly entangled.

The boy envied her freedom. The fact that she could wander at her pleasing.

He couldn't go further than the edge of the woods. It was as if the blood in his veins drained away. His strength dissolved, leaving only mute despair clinging to his tongue.

But he had tried. Oh yes, he had tried. Back at the beginning when he had managed to race on ahead of their hunting pack. Visions of bursting out from the trees, to batter on the door of the cottage *Let me in, let me in, I promise I'll be good.*

What hope he had nurtured, clasped in his hand, like a quivering heartbeat.

A tight smile appeared on his face. He held his dirty hand out to the flame. Let the heat creep into his fingertips.

A sound came from the hallway, filtering through the damp air. The squeak of metal. He drifted to the door, glanced down into the darkness, following the slow screech of the doll's carriage on its nightly journey. Sometimes he caught a glimpse of her face hidden behind the dark veil.

The boy shivered. It was pointless to follow her; she was as trapped as he was.

It was full dark now, the air thick with the night song of the forest, and the storm had dwindled, although he could still hear angry rumbles of thunder over the hills. But he did not have the stomach for the chase tonight, despite the hunger gnawing at his belly.

He slipped into another room, his feet making no sound on the moth-eaten carpet. A peeling harpsichord stood on a rotted rug, a mildewed velvet chair with curved Queen Anne legs by its keys.

Some nights its lonely refrain vibrated through the empty rooms.

The boy crossed to the window where the heavy drapes hung, stiff with dust and decay. Outside, the black film of the lake devoured the light of the moon.

His fingers curled, resting against the old glass, his mind a turmoil of half-formed pictures, like a story from a dream. There were ghosts here and one was his memory.

Agitation itched under his skin. Something felt different. Something was stirring within the walls of this cursed house.

Ever since he had seen the woman in the cottage, the edges of what he perceived had twisted. There were distant images behind them, a tantalising glimpse of another world. Another time.

He couldn't remember being anywhere else but here, but he knew the scent of change. The scent of a world collapsing.

He closed his eyes, the sound of Corrigan's wings against the walls of the corridor shifting the weariness from his bones.

What would he give to be free? The question dangled in front of his eyes like the shadow of the noose that sometimes hung over the great hall.

And the answer arose from the little pot of hope he kept locked inside his heart, that small part of him that was still the boy who looked for fairies in the wood.

Anything.

TWENTY-ONE

Faye awoke as the dream crashed down in her head. She fought to hang on to the threads, because it had been about Toby, and he was right there, rolling his eyes at something she said, a slice of half-eaten toast in his hand. His bed-head hair, so like hers, was all curls and tangles, half over his face, and that grin she knew would break a thousand hearts, played on his lips.

The dream dissolved into nothingness as dreams always do, and she was left with the edge of the sheet clutched between her fingers.

She hadn't been home on the day that gutted her life. Dan was working from the study by the front door and she was out running errands—queuing at the post office, irritated by the fact a man at the counter was taking an age to write a customs label—when her son closed the door for the last time. She hadn't been there to pull Toby into a hug, to tell him to send a quick text if he decided to change his plans.

But it wasn't his choice to change. The car had pulled out from a junction as Toby crossed the road. Eye witnesses said the driver was on the phone. Eye witnesses said that the crunch of splintered bones as Toby was flung over the bonnet and onto the road was something they would never forget.

Silent tears rolled down her face. Dan was the last one to

see their son and she couldn't forgive him for that. She had seen the guilt in his eyes as she'd asked him first what Toby's last words were, and then whether Dan had even talked to him before he slipped out of their lives forever.

From the room across the corridor, Dan's gentle snores split the silence. Her lips tightened. Why should he be able to sleep so easily?

Faye swung her legs out of bed. Through the window the glint of a thousand stars and the cold light of an almost-full thunder moon. She padded across and hopped onto the sill, pulling her knees to her chest. The window was open, the night air cool against her skin. *Keep it closed,* Dan had said, and there was something about his eyes as the words left his mouth. Something that might have been fear.

A movement in the tree line at the edge of the woods. Faye fixed her eyes on the spot, reaching for her sketch pad then realising it was back at the old house. This time it definitely wasn't the stag. This time the blurred shape had more distinct edges. And she could swear she could hear the tinkling of a bell.

Her hand flew to her mouth as, for the briefest of moments, the shape became a boy. A boy who had the same build as her son.

Her heart leapt, then settled into a pattering frenzy, but as quickly as he had appeared, he was gone.

She jumped down from the sill, raced across the room, clattering down the stairs, not caring if she woke Dan, every fibre of her being concentrating on getting to where she had seen the figure. Her fingers fumbled on the bolt on the door as she tried to slide it free. At last it gave, and she was out, running barefoot down the path under the sunflowers.

Through the gate and across the small patch of land between the cottage and the woods, logic warring with her heart-hope that, somehow, this was her son returned to her.

Tiny stones and twigs dug into the soles of her feet as she stumbled across to the edge of the wood. The space where he had been was empty.

She called his name and sent it spinning like a prayer into the darkness. But the rush of the night breeze in the trees was her only answer.

She stood in the dark with her son's name on her lips, and the cottage of her husband's childhood summers at her back. Everything good lived in the past. A sob caught in her throat, despair digging its claws into the hope she had dared to hold aloft.

Faye took a couple of steps into the inky gloom of the woods, only a couple of steps yet the forest seemed to close in around her.

She took a few steps more. Everything was black and deep like the very bottom of the ocean. Faye was aware of her own tiny insignificance in a world where other things breathed. Something rustled in the undergrowth and then darted away. Gradually, her eyes adjusted to the darkness, the deep black becoming shades and shadows. A large, gnarled oak stood about ten feet away with something pale at its base. Faye crept across, wincing as twigs and acorn cups dug into her feet. A cluster of tiny mushrooms nestled at the foot of the giant tree. Bright red domes with pale speckles. *A fairy village.* The memory came sweeping back, brushed away the years, and, for a moment, she was a small girl, lying on her front with her eyes fixed, waiting for that first glimpse of magic...

She remembered reading Toby stories, curled up on her

knee with his thumb lodged in his mouth, his damp baby curls fresh from a bath, tickling her skin.

Anger flared, lodged behind the lump in her throat. The naïve beliefs of an innocent girl did not belong in the real world. The real world had teeth and claws and wasn't afraid to use them to grind you down into a minced-up version of who you had once been.

In her peripheral vision something pale shifted. Panic seared through her veins. She stumbled backwards and landed heavily on the clump of mushrooms, smashing them into a slimy pulp.

The destruction of a dream clung to her fingers.

The something pale wasn't the boy. It wasn't a stalker hell-bent on cutting her throat. Swinging from a branch, as though it had grown there, was the bag she had left at Barrington Hall.

$$+$$

Faye closed the cottage door behind her, sliding the bolt into its catch. She cast a glance up the stairs, almost sure she'd see Dan at the top.

She tiptoed to the kitchen and cupped her hands under the cold water tap, splashing her face. Her stomach was a nervous mass of startled butterflies. If this were a dream, right about now would be a good place to wake up.

What had she seen in the forest? A figment of her own imagination? But her bag was proof someone had been there. And she knew now that the figure she had glimpsed had not been her son. It was the boy from Barrington Hall.

She clutched the back of one of the kitchen chairs, her knuckles white.

A shaft of moonlight cast a pale glow through the

window, diamond-shaped patterns painting the table. Faye reached out with one hand, sliding her fingers across its surface. The wood was uneven under her fingertips, tiny ridges and hollows from decades of use. Her fingers closed around the urn.

Inside was all that remained of the woman who had lived here. Flesh and blood and bones reduced to a handful of ash.

The patch of moonlight darkened for an instant and Faye wheeled, her eyes to the window, her nerves rubbed raw from her strange encounter.

But only the creeping ivy tendrils moved in the night breeze.

Carefully, she released the urn, turning to the door that led to the stairs, the tote bag clutched to her chest. The staircase was in darkness and she didn't want to flick on the light, in case it woke Dan. She didn't want to tell him about the fleeting glimpse of the boy, because she knew he wouldn't believe her.

Her hand brushed over the pitted, painted wall as she edged her way up, the old boards cool under her feet.

Three steps from the top, the hair stood on end in the nape of her neck. She turned, eyes wide, the bitter scent of green floating towards her.

A slow creak breathed into the darkness. The door to Lucinda's room.

Faye shot into her bedroom. She banged the door closed so quickly a rain of plaster fell behind the stout wall. Her fingers trembled as she slid the latch home, her heart lodged somewhere in her throat.

Backing away from the door, she listened, honing every ounce of her concentration into one sense.

But only silence sang in the air around her.

She waited for Dan to shout out. He must have heard the door slam. But all was quiet. Faye's eyes flicked to the window, remembering Dan's insistence about keeping it closed. Moths, he had said. But now she knew he didn't mean moths at all.

Something had happened here all of those years ago.

But, if that were true, why had he brought her here? A sob rose in her throat and she let it free. A tiny noise in the world of night. The darkness swallowed it with starving jaws.

She grabbed the window handle and pulled it closed. Or tried to. It banged against the frame, refusing to sit inside it like a stubborn child. She tried again, desperate.

With a final yelp of frustration, she pushed it away and sent it hurtling back against the outside wall. The night air cooled her flushed skin and she found herself scanning the forest, feeling the pull of its ancient bones. It was majorly messed-up when being out there in the dark seemed safer than staying where she was.

There was still no sound from across the hall. Dan wasn't a sound sleeper; she'd heard him many times tossing and turning as he muttered through his dreams. But tonight he was sleeping like a dead man. The thought grabbed hold and squeezed. She crossed her arms across her chest and hugged her elbows, telling herself not to be so stupid.

Her eyes fell on her headphones, lying in a tangle on the bottom of the bed. She could escape, imagine she was tucked up at home with the city humming its night song under her window.

But what good would hiding do now?

Faye climbed up onto the old bed with its sagging mattress. The one Dan had slept on as a boy. She longed to ask him what had happened. But he had clammed up in the kitchen after she'd fallen off the chair. When she had finally tried to reach out.

She needed to find out what was inside the glass case and why it was there.

That flash of blue, which seemed to haunt this place.

Faye stuffed a pillow behind her and sat back against the headboard. She pulled her bag into her lap. The canvas was still damp, smeared with mud.

She drew out her sketch pad. It was open on the page of Barrington Hall, the paper slightly crinkled from the rain. Her breath halted in her throat as her eyes scanned the lines and curves, the smudges amidst the imprint of raindrops. She looked at it for a long time.

Every artist is a critic, especially of their own work, but as Faye continued to stare at what had come from her fingertips, she knew this was one of her finest pieces. The rawness of it bled like an open wound.

Because that's what she was. A matted facsimile of who she had been, going through the motions of everyday life because she didn't know any other way. She had been numb for so long it had become her normal.

But when she had seen the strange boy a small spark had ignited deep inside. She could feel it now, a tiny flickering light in her darkness.

The memory of her son lived in that flame.

TWENTY-TWO

He swims through the darkened forest, his arms circling, the pressure of cold liquid against his ears. He can see the tops of the trees rippling through the surface, but when he reaches for them, they dissolve into nothing. A mournful cry sounds far away, the noise distorted as it falls through the water. He can't breathe. Can't see any way out.

Please, don't let me die.

And then he is floating upwards as the sun's rays spike through the surface, floating towards two great doors, the blackness beyond as deep as a grave.

Dan's fingers clawed at his pillow as he awoke, gasping for air. Sweat trickled down his back as he fought with the remnants of his dream, as it hovered at the edges of his consciousness, its reality a thing that was both present and ever fading.

'Fuck.' He wiped his sweating palms on the sheet and swung his legs out of bed. Hanging his head, he willed his heartbeat to stop its rapid trip hammer.

He hadn't expected to sleep after the events of the day, but he had fallen into that strange fugue between slumber and wakefulness as soon as his head hit the pillow. It felt like it did when he was on a night flight, some part of his brain still trained on the present.

He reached for the water at the side of the bed and curled his fingers around the solidity of it. Bringing the glass to his lips, he inhaled a few deep breaths, the reassuring coolness entering his lungs.

But what touched his lips as he tipped back the glass wasn't water. There was a brush of papery wings against his upper lip, and then it was there, battering against his face in a frenzied dance. Dan yelped and dropped the glass, recoiling as the moth skittered against the wall, the ceiling, every fucking place, sending his stomach into a crushing, bilious roil. He reached out for the lamp, misjudged where it was in the dark, and sent it crashing to the floor. He heard the light bulb shatter.

Dan flung himself across to the door, his fingers running frantically over the wall, looking for the toggle on the light switch. He found it.

Light flooded the room from the simple chintz-covered pendant on the ceiling, and the moth dived towards it, continuing its manic flight, happy to batter itself senseless in the process.

Dan could still feel it on his upper lip. His brain galloped into the horrific realm of it crawling in his mouth. He stood on the bare floorboards, one hand still fastened against the light switch, wondering how things could have got so ridiculously screwed up in just a couple of days.

And all the while his wife slept in the next room, which was number one on the list of screwed-up things.

He wanted to creep out and go check up on her. Open her door and peek around the corner, watch her as she slept, taking those few, brief moments to let the love swell in his heart. But he could imagine her face if she woke up and found him there.

She blamed him for Toby's death, he knew she did. And underneath it all, he blamed himself. If only he'd offered his son a lift.

Slowly, he opened the door and listened, but all was quiet.

He thought about the urn downstairs on the table. It might as well have had a huge flashing neon sign above it. Dan knew he couldn't ignore it any longer. Faye was already silently questioning him about it and he was running out of excuses to himself. And what about Albert? If he called again, what was Dan supposed to say? 'You see, Albert, it's like this. Dead things scare me senseless. So there's no way in hell I'm taking that urn and scattering what's inside. Especially in the lake, with that bloody, awful house looming over me.'

Something that might have been a laugh rose in Dan's throat. He'd spent hours trying to find his Aunt's solicitor; maybe it wouldn't be a bad thing if he did turn up.

The moth had settled itself behind the old mahogany wardrobe. Dan's throat was dry but he wasn't about to drink anything out of that glass. And now he was wide awake. He righted the lamp, and swept the shattered bulb against the skirting board with the side of his shoe.

Carefully, he crept down the stairs, wincing as the old boards shifted under his weight. The door to Lucinda's room was open. Only a little bit, just enough for the darkness inside to bleed out into the hallway. Dan was positive he had shut it before coming up to bed. He ran his tongue over his front teeth.

He crossed the kitchen, moonlight painting the old quarry tiles with a silver wash. Taking a glass from the shelf above the sink, he filled it with water and gulped it down.

Out of the silence came a terrible noise. Dan wheeled, his eyes flying to the window. Rapid movement on the track where his car had stood. The sound amplified, an awful, demonic snarling that twisted his nerves into knots and raised goosebumps all along his arms.

The gate crashed open and a blur of shapes raced up the path. Dan caught a glimpse of a tail. And then two foxes, whirling like spinning tops, crashed over the lavender border, the noise all pain-filled fury. They scattered dried leaves like confetti as they fought, tooth and claw, rolling across the cottage garden as one.

Dan moved closer, his breath fogging the lead-lighted window. A flash of white underbelly and a yelp of pain. A tangle of red fur and teeth and savagery.

They were under the apple trees at the side of the kitchen window now, whirling away from him, neither one of them willing to give in. But that awful noise still rang in Dan's ears.

He backed away from the window, watching the darkness beyond, where the forest met the track. Something was out there. He could feel it in his very marrow.

He licked his lips, his heart ramming against his ribcage as though he'd just finished a marathon. *Not a marathon, Danny. Just running away.*

The edge of the table met the base of his spine, right at the point where his nerves rested. He crumpled slightly, his elbow sweeping over the table, and even as it hit the side of the urn Dan knew it was hopeless to try and stop what was happening.

The urn toppled, rolling in a swift trajectory, then plummeted from the table like a dead bird. It crashed onto the floor, the lid flying off.

Lucinda Latimer's ashes scattered across the red tiles she had walked upon. A soft cloud billowed upwards.

The front door flew open. It crashed back against the wall and Dan crouched in terror, his fingers clinging to the edge of the table, his limbs locked in paralysis. A gust of wind hurtled in, lifting the ashes from the floor. Dan felt them hit his face as the windows rattled behind him. The blast hit the side wall of the kitchen, knocking the copper saucepans which hung over the old range, the raucous clang of metal against metal as they swung precariously.

Then all was quiet.

Dan looked around in wide-eyed horror. There was nothing left of the pile of ashes, just the urn, slowly rolling to a halt. He ran the back of his hand over his mouth, felt the grit on his lips. Gagging, he raced for the sink, throwing up a watery sludge.

The front door stood open. As he crossed the kitchen to close it, Dan paused on the threshold. There wasn't a breath of wind outside, only the pleasant chill of a summer night.

He hadn't wanted to scatter the ashes in the lake but something out there had had no intention of letting him try.

115

TWENTY-THREE

Sunlight stroked her cheek. Faye opened one eye and stretched her arms above her head, her fingers catching the carved indentations of the headboard. Soft summer warmth drifted through the open window.

Then she remembered what had happened the night before. But in the golden hue of a new dawn, the shape in the shadows almost seemed like the fragments of a dream.

Yet dreams didn't return lost property.

A gentle knock sounded on her bedroom door. It cracked open a little.

'Faye? Are you awake?'

She raised herself up onto one elbow. Dan's head peeked around the corner, his hair dishevelled, dark hollows under his eyes.

He came in and sat at the end of her bed. 'Did I wake you last night?' He rubbed his palms along his shorts. 'I went down for some water, knocked a few things over.' His smile was forced, any warmth swallowed by its closed-lip tightness.

'I went down, too.' She glanced at her bag, saw it in her mind's eye lying on the chair by the door in Barrington Hall. 'Couldn't sleep.'

'Strange rooms always do that.' Sweat trickled down the side of his face. 'I have to go into the village and see about getting my car unclamped. But I want you to come with me.' His eyes were slightly glazed as he looked out of the window.

'I'll be fine here.' She clenched her fists under the covers. 'Promise I won't go standing on any more chairs.'

'Faye. Please.' There was a quiet plea in his voice.

A lump formed in her throat. He was frightened. She found herself nodding and the tension fell from his shoulders.

'Is there a library here? I could go get some books out.' The idea flitted across her mind and she grabbed it with both hands. 'I have to do something to pass the time.' She averted her eyes, because the lie sounded cracked around the edges, and she was sure he would see through it.

But inside, her heart began to race. Yes, she'd go to the library, but not for books. They had public computers.

His hand strayed across the covers, lingered there for a moment.

She wanted to ask him about his childhood. About all of the messed-up things, but she couldn't find the right words. They were lodged in her throat, their roots strangling her voice.

Something awful had happened here. Something Dan had been caught up in. Something that wanted her to be a part of it.

+

Faye turned the handles of the old-fashioned taps. They were the kind with rounded metal points on a horizontal disc, and as the water flowed into the bath she breathed in the steam and made a silent pact that this would be the day she would find answers. The pipes in the wall creaked and clanged and Faye was glad of the light burning behind the glass shade. The small window was almost entirely obscured by some kind of creeping ivy.

Showering was a long, drawn-out affair as the water pressure in the cottage was useless. And Faye desperately wanted the warmth of the water to surround her. To cleanse her. She couldn't dislodge the memory of Barrington Hall. Its chill had seeped through her skin and was pushing up against her bones.

A search through the drawers in Lucinda's bedroom turned up a tub of rose-scented bath petals. She dumped a handful into the swirling water. The heat melted them instantly.

Gone. Just like Toby.

A hard lump formed in her throat. She grabbed a towel from the rail and buried her face into the well-used cotton. Grief howled inside her heart.

If Dan had brought her here to rebuild what was shattered, it was a dismal failure. The glimpses of the boy in the wood—*in the house*—had only brought back the aching loneliness and the fury. The boy wasn't her son, yet there was something about him she couldn't shake off, some kind of connection.

Her mothering instinct, for so long trapped behind the jagged reality of loss, was fighting for release. He might be a runaway, hiding all alone in that God-awful house. Her heart ached to think of it.

'Faye…'

She dropped the towel, a flush rising to her face as though she'd been caught doing something she shouldn't.

'I think you might have enough in there.' Dan nodded and her gaze fell to the bath. The water had reached almost to the top. Rose-scented steam wafted out of the depths.

'I'll be downstairs if you need me.' He paused, his fingers curled around the edge of the door.

'I won't.' The answer came out too short and too curt, and she wanted to take it back, but he was already gone, the stairs creaking under his retreat.

Undressing quickly, Faye stepped into the warmth of the water. She gasped as the burn hit her skin. It was far too hot, but she slid under its surface until it reached her neck, her skin tingling as her circulation quickened. Curls corkscrewed in the damp heat, and she was filled with a strange cocktail of emotion, the electricity of it zapping through her blood as though a needle had punched into her veins. Eagerness and a crazed delight. Vulnerability, painted over with fear. She found herself thinking about the lake and what she'd seen there. Did this water come from that lake?

'Stupid, stupid.' She spat the words into the water, tiny ripples fanning out across its surface.

But that noise she had heard tinkling in the wind. A tiny bell? A wind chime? Whatever it was she wanted to stifle it. To close her hand over it, to suffocate the sound because it felt like madness, and it was imbedded in her brain. She heard it now when it wasn't really there.

The boy with his edges swallowed by the shadows. She wanted to follow him into the darkness. To rescue him.

And all the while these thoughts churned through her brain, Faye knew they made no sense at all.

She closed her eyes, let her limbs go light. Let them float to the surface of the water. The weightlessness wrapped her in tender arms and a small sigh escaped her lips.

Death is a blessing.

The words jackhammered through her skull and her eyes

flew open. A sudden crack and the glass shade exploded, plunging the tiny bathroom into almost pitch darkness.

She sat bolt upright, telling herself it was only an old light. The unexpected heat had probably made it shatter.

A shiver ran across her damp, exposed skin. The air in the small room chilled. She reached for the towel she'd left at the end of the bath but it wasn't there.

Behind her, very slowly, the bathroom door opened, letting a chink of wan daylight through.

Faye turned, but there was nobody there.

She let out a small exhale of relief and brought her knees up to her chest. The water, which minutes ago had been unbearably hot, was now barely more than warm. The thin light caught something dark floating on the water. She cupped her palms and caught it, bringing it closer.

A dead fly.

The blood rushed to her head as she stood far too quickly. She reached out and pushed the door fully open.

The surface of the water was covered in flies, some of them still alive, tiny wings beating uselessly against the current she'd created. Revulsion rose in her throat and she leapt out of the bath, wincing as a shard of shattered glass bit into the sole of her foot. The jagged sliver slid into her soft, warm skin, and she stumbled, her eyes still glued to the horror of what was in the water.

Grabbing the towel from the floor, she wrapped it around her body and fled from the room. She closed the bedroom door, backing away, the stain of her crimson footprints following her like a lost wraith.

TWENTY-FOUR

Dan swept the glass from the bathroom floor with a dustpan and brush he'd found in the cupboard under the kitchen sink. He'd been going through some old papers of Lucinda's—a copy of the codicil he'd signed without really reading all the small print— when he heard Faye's dash from the bathroom.

The sight of her scarlet footprints on the floorboards churned up memories of the deer he'd left to die. He'd had to pull the shard of glass from Faye's foot. Even now he thought he could still smell her blood on his fingers.

He grimaced and stood, easing the ache from his back. On the surface of the cold bathwater, the flies floated; little black bodies, little translucent wings. Dan had told Faye that they must have been in the glass light fitting, and the explosion had rocketed them into the water. But there were too many for that. They both knew it.

He tried to forget the sketch he had seen. Tried to forget he had sneaked into Faye's room whilst she was in the bath, all guile and guilt, to check what she had been doing.

Gingerly, he pulled the plug up by the chain, watching as the water level fell. How the hell he was supposed to get them out of the plughole he didn't know. He would get to that when it happened.

The contents of his stomach rose in a nauseous soup and

he swallowed the build-up of saliva in his mouth.

Dan tipped the glass fragments into a plastic bag as the vortex from the water pulled dozens of winged bodies into its current.

Don't ever kill anything in these woods, Danny. Especially if it has wings. Lucinda's voice, so clear Dan actually spun around, half expecting her to be stood in the doorway.

The ramblings of an old woman, he thought After all, living alone in the back end of nowhere had to have some effect on how your brain worked. Every night she had sat in the rocking chair with her knitting bag on her knee, tying knots in balls of wool. If that didn't say half crazy, what did?

Yet Dan didn't remember thinking that when he was a boy. He only remembered the freedom she gave him. But that freedom came with rules, and he was quite happy to keep them if it meant he could do what he wanted during the day.

He feels the warmth of the sun on the back of his neck as he climbs the twisted oak in the forest, the thick, green leaves swishing past his face as he clambers ever higher. The branches seem made for a boy's feet to rest upon, always in the right place to ease his body towards the sky. He doesn't worry about falling. There is something in his blood that needs to reach the top.

He remembers looking down through the leaves, seeing a tiny figure on the ground with an upturned face, the worry evident even from this distance. Sunlight wicks from the lake and he shields his eyes, his gaze sweeping across...

The first glimpse of Barrington Hall. He can't take his eyes from its thick, black stones. His gaze travels along its roofline to the tall chimneys pointing to the sky like accusing fingers, the dark windows glistening like open wounds. It calls to him as seductively as any ocean siren.

Time stands still as he rests his cheek against the rough bark of the oak. The scent of green fills his senses, so potent he swears he can taste flowers on the back of his tongue.

And then his foot slips from the bough he is perched upon and, for a moment, he is dangling by one hand, like a monkey in the jungle. Panic shoots through his veins as he clutches at a batch of leaves, a shout from the ground to hang on. But even as his fingers close over the edge of a slim branch, the lure of Barrington Hall pounds in his brain.

'Dan?' Faye's voice pulled him from his thoughts. He cleared his throat, found her standing in the doorway, her injured foot clothed in a sock.

'I think I've got all the glass up, but don't come in here until I double check.' The common sense of his brain locked into place, words spilling out almost on autopilot, though he could still taste flowers on the back of his tongue.

She gave him an appraising glance. 'You looked like you were deep in thought.'

'Really?' He forced a laugh. 'Just going over what I'll say to this guy Porter when he finally unclamps our car.' It was the lamest of excuses.

She twisted her lips to one side, her gaze falling to the bath.

Dan didn't want to look at the heap of wet, black bodies clustered thickly in the plughole.

She folded her arms across her body. 'It's a good thing you didn't have to scoop them out.'

Dan caught his mouth before it fell open, and forced himself to look. There were no flies at all. Because the plughole had had its metal guard removed. All that remained was a deep, black hole.

Dan knew, at that instant, this had happened before.

An image of the pipework lined with decaying flies punched into his head. He ground his teeth together, his jaw clenching as the image turned into a moving screen. But this time the flies weren't dead; they lay on their backs, their legs curling uselessly, their wings stuck fast to the sludge in the pipes.

He grabbed the edge of the bath, made a show of checking the small black hole. Sweat ran down his spine.

'I'll get a new light fitting when we go into the village, maybe a spot bank so there's nowhere for anything to hide.' His voice sounded faraway to his own ears.

He reached across, needing to close that awful hole. His fingers curled around the chain. The plug swung from side to side like a hypnotist's watch. *Like something hanging from the end of a rope.*

Dan lowered the plug, the action slow and deliberate.

Something moved deep within the black hole. *Impossible*, his mind said.

But his eyes saw.

TWENTY-FIVE

When Faye went down for breakfast, the urn wasn't on the table. Damp patches spotted the tiled floor.

'Spilled some orange juice earlier, so thought it was a good idea to mop the floor. Don't want the flies to think we're putting on a banquet.' Dan buttered a slice of toast. His tone was light but she could see his fingers shaking.

She cleared her throat.

He half turned, his two-day stubble dark against his pale skin. She'd never seen him like this. Some small part of her wanted to reach out, to cover his hand with hers, tell him it would be okay.

But nothing would ever be okay again.

'I think there's a boy living in Barrington Hall.' The words left her lips in a tumble, each one falling into the next. She hadn't wanted to tell him, had wanted to keep the boy a secret. Keep him to herself. But she also needed Dan to tell her she wasn't going crazy.

His throat rippled. 'That's ridiculous, Faye.' She recoiled at the harshness of his answer. Shadow passed over his eyes. 'You know as well as I do that the place isn't fit for rats to live in. It's got no electricity or mains water, how could someone be living there?'

She fixed her eyes on a spot on the floor where a sunbeam

danced. 'I thought I saw someone in the woods...' Even as she spoke, Faye's anger at her own inadequacy burned in her throat. She didn't think; she had definitely seen.

'You're just hurting.' This time Dan's words were softer. He reached out and tucked a curl behind her ear. 'Grief can make you see all kinds of things.'

'But what if it's true?' She hated the way she sounded half hysterical, hated the sting of tears behind her eyes. 'What if I'm right and he's all alone and needs help.'

Dan looked away, smacking his lips together like he always did when he was trying to keep his temper. 'You can't replace Toby, however much you want to. Your imagination is just playing tricks, and deep down, you know that.'

She wanted to launch herself across the small space separating them and pound her fists against his chest. She wasn't imagining things, she wasn't. She needed him to believe her and he had just dismissed her thoughts as the raving of a grief-stricken woman. Right at that moment she hated him so much she could taste it on her tongue. A worm eating away what was left of their marriage.

The sound of the gate latch came through the open window, disturbing the wall of bitten-back words. Feet on the path and then a single rap at the door.

Faye headed into the hallway, glad to have something to do with her hands. Her limbs burned with pent-up adrenaline as she opened the door.

Robert McCallum loomed over the threshold.

'Mrs. Morgan, I believe?' The huge man dipped his head, his shadow falling on the hallway floor.

'Robert. What can I do for you?' Dan appeared, and his presence felt like it wanted to pick her apart and discard the things he didn't like.

'More like what I can do for you, Danny.'

Faye turned away from Robert's penetrating gaze, sure that everything she had said had been overheard and was now logged inside the gamekeeper's mind. Someone else who would think she was crazy.

'Your car was clamped yesterday, which wasn't all that welcoming.' Robert rubbed his beard with his thumb and forefinger.

Dan muttered something.

'But I'm afraid I've got some more bad news.' There was a pause and Faye held her breath, looking between the two men. 'A lorry side swiped it last night, caved in all along one side.'

'Jesus Christ!' Dan flung his hands into the air. 'What else can go wrong here?'

Robert watched Dan explode with an expression Faye couldn't read. 'What do you mean?' She waited, leaning against the door with the warm sun on her face, but there was an icy chill in her veins.

The seconds ticked away.

'Just irritating stuff.' Dan's voice was clipped. 'I guess I'm not used to living out in the sticks.'

Robert nodded. 'Takes a bit of getting used to. Especially around here. Newcomers don't seem to stay for long. Most families have been around for generations, and the old ways have passed down.'

'What old ways?' Faye asked.

'Knowing that there's give and take. That there are certain things they don't do and certain things they must do. The forest was here long before us and it'll be here long after us. We respect it, and those who live within it.' His eyes roamed past her, into the room where the glass case stood. Stuffing wild animals didn't sound much like respect to Faye.

'That may well be, but sometimes the future can't be held back.' Dan had that look in his eye, the kind he used to give Toby when something wasn't up for discussion.

'Only answering Mrs. Morgan's question. No slight intended.'

An awkward pause followed where the two men sized each other up. Faye retreated inside herself and watched as a fat honey bee gathered pollen from the lavender bush by the door.

'Thought you might like a lift into town. See about getting your car fixed up.' Robert broke the silence and some of the tension left Dan's shoulders.

'That would be great, Robert, thank you. Are you ready, love?'

And just like that it was as if their heated words had never happened.

'Give me two minutes.'

With her toothbrush jammed inside her mouth, she gathered her things and shoved them into her tote bag.

There might not be any answers at the library but she was determined to try.

TWENTY-SIX

Barrington Hall had not always been a place of darkness. Built by William Kidd in 1848, who hankered after a family home in the country, and who left blueprints for the Hall's construction whilst taking his children around Europe on a grand tour. On his return, he discovered that his designer had spun a different vision from the plans.

Barrington Hall was an ungodly mix of gothic and modern, with a splash of ecclesiastical in its towering spires. Built of black granite, quarried in Dartmoor, it was a scar upon the acre of forest from which it rose.

But for all its ugliness, it had a certain draw, a rough mish-mash of brooding style and elegant dourness. William fell in love with it immediately, moving his family down from Bath, integrating himself into the surrounding countryside and the people who lived there. He was a fair master, leasing his cottages to his workers for only pennies a month. They, in turn, worked hard for him, felling trees to send to the newly built sawmill.

His children—Jane, the eldest; Mary, three years younger; and Elliot, a year adrift in age from Mary and the apple of his sisters' eyes—ran wild in the woods, playing with the children of his workers. It was a rare classless society, but the workers never forgot who their master was.

William preferred a hands-on approach and was often seen working in his timber yard, loading the logs onto carts, and the children were left in the care of their nanny, Charlotte.

One summer night, as she called them in from play, Elliot lagged behind the two girls. He was an angel-faced child, with straw-coloured hair and a dimple right in the place that had all the old ladies pinching his cheeks.

'Well now, Master Elliot, what do you have there?' Charlotte loved him with all of her heart but she was a shrewd woman and knew cunning when it came to play.

The girls stopped chattering and went into the house, casting furtive glances over their shoulders, picking up their skirts as they tripped up the wide steps to the great doors.

Elliot stood, clasping a jar to his chest, his hands hiding the contents, his upturned face all pink cheeks and summer dust. ''Tis nothing, Lottie. Simply something I caught in the woods. I'll let it go after supper. I want to draw it.'

Charlotte narrowed her eyes, her hands on her hips. 'Just you be sure to let it go. I won't have creatures dying in this house because you wandered off and got into more mischief.'

'I do promise, Lottie.' He beamed up at her, a vision of childhood in a tweed waistcoat and pale yellow breeches. Smudges of dirt clung to his brow.

Charlotte watched as the small boy skipped into the house, making a mental note to check the nursery whilst he was sleeping.

Elliot paused at the curve in the winding staircase, the glitter of the chandelier catching the early evening light.

'You will let it go, won't you?' Mary's voice drifted down from the upstairs gallery. Elliot could see her face through the rails, her cheeks pressed up against them, the white of her lace collar bright in the shadows.

'Of course I will.' A butter-wouldn't-melt-in-his-mouth smile.

'Annie says you shouldn't take them from the forest. Bad things will happen.'

'I only want to draw it, Mae Mae.' He used her pet name like a song.

She receded into the shadows and he heard her rapid footfall on the stairs leading up to the nursery.

Elliot held up the jar, tapping his dirty fingers against it. A shimmer of translucent wings, and a tiny creature threw itself repeatedly against the glass sides.

He had spent months laying his trap, leaving trails of sugar water, watching from the undergrowth as they flitted about, long tongues curling into the sweetness, his jar balanced upside down on a fork of twigs.

A patient man earns his prizes, his father had once told him.

Elliot grinned, and it wasn't the grin of a cherubic child. He had no intention of letting anything go.

After supper, Charlotte called him into the drawing room.

He had made sure to scrub his hands and face, wetting his hair and combing it back like he did on a Sunday before they went to church. Tucked under his arm was a small leather bible.

Elliot knew what she was going to say. It had to do with what he had caught in the jar. Charlotte had been born in the village, had grown up with tales of superstition and whimsy.

She stood in the evening light, her hands primly folded over her black dress, a few strands of hair escaping from the coiled plait she always wore. It made her look older, more severe, but Elliot had seen her as she slept, auburn hair cascading over the pillow slip. She wasn't anyone to be afraid of.

'You called me, Lottie?' He made sure his tone was respectful.

'You haven't forgotten what I said about the jar, have you, young master?' She met his gaze, one eyebrow slightly raised.

'Of course not.' He graced her with a radiant smile. 'I am to learn my scripture for when Papa gets home.' He stroked the cover of the bible lovingly. 'Then I will draw before our evening bathing time. I'll make sure to leave the jar on its side on the grass before I say my prayers.'

Charlotte inclined her head, her outline caught between light and shadow. Elliot stood his ground, his face tipped up towards her. A strand of blond hair fell over his brow. She smiled, and right then Elliot learned a vital lesson in deception.

She dismissed him, watching silently as he closed the door. The smile fell from his face as he tripped up the stairs, hearing his sisters' idle chatter as they played with their doll's house in the nursery.

Elliot climbed the stairs to the very top of the house, where the servant's quarters were. The air was hot and stuffy, the utilitarian row of doors in stark contrast to the opulence below. He came to the end of the hallway, where a square hatch was set into the wall. The hatch opened inwards and led to a small space between the rafters. Elliot had found it whilst playing hide-and-seek and had hidden there, delighting in the ever-increasing crossness of his sisters when they failed to find him.

The jar sat on a milking stool he had brought up from the stables. He crouched and shook it with one hand, the creature within rebounding from side to side. Delicate antennae twitched from side to side as its wings opened. Elliot pressed his nose against the glass, a chortle escaping from his lips. Oh yes, this was what he had been trying to capture for months: the elusive fae of the forest, the creatures the villagers all revered.

Pinned to the sloping rafters were other unfortunates. A selection of butterflies, their once-bright wings dimmed and dusty. The remains of a chaffinch he had tried to gut and stuff, its head hanging to one side, one tiny clawed foot erupting from its bloody feathers. Two baby bats he had found on the ground under the old willow by the lake. They had been dead already, but he took great pride in nailing them to the rafters by their dried-out wing husks.

He had always been fond of the macabre, and found great delight in chasing his sisters with anything he found that was dead. It was easy in the forest. Things died there all the time. Sometimes he followed the gamekeeper as the man set about checking his traps, a rifle slung over his back. Elliot always thought that was a coward's way of killing. If you were to take a life, you should be able to feel it die under your fingertips.

The first thing he had killed had been a small frog. It had hopped from the lake and was sunning itself on the grass as Elliot sat with his fishing net dangling idly in the water. His sisters had left him, following the trail of a silver carp as it swam through the clear water. He could see them on the jetty, Mae Mae peering over the sides, her ringlets obscuring her face. Elliot loved his sisters but he didn't think they had much in the way of brains.

He fully expected the frog to move as he raised his net, but its round eyes were closed, its throat softly bobbing.

The net came down as quietly as the fall of night. And then it was in his hand, the yellow string of the net encircling its body, but the more it squirmed, the more it entangled itself. Elliot waited until it was exhausted, his cheeks flushing.

He didn't really remember picking up the rock. But what he did remember was the exhilaration in his veins as his hand came down hard on the tiny body. A cleft tongue slipped out, the protruding eyes as round as marbles. Its skull caved in first, the oozing matter squirting out between his fingers.

Elliot closed his eyes at the vivid recollection, biting the edge of his lip.

And as he gazed down at the tiny figure in the jar, with its soundless, desperate attempts to break free, he realised this was a turning point.

Superstition was for the dim-witted. The future belonged to industry and medicine. His father had said so one afternoon as they had rode through the forest together, Elliot's pony trotting alongside his father's thoroughbred.

Elliot drew a jagged metal nail from the inside of his waistcoat and unscrewed the lid of the jar.

TWENTY-SEVEN

The inside of Robert's old SUV smelled faintly of wet dog. The gamekeeper made small talk as they drove to the village, with Dan adding words that felt hollow and faded. Faye stared out of the window, her eyes on the passing trees.

Robert dropped them off by the cenotaph, last year's poppy wreaths still scarlet-brave against the old stone.

They crossed the road to the library and Dan hesitated; his earlier argument with Faye weighed heavy on his shoulders. He hadn't meant to be so cruel. So dismissive. But she had already turned away from him. A sign on the door proclaimed that it opened at 10 a.m. but it was clear she didn't want him to wait with her.

Dan stepped back into the road, then lurched forwards as the blare of a car horn sounded right behind him. Adrenaline arrowed through his veins.

An arm jerked out of a van window, giving him the middle finger. His lips tightened. This bloody village seemed determined to fuck up his blood pressure.

Faye watched as he crossed the road, her bag clutched tightly against her chest, her eyes darting to the disappearing white van.

He thought about the urn and the sudden wind that had come out of nowhere, gusting through the cottage. Unease churned in his gut as he walked under the awnings outside the flower shop and the greengrocers next door. Buckets of summer blooms rested in the shade, the scent of roses coming from the open door. Trays of bright fruits and vegetables sat in uniform rows in quaint wooden boxes. It was a quintessential British scene, right out of a children's story book, but Dan could feel something rotten lurking, the decay skulking just out of sight.

But he simply might be reacting to all of the fucked-up things that had happened. The rational man who dealt with multi-million-pound companies on a daily level had had the rug pulled out from under his feet by a childhood summer he couldn't quite remember and the wishes of a deceased relative.

And now his wife was seeing strange boys in the woods. *In that house.* So much for any sense of healing he had hoped might blossom.

It was utterly and severely crazy. And Dan hated how he had reacted to Faye's words. Hated what he had become.

His car sat forlornly at the kerb where he'd left it. Even from across the street Dan could see the dented metal. From the front wing to the back wheel arch, something had redesigned his car as though it was made of clay.

A rusty pick-up truck sat behind it, *Jem Porter – Repairs and Servicing* painted on the driver's door. A man sat behind the wheel, his face hidden by an open newspaper.

'Like a bloody vulture,' Dan muttered as he crossed the street, this time making sure nothing wanted to turn him into roadkill. 'Jem, is it? Dan Morgan. That's my ruined car in front of you.' Dan wasn't up for small talk. He just wanted to get this over with.

The man lowered the newspaper aggravatingly slowly.

His face was as lined and weather beaten as an old walnut, but the sharpness of his eyes were like cut glass. He looked Dan up and down.

Dan felt his temper rising like a tidal wave, but he managed to clamp it behind gritted teeth.

Jem pushed open the door and slid out from the cracked, vinyl seat. He was a small, wiry man with a slightly curved spine, wearing a red-checked flannel shirt despite the warmth of the day. He sucked in air between his teeth as he walked the length of the car. Dan might as well have been invisible.

'It's a big job. Those panels will need to be ordered in specially. And the paint.'

Dan slid his fingers into the pockets of his jeans. That way he couldn't strangle Jem.

'Of course.' Dan glanced across the street where a few people had stopped to watch the show. 'Look, I don't care if it's not a perfect paint match. Just get me mobile again. The cost doesn't matter.'

Jem turned his head, those shrewd eyes drilling through Dan. 'The cost always matters, Danny. In all things.'

There was the kind of silence where the world seems to stop and inhale. And then Jem cracked the veneer by clapping his hands together once, an action that seemed to Dan like the opening shot in a battle.

'How long?' Dan forced two words from lips holding far more behind them.

Jem ran his palm gently across the dented bodywork as if it were a horse's flank.

'A week. Maybe more. Depends on how quick the suppliers can get stuff to me out here.'

Jem spoke like the village was at the end of the world,

and for a moment, Dan felt as if he'd fallen into some kind of alternate universe. He wondered if somewhere else, a version of him was connecting with his wife in an exact replica of the cottage.

'You in a hurry to get back to London?' Jem addressed the front wing of the car. His knees creaked as he crouched to look at it from a different angle.

Dan was in a hurry to get anywhere else but here, but it was obvious that wasn't going to happen. 'I've got time.'

'It's a funny thing, time.' Jem raised his eyes to meet Dan's. 'It seems to run at its own speed. Young folk never think about it. Time passes slow for them. But when you get to be my age, well'—he wiped the back of his hand across his nose—'it fair flies by. But for some it stands still.'

A sudden breeze tunnelled down the street, bringing with it the scent of the summer forest. Dan's scalp prickled. Jem's words seemed very pointed, as though something else hid behind them and it was up to Dan to decipher the clues.

'Have you lived here long?'

'Could say that. I was born in the cottage by the war memorial. It used to be the blacksmith's place, when a man could earn an honest living from a trade like that. My father was born there too. Lived here for generations we have. And seen a lot of things.'

'I suppose you've seen a lot of changes?' Dan was happy to steer the conversation away from whatever Jem had been hinting at.

'Oh, yes, a lot of changes. Most of them not for the better. Places like this don't survive well in modern times, but there's families here, like mine, who go back a long way. We band together, look out for each other. And the forest. We listen to it, you see, because we owe a huge debt. Although I don't expect you city folk to ever understand. You're all too busy running around in circles chasing your own tails.'

Part of Dan wanted to object, but if he really thought about it, Jem was right. What Dan did only put more zeros on the bank accounts of people he never met, digitally increasing their wealth. He doubted if any of them knew he existed.

'You have a wife, don't you, Danny?' Jem's eyes softened. 'You need to make sure you know where she is. Don't let her go a wandering. It's easy to get lost in the forest. To be drawn to things she doesn't understand.'

The moisture left Dan's mouth. 'What are you saying?' Anger clawed its way up his throat.

'No point in using up energy on me. I've said enough. And I think you've had enough hints.'

If Jem had been a younger man, Dan would have pinned him up against his truck and forced the answers from him. But he was savvy enough to know abusing an old man in broad daylight, with an audience, wasn't a sensible thing to do.

Jem's words thudded through his skull. *Don't let her go a wandering.*

Hadn't he done that very thing? Left her alone when he went to find Albert Jenkins, the man who had fallen off the face of the earth after being everywhere the day after they arrived. Left her in the cottage with the glass case, the one Lucinda had guarded so well.

Dan's legs turned to jelly. He grabbed for the roof of his car, dimly aware that Jem had climbed back into his truck.

'Don't worry about paying me to unclamp your car. It was an honest mistake parking here.' Jem leaned an elbow on his rolled down window. 'I'll come by the cottage when your car's done.' His old diesel engine stuttered to life.

Barrington Hall. The shadow memory of it passed over Dan's head like a storm cloud. Whatever had happened here, in that distant summer, was all linked to that place of black, sinister stone. He couldn't remember because something didn't want him to.

He had come here to try to soften the grief in his life, but the tattered threads that held Faye and him together were dissolving like ice in water, slowly, invisibly, never to return.

TWENTY-EIGHT

Faye sat on the low wall by the library door, last autumn's leaves clustered at its base. She could see the outline of the librarian inside, stacking books on the shelves from a small trolley. It wasn't much of a place, just an ugly pre-fabricated oblong of concrete with a grey, tiled roof. On a few of the windows were papers advertising local shows and jumble sales. But the dates were so old Faye could hardly read them. She stood and ambled past the window, letting the woman inside know there was somebody waiting.

The minutes ticked by agonisingly slowly. Faye planted herself on the coir door mat outside the glass doors, determined not to be put off.

The librarian, a woman in an austere black dress, her hair swept up into a bun and held in place by a large tortoiseshell clip, unlocked the doors. Her eyes met Faye's and she nodded curtly. It was the woman who had been in the forest with Albert Jenkins. 'Good morning. Please don't eat or drink in the library. And there are no mobile telephones allowed.'

Faye forced her own greeting through gritted teeth. As she had none of those things in her possession, she wondered if the woman was trying to annoy her on purpose. She walked to the desk, placing her hands on the counter. 'I'm here to find out more about local history. Can I use the library computers?'

She graced the librarian with her best smile.

The woman, whose lanyard named her as Lydia Koster, looked at Faye over the top of the wire-framed glasses she had just perched on her nose.

'I won't be long.' Faye delved into her bag and brought out her purse. 'And I can pay.'

'I suppose I could let you.' Lydia sighed, as though the thought was a personal affront. 'But don't go on any disreputable sites.'

Faye bristled but found her voice saying that would be fine, despite feeling insulted.

Lydia brought out an ancient silver laptop from one of the drawers of her desk. Faye watched as the librarian booted it up. The screen took an impossibly long time to load.

'You'll be Danny Morgan's wife, then.' Lydia's eyes were fixed on the laptop, but Faye caught a furtive glance across. It was a strange thing to say as Lydia had obviously seen her with Dan when they were lost in the woods.

It was true what they said about small villages. Everyone knew everyone else's business. Faye wondered if she and Dan were the most exciting things to have happened here this year.

'I remember him.' Lydia removed her glasses and studied one of the lenses, and Faye held her breath, waiting for the librarian to continue. But Lydia was cleaning the lens with a cloth, as though she wanted to wipe her last words away.

'You knew Dan as a boy?' She asked it casually, but inside she was desperate for any morsels of information Lydia could feed her.

Lydia angled the screen towards Faye and pointed to the end of the desk. 'It's a slow machine so don't expect all those modern bells and whistles. But there's a nice site about the village and its mention in the Magna Carta. That should keep you occupied.'

Faye wanted to say the Magna Carta wasn't exactly what she was looking for; she wanted an answer to her question. But it was clear it had fallen on stony ground. She swallowed her frustration and slid the laptop over to the end of the desk, where a fold-up chair rested.

Lydia wasn't kidding when she said the machine was slow. It chugged and clicked as it loaded pages painfully slowly. Faye logged on to the local history site, where the information about the Magna Carta made the front page.

Occasionally, Lydia would slip past with her arms full of books, checking what Faye was looking at. Faye brought out her sketch pad and turned to a clean page, making scribbled notes that she knew she would never use.

As the clock ticked its way to half past the hour, the phone on the desk began to ring. Lydia looked at it as though it was some small creature with dirty feet. After at least a dozen rings, she picked it up, turning away from Faye as she spoke quietly.

Faye didn't need a second chance. She clicked through the history site, following links until she came to one saying Barrington Hall. The button was greyed out, the link broken.

She opened a new search engine and typed in the name. Barrington Hall was there with numerous tantalising mentions, but every time she clicked on one it brought up the same page. *Unsafe link. Use your back button.*

Lydia's conversation was coming to an end. Faye scanned the page, hoping to snatch a small amount of information from those first few lines, but all she could see was a description of the building and one line. *Commissioned by William Kidd.*

As her finger hovered on the return key and Lydia finished her call, Faye caught a few words on the last link. *A village mourns.*

'Did something happen here, with the old house by the lake?' Faye tried to keep her voice light, but an urgent need burned in her throat. Her pencil rolled onto the floor and Faye stooped to pick it up from the worn parquet tiles. The library door opened, the little bell above it tinkling, the sound brushing up against her memory. A gust of wind cooled the back of Faye's neck.

'When did you do this?' Lydia's words met Faye as she straightened. The librarian's eyes were wide behind her glasses.

The wind had ruffled the pages. Barrington Hall stared back at her with all of its brooding menace.

It was pointless to lie. The sketch was there.

'Yesterday, just before the thunderstorm.'

The man who had entered grunted, wiping his hands on an oily rag he pulled from his pocket. 'Hasn't rained here in the village for weeks.' He exchanged a glance with Lydia. 'Best be keeping to your cottage, my dear. You and Danny.'

His words were quiet and solemn.

'Why?' Faye's voice wavered as she fought with the sudden surge of exasperated anger.

'There are things here you wouldn't understand. Best to let the past be the past. It's never wise to go poking about in it.' He nodded at her.

Faye gathered up her things and slid them inside her bag. She wasn't sure what she was supposed to say to that. Two pairs of eyes drilled into her back as she made for the door, exiting into bright sunshine and much fresher air.

She had come to find out more about Barrington Hall.

But what she had discovered was almost more disturbing than the stark, black stones.

Whatever it was, whatever it had been, was cloaked in the thickest shroud of secrecy. And Lydia had never answered her questions.

TWENTY-NINE

The cherubic son of William Kidd wasn't sure what gave him more pleasure. Piercing their tiny bodies with the nails he stole from the stables or tearing off their wings.

The first time was the best, as it always was, and years later he would still remember the softness of her slightly distended abdomen as the fine point pressed against it. Her shrill scream as the contents of that abdomen spilled out, a thick, sticky goo-like jelly. Elliot had licked his fingers, then spat on the ground. And the guilt he felt was all about the latter.

His first didn't live for long. Her desperate attempts to escape, despite the needle pinning her to the rafter beam, lasted only until the wax from the candle had started to pool on the tea chest Elliot had set it upon. He had watched her last moments, the cries replaced by a kind of bird-like whimpering. And when she finally stilled he examined her under the magnifying glass he had taken from Charlotte's nature-study desk.

A creature that defied all of the texts in the leather-bound tomes in his father's library.

Fae. Fairy. Sprite. Names from the books his sisters read by the light of a candle, the shadows on the nursery wall rising and falling in the flickering glow.

But Elliot didn't care what they called these things. The dim-witted people in the village brought gifts to these creatures, held them in some kind of high esteem, and, as far as Elliot was concerned, this meant they were not giving their full attention to their work.

His father was a good man—too good, Elliot thought. To think that the villagers were taking advantage of his kindness by worshipping disgusting little abominations made Elliot's stomach flip over. Best that he started to cull them now, before he himself took over the family business. His father always introduced him as 'my honourable heir' and Elliot saw no reason why he shouldn't start to clear the pathway to his own success as early as he could.

Tearing off their wings came with his second capture—two tiny creatures caught together. They clung to each other in the jar, the wings of the tallest one wrapped around the smaller. This time Elliot used harsh twine, stolen from the gardener's shed, wrapping it tightly around their abdomens and hanging them from a nail in the rafters. He watched them spin, fascinated by the manic fluttering of those translucent wings as the light from the candle guttered in the shadows. He unhooked the tallest one and lowered it to the flame, watching with fascination as the fragile wings crisped to nothing in the blink of an eye.

What remained spun slowly on the string hanging from his fingers, its feelers twisting together in agony. He sighed and wound the twine back around the nail.

It was too quick. He had learned that he needed to extend his experiments, to savour each moment.

The smallest one, no bigger than his thumb, was silent. Like a duckling hiding amidst a nest of reeds, it knew when a predator was about.

Taking a small pair of wooden surgical tweezers, Elliot unhooked the twine, fastening it around his fingers until the tiny body lay across his palm. This one was pale green in colour with fuzzy down coating its body and head. Two tiny black eyes stared into his.

Elliot paused, his mind pre-occupied for a moment. This one almost certainly was more youthful than the others, the fuzzy mass akin to his own crown of curls.

'Are you special?' he crooned to the life held prisoner on his hand. 'Papa says I'm special.'

The tiny eyes blinked once.

Elliot held the tweezers aloft, his tongue protruding slightly from his mouth in concentration.

And then he began to tear.

THIRTY

Faye was standing on the street corner, by the library, when Dan crossed the road. Under his arm was the box containing the new light fitting he had bought at the ironmonger's on the high street.

The late morning sun beat down upon his back and he could feel sweat starting to trickle down his neck. It was the sticky, oppressive warmth of a British summer, when heat has overstayed its welcome. He glanced at the sky. To the west, over the woods, dark thunderclouds hung, swallowing the blue bite by bite.

Something stirred in the dry earth of his memories. Another summer's day long ago. He looked down at his hands, and for a moment they weren't the hands of a man, but those of a child, clasped in prayer. He was on his knees in the mud. And the rain, the dark and painful rain, fell from the sky in a solid blanket of despair.

'Dan, are you okay?' Faye's worried voice cut into his thoughts. 'You're really pale.'

'Of course I am,' he lied. But the smile on his face was as thin as paper. 'Did you get any books?'

She paused and looked away, wetting her bottom lip with the tip of her tongue. 'No. They didn't have anything I wanted. Not much choice in a place like this.'

Dan knew she was lying. Faye knew she was lying. The uncomfortable wedge slid between them like a thorn through flesh.

┼

It had been another screw up of a day.

From his argument with Faye to the van that had tried to mow him down, to his frustrating conversation with Jem Porter. The feeling that shrouded Dan now was one he really didn't like to admit to. Helplessness.

His insistence that he take Faye for pizza had nothing at all to do with his appetite. They both knew, as they sat at the table by the window overlooking the park, with its cheerful red and white checked tablecloths, that they were postponing the inevitable. Returning to the cottage and the questions that hung there.

Faye had been so quiet, picking at the crust of her pizza like a mouse, whilst Dan had rambled on ridiculously about anything that came into his head. No one mentioned their fight from earlier. But as they sat there and the world turned around them, Dan made a decision. Tomorrow, they would take a taxi and drive to wherever the hell his phone had signal. He would hire a car and they would go home to the city. Fuck the cottage and fuck Barrington Hall. He didn't care if he never set eyes on either of them again.

Lucinda's will had forbidden him to sell the cottage but it said nothing about leaving it to rot in its own juices.

They spent the afternoon in the park again, Faye absorbed in a book she had bought at a charity shop next to the pizza parlour. It hadn't escaped his notice that she wasn't wearing her headphones. If Dan closed his eyes he could hear the laughter of children in the playground across the river, and,

150

in the far-off distance, the chimes of an ice-cream van. It was all so normal. So safe.

But as the people walking by the river dwindled, and the sun began its descent towards the hills overlooking the village, Dan knew they must go back. Just one more night, he told himself. One more night. He'd wait up if necessary, park himself outside Faye's door to make sure...*what? He wasn't even sure what he was afraid of.*

The thunderclouds still hung in the sky but they had congregated into one black mass, an anti-social hulk of aerial gloom.

As they walked down the pathway into the woods and the sound of the village died away, Faye finally found her voice. He could feel her studying his profile before the words spilled out.

'Tell me about your summers here. What did you do with all this space?' Her eyes flicked towards the trees.

Faye's question lifted all the hairs along his arms. His stomach flipped over.

In the undergrowth, an angry blackbird chittered, and high above, the molten silver line of a plane caught by the setting sun.

'I hung out with a few of the village kids usually. I think we got on well because there wasn't many of us, but as I got older, we kind of drifted apart, like kids do.' The blatant lie stuck in Dan's throat like a fish bone. 'We fished in the stream and played tag in the woods.' Dan's memories streamed past his mind's eye. He wanted to say that they went swimming in the lake, that they crept inside Barrington Hall when they had been told not to, but the words all glued together on his tongue.

The expression on her face made Dan's heart sink. Lips slightly parted. Fervour in her eyes. This was what she wanted from him. His sinful past.

A loud crack echoed through the forest. A group of crows took flight from the canopy of a huge oak, cawing in indignation as the sharp sound ricocheted through the trees.

'Was that a gun shot?' Faye's eyes widened. It actually did sound like a gun, if all the movies Dan had ever watched were true. But it was more likely an old car back firing. This village was filled with antiques of every kind.

The undergrowth rustled behind them and Dan spun, putting out his arm in front of Faye. Robert McCallum strode from the thicket, holding the body of a fox by its tail. A shotgun hung from a strap on the gamekeeper's back.

Dead. Dead. Dead. The word hammered against Dan's skull as though determined to crack it open.

One of the fox's hind legs was bloody and raw, the fur stripped away.

'I've been after this old dog fox for months. Been making a real nuisance of himself with the folks who run the chicken farm up past the old sawmill. He was a wily old critter.' Dan thought Robert's voice held a touch of sadness. 'He got himself all caught up in my snare at long last, tried to chew his leg off to get free.'

Beside him, Faye shivered, and Dan put himself in her line of sight.

'Apologies if I scared you with the shot. Had to put him out of his misery quickly, you understand.'

Dan had a mouthful of questions, all to do with the legalities of firing a gun in the middle of a public space, but he doubted the niceties of law had much sway out here in the sticks.

And he was more than a little bit grateful Robert's sudden appearance had stemmed Faye's interest in his childhood. For now.

He wondered why he hadn't told her about his plan for tomorrow. Maybe he was hedging his bets in case he changed his mind. Or in case something changed it for him.

The gamekeeper slung the fox over his arm like some kind of macabre fashion accessory, and fell into step beside Dan.

'I'll walk you back to the cottage. It gets dark here quickly.'

Part of Dan wanted to say he wasn't scared of the night and that he knew his way by now, but another part, the part that had stayed with him since he was a boy, was more than thankful for Robert's company.

Robert seemed content to talk, the soft burr of his accent soothing Dan's tattered nerves as, overhead, the sky gradually lost its light, the bruise-coloured twilight deepening as they walked. Through the canopies of the trees, tiny star pinpricks glittered. Above their heads, a coven of pipistrelle bats began their nightly feed.

Faye walked in front of them, her shoulders hunched, her bag dangling from one shoulder. She gripped the strap tightly with one hand, as though she were frightened someone might spirit it away.

'I didn't think there'd be much call for your profession these days.' Dan inserted a comment into a sudden lull, trying to stop his eyes from fixating on the matted blood trail leading from the hole in the fox's skull.

Robert's keen gaze swung into the shadows, his arm

reaching to halt Dan in his tracks.

Dan held his breath as the night pressed its fingers against his throat. In the undergrowth, at the side of the path, something moved. The rustle of leaves in a low lying bough.

Robert waited until whatever it had been disappeared. 'These woods still need looking after, much as they always have.' He answered Dan's question as though the last minute had never happened. 'I do what I can to keep the peace.' He nodded towards Dan as though Dan was part of this secret village club. But Dan had left halfway through this movie and when he returned he'd missed a crucial plot point.

Robert produced a heavy-weight torch from the pocket of his gamekeeper's jacket and flicked it on. The strong beam shone fiercely along the path, the night insects like manic snowfall in its glare.

An owl screeched high in the trees and Dan's heart skipped a beat. Everything here was so ridiculously normal, but on the edge of reality, a darkness that had nothing to do with night preyed.

They walked in silence for a few minutes, then Robert started whistling softly, a tune Dan didn't know. Faye's steps quickened as they neared the cottage. Dan knew she had felt it too, this indescribable wrongness lingering here tonight.

Thunder rolled somewhere over the hills.

The trees thinned and the top of the thatch came into view, the moon on its shoulder. The clearing lay covered in a pale light, all colour washed from the ground.

Dan watched as Faye made her way through the gate. Out of the corner of his eye he thought he saw something move on the thatch ridge, something retreating back against the chimney's shadow.

A chill crept across his skin and he shivered, despite the clamminess of the night.

'Do you want a nightcap, Robert? I'm sure there's a good malt hiding in a cupboard somewhere.' The words rushed out of his mouth in a jumble.

Robert pursed his lips, then grinned. 'I wouldn't be a Scotsman if I refused a wee dram, now would I?'

Dan clapped him on the back, the tail of the fox brushing against his arm. 'You're welcome, but leave this guy outside. I don't think he's house trained.'

Robert laughed and they followed Faye up the garden path towards the sleeping cottage. Under the bowed heads of the sunflowers Dan risked a glance towards the roof, but there was nothing there.

So why did he feel like there was something watching?

THIRTY-ONE

You feel the movement of the earth as he breaks through the soil. Just as you felt his worm-like stirrings last night. It feels like your skin is being ripped from your body, but you know that's only the memory of what he did to your children. You buried his wickedness and created your own. Revenge is a dish best served cold, and you have had many years to dwell upon your own reasoning. How he not only slaughtered your kin but poisoned what you once were. The cancer of him devoured your purity.

You don't understand how he has come to be again. You made sure he was dead. But only after he had been buried for days. You can still hear his screams as they lowered his coffin into the ground. Still hear the pounding of small fists against the lid.

Taking flight, your wings a blur in the forest gloom, you weave between the ancient trees, their heartbeat in tune with your own. The moon follows your path, winks down through the sleeping leaves. As you grow closer you feel it in the air, an inverted ripple of wrongness. And, in your blood, you feel Barrington Hall answer.

The grave is different, paler in the diffused moonlight. You flit down, hover above it, not wanting to taint yourself by touching it.

His name is gone and something inside you breaks apart. At the base of the stone, a small posy of wilted flowers, the bright pink of a dog rose surrounding a single stem topped with blue. It is too late for that bloom to flower. But there are always some here, as if they are keeping watch. The place your mate was taken.

The name is gone. The hard fact of it vibrates from the wrongness, from each blade of grass, each fragment of weathered bark. Your magic aches in your veins and you can feel the flow of it thickening.

A name that is scrubbed from a grave sets the spirit free. The monster of Barrington Hall is going home.

THIRTY-TWO

Dan stood in the kitchen, his hand clamped around a whisky tumbler, his palm sweating against the glass as he raised it to his lips.

Robert pulled up a chair and settled his considerable form upon it. His hands were mottled with dried blood but it didn't seem to bother him. He fixed Dan with an unnervingly focussed stare, his glass untouched before him.

'I take it you're thinking of heading back to the city, Danny?'

Dan stopped mid-swallow, the liquid burning his throat. He spluttered, coughed into his hand, but before he could reply Robert spoke again.

'I know that look on your face. I've seen it before. It's a look that says 'if I run it will all be okay.' But it doesn't work like that. If you run it will call you back eventually. Unfinished business always catches up to you in the end.'

Dan's heart fell into his stomach. He wanted to protest, to tell the older man that he didn't know what he was talking about, but he couldn't find a shred of courage from the whispering of dread running in his veins.

'This place.' Dan ran his tongue over lips that suddenly felt as parched as desert sand. 'It feels cursed.'

Robert picked up his glass and took a long sip. The

seconds stretched out between them.

Dan was fully prepared for Robert's scorn, or to be labelled as mildly hysterical, but part of him was glad he had finally said the words grating against his bones.

'You think we're all simple folk here, don't you? That whilst you're living in your steel and concrete boxes, making money and craving more, you're better than us?'

There was no accusation in Robert's voice, which had dropped into its soft burr.

'But there are things here you have no idea of, things that have existed for centuries, things that won't die, no matter how much logic you apply to them.'

'What are you telling me?' The edges of Dan's words trembled.

'That it's pointless going home. You need to face up to what's out there, because it won't let go.'

'And what exactly *is* out there?' Dan's heart was slamming against the walls of his chest so loudly that he would be surprised if Robert couldn't hear it.

A shadow fell over the kitchen floor. Faye stood in the doorway, curled fingers resting against her lips.

'You don't remember what happened that last summer, do you?'

Here it was, the words he both wanted to hear, and wanted to run screaming from.

'I think there was some kind of accident.' Dan forced the words through his dried lips.

Despite the sultry heat of the summer night, his fingertips were freezing.

'It wasn't an accident.' Robert paused, and took a long swallow of whisky. 'You disrespected Barrington Hall.

Disrespected the lake. And you'd already gone into the house, despite being told not to.'

It is so cold in that hallway.

'Can you hear that?' the boy says, his face bone-white in the sudden lightning glare. 'I can hear something breathing'…

'Barrington Hall is, to use your own words, Danny, cursed. And that might not sit well amongst your fancy ideas of what exists and what doesn't. It's been cursed for generations. The people who've owned it have been cursed. And your family is part of it.'

'That sounds'—Dan wanted to say ridiculous—'very far-fetched.'

Robert shook his head slowly. 'Far-fetched it might sound but it's all the truth. And you know it. It's why you invited me in, because you didn't want to be alone. Because you wanted answers.'

Nausea rose in Dan's throat. He had come back here and found ghosts of memory that wouldn't stay dead. And now they wanted their pound of flesh.

Robert pushed his chair away and stood, his frame blocking out the light from the hallway.

'I'd best be on my way. You've got things to talk about. Things to remember.'

Part of Dan wanted to ask the gamekeeper to stay, because if he was left alone with Faye it would mean they would have to speak about things that he had buried for so long.

Faye stepped back into the shadows, her silence saying much more than words.

Robert paused at the open door to Lucinda's room, his eyes darting across the gloom. Dan followed his line of sight.

And found the glass case. He recalled the way Lucinda had sat in her rocking chair, her eyes fixed upon it, her fingers deftly tying the knots in those balls of wool.

Dan remembered Faye's accident, her need to see inside it, and his throat tightened.

Robert opened the front door. The summer night rushed in with the scent of rose and forest green. He hoisted his shotgun over his shoulder.

The gamekeeper paused at the gate, framed by the bowed heads of the sunflowers.

'Do the right thing, go and say you're sorry.' Robert went through the gate and Dan watched as he disappeared into the dark arms of the forest.

Faye came to stand at his side. 'He didn't say goodbye.'

Dan slid an arm around her shoulders and for once she didn't pull away. 'He didn't need to. He did what he had to do.'

THIRTY-THREE

As the front door closed against the night, the suffocating weight of claustrophobia knelt on Faye's shoulders. She had crept down the narrow stairs and listened to the conversation between the two men in the kitchen. She had heard the cold fear in Dan's voice, the matter-of-fact speech from Robert's lips, and the overwhelming pressure of knowing she was right all along about Barrington Hall, numbed all her senses.

'Jesus.' Dan clawed at his skull, backing away from the door. His steps led him into the kitchen. Into the light.

'Faye...' Dan held out his hand. She shuffled to the kitchen doorway. Her feet seemed glued to the floor.

He wiped his hand over his mouth, then looked at his fingers as though he expected his words to be stuck there, bloody letters filled with guilt. Faye watched him as though she were watching a stranger, watched as his walls all came tumbling down. How long had she hoped that he would open up to her, would show her some vulnerability, and now that he was, she was terrified.

She hugged her arms across her body, suddenly chilled to the core.

'What happened to you?' Her voice didn't sound like her own. It rang against her ears, filled with disbelief and the sharp tang of accusation. She wanted to scream at him, anger building in her throat for bringing this danger to their door. But underneath that fury was the knowledge that being here had unfurled all of her senses, like a flower before the sun.

Her husband gripped the back of one of the kitchen chairs, his knuckles bone-white. She had the distinct impression that it was holding him up.

'I don't remember,' he said. 'But there was an awful accident. And I think it was my fault.'

'Robert said it wasn't an accident.' She dug her fingernails into the soft flesh of her arms. 'That you disrespected the house.'

The air thickened around them as the walls of the cottage seemed to exhale. And in the dense silence that followed, Dan's head snapped up, grim determination replacing the slack mask of helplessness. He moved towards her slowly, taking her hand in his.

She looked down at their clasped hands, remembered how she always curled her fingers inside his palm as they walked.

'We're leaving tomorrow,' he whispered, and she knew why. The bones of this place were listening.

But part of her wanted to protest. Robert had told him not to run away again. And what if something followed them home?

A nervous pang rolled through her stomach. The image of the boy settled, butterfly soft.

Despite everything she was exhausted. It seemed like days since she had gone into Barrington Hall. Where was the boy tonight, huddled in the dark belly of that house or waiting for her to appear at her window?

'Come on.' He led her across to the hallway, checking

that the bolt on the door was firmly across and that it was locked. He reached for the handle of Lucinda's room and closed the door. The click echoed in the stillness.

'What about that thing in the case?' she whispered, a chill raising gooseflesh on her arms.

He glanced towards the closed door, his lips set into a thin line. 'It's in there for a reason, and that's where it's staying.'

She wanted to ask if letting it out would help them or condemn them, but the words crawled into her throat and refused to go any further.

'Do you want to sleep in my bed tonight, no strings attached?' Faye nodded and he smiled. 'I'll try not to snore, but if I do, poke me.'

A little light-hearted quip, but it only touched the surface of her apprehension.

They crept up the stairs, the old wood creaking, her hand tightly gripping her husband's fingers. In the hallway below she sensed the shadows deepen, but she didn't look back, because all the books told you not to.

Lucinda's bedroom smelt faintly of old roses and dust, but as Dan drew the chintz curtains with the little flowers scattered across the fabric, and she kicked off her trainers, she found herself wondering about the woman who had cared for Dan and the secrets she, too, had kept. Faye couldn't imagine living alone in this cottage, unless Lucinda had had no choice.

She crawled into bed, fully clothed, and pulled the satin-edged coverlet up to her chin. Dan bunched the pillows up against the white iron bed head and squeezed her hand. 'I'm not sleeping. So you can.' He bent down and pressed a kiss to her brow.

She had so many questions, but right now, as the tiredness weighted her bones, they settled in her mind.

And as the shadow of sleep descended, her last thoughts were of the strange boy who lived in Barrington Hall and how much she wanted to protect him.

✝

Faye had been dreaming. Something weirdly surreal about a kitten with feet like a dragon. She could still hear it on the edge of her dream, a slight scratching of claws on a wooden floor.

She opened her eyes, aware that her arm was chilled, and pushed herself up onto one elbow. The room was dark, the lamp that had been lit as she drifted off to sleep no longer bright.

And slumped across the pillows with his head at an awkward angle was Dan. Fast asleep.

I'm not sleeping. So you can, he had said and she had felt safe. But that safety was draining away like water down a plughole. She remembered how the dead flies had been sucked into the vortex of the bath water, imitating her own spiral of darkness.

She rubbed her chilled skin with her other hand, shivering as the bed covers slipped to her waist. The temperature in the room felt like a December day, a frost-bound cold like the touch of winter fog. The kind that clings to everything.

Faye let out a shaky breath, almost sure she could see it in the dark. The scratching came again. But this was no dream. It was coming from the other bedroom.

'Dan,' she whispered into the darkness, nudging his arm with her hand. There was no response. 'Dan, wake up!' Her voice spun out into the silence, but even as she shook his arm and pleaded, some part of her knew that he wasn't going to wake up.

Very slowly, she slid her legs out of bed, pushing her feet into her trainers. Icicles of fear spiked through her veins, numbing her fingers as she struggled with her laces.

The bedroom door creaked open. Faye listened with her heart lodged in her throat, listened for movement, her brain conjuring images of terrible things looming in the shadowy hallway.

And as her eyes fell on the open door she remembered that Dan had shut it. Had locked it from the inside.

Which meant that whoever or whatever had unlocked it had somehow been in this room whilst they slept. A small whimper escaped through her lips.

She stole across the floor, her fingers trembling as they curled around the edge of the door, half expecting to see a monster. But all she saw was darkness. And that was somehow worse.

The blackened maw of the staircase yawned to her left, but she didn't look, not even when the door to Lucinda's room opened with a loud click.

She ran across the small space between the rooms, sure that something would grab her ankle and yank her down the stairs. Slamming the door closed, she rested against it. Panic burned like wildfire through her veins. This room didn't have a lock, but that really didn't matter.

A sudden draught lifted her hair from her brow and she turned slowly to the window.

It was open to the night. Open to the teeth of the forest.

The strength dissolved from her legs and she staggered

across, desperate to close it, Dan's warning pounding in her head. Why wouldn't he wake up? The tightness in her throat was a physical pain.

As Faye reached for the handle, she pushed her fingers through something sticky. She stared down at the silvery strands floating from her fingers.

A clump of moss on the outside sill began to move.

Only it wasn't a clump of moss.

It took her brain a few moments to decipher what it was. And a few moments more to accept the horror as it uncoiled inside her head.

The silver strands tightened around her fingertips.

The creature that had spun the web unfolded its legs, raising itself up, swollen spidery body bristling with black hair. Its jaws glistened in the moonlight. Faye slammed the window shut so hard that the glass rattled.

The remnants of the threads drifted on her fingertips and she rubbed her hands frantically across her t-shirt.

The scratching came again.

Her eyes flew to the wooden headboard—something inside it was trying to get out.

She ran to the door, her fingers trembling as they fumbled on the latch, but the door refused to open.

Faye shrank back until she was pressed into the corner of the room opposite the bed. She slid bonelessly to the floor, dragging her knees into her chest, her arms around them, her whole body shaking violently.

Fixing her gaze on the dark wooden headboard, the thing she had slept beside, she bit down hard on her lower lip.

The surface of the wood was a squirming mass of movement. Things she couldn't identify slithered and coiled.

In the very centre a small circle began to turn. Faye couldn't take her eyes from its hypnotic swirl as it gained momentum. Moving faster and faster until her vision tunnelled and everything else faded into oblivion. The sound of water filled her head and for a moment she was in the lake again, struggling to free herself from the fingers of the weeds.

Then a loud crack came from the window, jolting her attention back to the present, although she could still feel the pressure of the water against her ears. The old glass shuddered under the burden of dozens of swollen spider bellies, hairline cracks etched upon the panes.

She forced her gaze away from the window, to movement on the old, country-rose-covered wallpaper. From the stems of each bloom trickled thick, black liquid. It twisted, spreading in vine-like veins, and to Faye's terror, it began to form letters.

The window frame shook and the glass gave way. The creatures tumbled into the room, crawling all over each other in their haste to reach her.

R said the letter scrawled on the wall.

A spike of pearled moonlight hit the floor and before she knew what she was doing, she was on her feet, squeals emitting from the creatures as she tore through them. Her foot came down on one as she launched herself towards the window sill, its body popping open like a crushed grape, pale innards gushing out.

U said the letter scrawled on the wall.

She bit back a revolted scream, her body hitting the wooden sill hard, knocking the air from her lungs. But the joyous freedom of the night was like an oasis in a desert, and she wanted to drink it in and never stop.

All thoughts of what she was going to do once she had climbed through the window were a haze of disconnected patterns, the only one that mattered was fleeing from this room. Small fragments of shattered glass dug into her knees and palms as she scrambled over the sill, her legs dangling against the side of the cottage.

For an instant, the ground looked a long way, too far to drop without breaking a bone. She risked one last look back over her shoulder, and saw the final letter.

RUN.

Faye pushed herself from the frame. One moment of gravity defying space. And then she fell.

THIRTY-FOUR

Faye's hip hit something solid and she yelped, a shooting pain vibrating along her spine. Her fingers scrabbled for grip but the porch roof slid underneath her grasping hands.

She slipped to the edge of the weather-worn tiles, legs swinging out into thin air. A glance towards her bedroom showed the spider creatures swarming on the sill, some already descending on silken threads that glinted like steel in the moonlight.

Faye ground her teeth together and let herself dangle over the porch. She let go. Her feet hit the ground in a bone-shaking jar that did nothing to ease the ache in her hip, but already her legs were stumbling down the garden path, the sunflower petals brushing against her hair.

She reached the gate and yanked it open, staggering out on to the patch of land before the forest. Wild-eyed and with a cold sweat prickling through her pores, Faye realised that she had nowhere safe to go.

Looking down the deserted track she prayed for a car, for Robert McCallum, even for Albert Jenkins, but nothing moved in this terrifying reality that had swallowed her whole. Everything everyone had told her came rushing back, the veiled warnings now crystal clear.

She had one choice and one choice only.

Sliding her phone from her pocket, she clicked on her torch and sprinted into the forest, gritting her teeth as the pain in her hip bit hard.

Everything looked different in the dark. The press of the trees seemed nearer, heavier, the pathway meandering in too many directions. But Faye knew the way. Knew where she was heading even though the thought of it was a pendulum blade, severing her sanity thread by thread.

She could feel its presence as she ran, its silent call as it pulled her forwards, until all that remained was the unstrung hammer of her heart against her ears and the bouncing pale beam of the phone, creating monstrous shapes out of fallen trees, leering faces alive in their bark. Tangles of undergrowth snatched at her feet, spindly branches caught in her hair, tearing strands out by the roots.

She refused to look back because none of that mattered anymore.

The stump of the lightning tree passed by in a blur and she veered right. A couple of times she fell to her knees over hidden tree roots, but always up on her feet in an instant, despite her lungs crying out for rest.

Something screeched above her, an ear-splitting sound, and Faye raised her head, catching a barn owl in soundless soar, its eyes as dark as ink against its pale plumage. On and on, past the tree where she had found the hapless rabbit, fear vibrating in her throat as her mind catapulted an image of herself caught in the trap, helpless and bleeding, as the spider creatures swarmed over her.

Her shoulder banged into something dangling from a low sprouting branch. A cold liquid splashed over her face and she shrieked, the sound eaten whole by the darkness.

On her lips a taste she knew. Sugar.

She angled her phone and found a hanging glass lantern. The same kind as Albert and Lydia had been filling. Another droplet splashed onto her skin.

Sugar water. The realisation came like a hard slap against her cheek: they had been feeding whatever lived in these words.

The tangled copse loomed ahead, its tumbleweed mass blocking her path. She paused, swinging her phone around in a circle, desperately searching for another way through.

The thought of the boy in the house, and whatever part he played, sang to her through the night. And on the back of this her son's image nipped at her heels, urging her onwards.

At the other side of the copse the leaves rustled.

Faye backed away a few steps. Something moved through the tangle of briars and her heart skittered like a needle across vinyl, the dead weight of her phone between her fingers.

The night coated her face, the cold disc of the moon criss-crossed with the dark veins of the branches.

A hand punched from the tangle. It grasped hers in an icy grip, yanking her into the copse. The tiny tinkle of a bell met her ears.

A chilled finger against her lips for the briefest instant. *Be quiet.*

Hawthorn and holly tore through her clothes, their razor-tipped points burning bloody welts against her skin. Faye hung onto the pain. Because it meant she was alive.

The darkness was absolute, apart from a few brief glimpses of moonlight through the canopies of leaves. But the light became a frightened thing as the trees closed in around them. In the distance, Faye thought she could hear the movement of water on the lake. But there was no wind.

She had a stitch in her side and her throbbing hip was a constant reminder of the horror she had fled from. Back in the cottage Dan slept like a dead man, oblivious to her nightmare.

Out of the corner of her eye a flash of blue glinted in the trees. Whatever was in the glass case in the cottage belonged here, in these woods, or in Barrington Hall.

The boy stopped abruptly, and she ran into his shoulder, once again aware of how fragile he seemed. A boy made of bone and flesh but as delicate as glass. She wondered what he ate, how he managed to scrape by living in the belly of that awful house.

She didn't really know him at all, but right now he was all she had, her strange and uncharted port in this terrifying storm, and she clung to him, the chill from his damp skin seeping into her own.

He glanced behind her, his eyes too big for his heart-shaped face, tangled strands of hair clinging to his throat. Then those eyes fell upon hers and she looked away, not wanting him to see her studying the dried blood on his jaw. She had been running away from monsters, but what was she running towards?

The trees around her began to fade out of focus, and for one awful minute Faye thought she was going to faint. The temperature dropped viciously, as though someone had opened the door to the Arctic Circle.

A creeping mist devoured the thick trunks of the trees, leaving only indistinct smudges, and when she glanced back at the boy his hair was frosted with tiny moisture droplets. His grip on her hand tightened.

'If I take you in, it won't ever let you go, you do realise

that, don't you?'

Faye wanted to say that it was only a ruin of a house, that it had a door she could go through whenever she wanted to. But something told her he was telling the truth. Because it had happened to him.

Before this place she had been a streetwise woman, plugged into the heartbeat of the city and the hamster wheel of social media, nursing a grudge against her husband and drowning in her own grief. In the span of only a few days, everything she thought she knew had been ripped apart.

'There's something in a glass case, at the cottage…' Her mouth was dry, the words caught on her parched lips.

From out of the mist a shrill clicking rolled towards them.

Faye watched in horror as the boy at her side answered in the same tongue.

He let go of her hand, his throat rippling. 'That's Corrigan,' he whispered. 'She's watching us.'

Goosebumps crawled across Faye's skin. 'Who is she?'

'Not who. What.'

Three small words. They sank their teeth into Faye's tenuous grip on reality.

'This is what she does,' he breathed, 'she feeds on your fear.' He was backing away, his form disappearing into the mist.

A frenzied rustling came from the undergrowth behind her and she tore her eyes away from his fading shape.

Something burst through the brambles and Faye stumbled backwards as it barrelled into her. A wet nose against her palm, a warm tongue.

Tilly. The dog began to bark, a rough, solid sound. A wonderfully normal sound.

Faye fell to her knees and wrapped her arms around Tilly's damp fur, letting the dog lick away her tears.

'Mrs. Morgan?' Robert's gruff voice boomed at the other side of the copse, and then the sound of his boots striking through, and the sweep of something parting the vicious thorns.

He emerged from the mist and Faye almost wanted to hug him.

'Why in the Dickens are you out in the middle of the night?' Robert's hand came to rest on her shoulder.

She wiped her nose on her arm, willing the tears to subside because she really didn't want to come across as unhinged. Even if she was. She made herself stand even though her legs were still wobbly, turning to look for the boy, because he might be able to explain better than she could.

But the boy had gone. Had slipped away into the darkness without a sound. And the mist had crawled after him.

'I couldn't wake Dan.' The words stuck in her throat. 'And there were things in my room...hideous things...'

Robert's eyes met hers, and it seemed like they held the colour of the shifting forest. She waited for the disbelief, but it didn't come. Because this was the man who knew what had happened to Dan all those summers ago.

Instead, he patted her shoulder with a hand large enough to be a bear paw.

'I want to show you something, Faye, something that not many people have seen.' He reached for her hand and placed it on the crook that was wedged under his arm. 'My father gave this to me, and his father before him. It was made when that house'—Robert nodded his head in the direction of Barrington Hall—'was built. My grandfather worked on the house, made this crook from a length of hazel wood. He didn't just take it, mind, no one back then took things from the forest. It didn't belong to them. The hazel shank was a gift to him. From the ones who protected the forest. It was my grandfather's most prized possession, and then my father's. And now it's mine and I never forget its message.' He ran a hand down the pale wood.

Faye's fingers curled around the shaft. *Superstition.* The word flitted through her mind. She had a fleeting image of the women at her yoga class looking into her little world, their whispers of contempt making her ears burn. But that part of her life seemed as distant as the milky face of the moon.

'Did you ever see them?' she whispered, 'the ones who protect the forest?'

Corrigan. If a thing has a name it makes it real.

He studied her for a moment, his bushy eyebrows shielding the fierce glint of his eyes. 'They had no need to show themselves to me.' Faye bit her lip. 'Because they know I believe in them.'

Robert set off into the darkness. She stumbled after him.

The gamekeeper drew a stout torch from his jacket and flicked on the beam, as though it was an afterthought. As though he didn't need the light at all.

They walked together, Robert occasionally sweeping bramble tangles aside with his crook. This was a pathway few people used. Barely a foot wide, it was covered with rising tree roots, and Faye had to concentrate to keep her footing. Tilly ran back a couple of times to check they were still following. She whined and worried, but Robert sent her on into the darkness.

A shiver flitted across her skin, the modern woman in her

knowing she was traipsing through a forest in the middle of the night with a strange man who could snap her neck with one hand.

She thought about the boy and the way he had just disappeared. The wet clay of doubt settled in her stomach. Doubt about Dan, and the cottage. About the boy and Barrington Hall. About what she had seen in her bedroom. What if she *was* losing her mind?

Robert stopped and pushed open a low metal gate. The hinges creaked, old metal pulled from its slumber.

Faye turned her head slightly. She could smell the thick, dank scent of old water.

'Robert, can I ask you something?'

He paused, ruffling Tilly's ears as she ran back to greet him.

Faye plucked one of the many questions swarming in her head. The one she truly wanted to ask, about Dan, was glued to the lining of her throat. 'Why did Lucinda tie those knots in the wool? What did they mean?'

'It was just her way of protecting the cottage,' Robert answered, his eyes on Tilly as she flopped down at his feet. 'A binding spell if you like. She thought she could keep it still, you see, keep it from calling out to its kin. But I told her it was as dead as a door nail, it had to be, after all this time. And that we had to keep it secret or else all hell would be let loose.'

His answer only raised more questions.

'Why did you have to keep it a secret?'

He shook his head as though he had said too much.

The path continued, veering to the left, following the course of a stream that had appeared as they passed through the gate. Their footsteps crunched on a carpet of old fallen leaves.

She stumbled over the edge of something hard, landing heavily on one knee. The ground beneath her hands was damp, that same scent of green she'd smelled in the cottage rising up.

Robert reached down and helped her to stand. Her trainer had slipped off her heel so she leant against a tree and pulled it back on. Robert angled his torch so she could see what she had tripped over.

A solitary fallen gravestone.

Her eyes scanned the shadows for more, but there was only this one, alone in the dark, with the ever-present rush of the stream behind its back.

'Local legend says this is where one of the children who used to live in Barrington Hall is buried. But I know for a fact that his bones aren't here.'

Faye glanced up, and behind the circle of light from Robert's torch his eyes were as dark as pitch.

THIRTY-FIVE

Dan awoke suddenly, sitting bolt upright in bed before his brain could shrug away the floating remnants of his dream. He'd been in the forest, close to twilight when all was shadow. Sounds came from beyond the trees, sounds that even now he could hear dying away like an echo. He rubbed his eyes with his fists, a strange clicking noise finally fading.

His head throbbed as though he'd just woken after a night out in the city, but he'd only had a small measure of whisky. Groggy with sleep, he reached across to flick on the lamp. And then it hit him, as the golden glow pierced the darkness—he had fallen asleep when he had promised Faye he wouldn't.

Even before Dan turned, he knew that his wife wasn't there. His hand flew to the sheets, hoping to find warmth signalling she had only just gone, but the bed was cold. He was up on his feet in an instant, pulling on his shoes, stumbling over untied laces as he wrenched open the bedroom door.

'Faye!' he called.

The echo that came back was such a forlorn sound. He had promised to look after her. And he had failed.

Pushing open the door to her room, he prayed that she was fast asleep, had only removed herself from his company, but there was nothing in that bed—the bed he had slept in as a child. His eyes flew to the window. Open. Of course it was open.

And then he saw the fractured glass covering the sill and floor.

A sob rose in his throat and he clutched his head with both hands, fear rising like a phoenix from the underbelly of his guilt. He ran to the window, his feet crunching on the glass fragments.

'Faye! For God's sake, answer me!' But God had no hand in what was happening.

She had gone to Barrington Hall. Or something from there had claimed her.

All of the warnings came back to him, toppling over each other in their haste to batter him to the ground.

Barrington Hall knew he was planning on leaving and so it had forced his hand, taking the one thing he loved more than life itself.

Everything that had happened was leading up to this.

Then something rose out of the ashes of his remorse. Something primal and protective.

Dan raced down the stairs, grabbing his rucksack from the kitchen. Pulling open cupboard doors and rifling through the contents in a frenzy, he threw in a torch that had belonged to Lucinda and a coil of rope with frayed edges. *All the best adventures end with a rope.* A voice from long ago.

Focus, Danny, focus.

He grabbed his old wooden catapult and tossed it into his bag, along with a pair of thick gardening gloves with a hole in one thumb. Dan had no idea why. He was running on instinct, hyper aware each second he was taking was keeping him from Faye. And hyper aware that he needed something to protect himself with.

But what he was looking for wasn't in any of the cupboards. He stopped, a gasp of strangled air hitching in his throat. His heart thudded against his ribcage.

Where would Lucinda have put it? He knew for definite that she would never have thrown it away. Memories of his aunt resurfaced from his racing mind. Standing in the garden, an apron dotted in tiny flowers covering her dress. Her face in shadow from a wide-brimmed straw hat. The scent of roses pricked his nostrils.

The outhouse. Dan slid the bolts on the front door, grunting in frustration as one refused to budge. He kicked it with his heel and it gave.

Yanking open the door, he ran into the night, praying that the outhouse wasn't locked.

His foot struck something solid, submerged in shadow on the path, and he stumbled, but his eyes were trained on the pale wood of the old shack at the edge of the garden. Peeling paint drifted from the door as he drove his shoulder into it.

God help him, he would tear it down with his bare hands if he had to.

His fingers curled around the metal handle, and memory took over. He twisted it first to the left, then to the right, then pulled up, and the door opened easily. Curtains of cobwebs drifted over his face, and the old familiar fear of death dug a knife into his gut. He flailed at the webs, trying not to imagine fat flies wrapped up in their strands. Just waiting to be eaten.

Why the hell hadn't he brought the torch?

But as his eyes began to make sense of the jumbled shapes in the outhouse, he saw what he was looking for. At the side of the door, in full view, as though Lucinda had known all along.

181

Dan grabbed hold of the handle, the weight of it somehow comforting in his hands.

'Don't you ever use this, Danny. Until you need to.'

Back then he hadn't given much thought to her odd wording, his arrogant teenage self dismissing it as muddled rambling. But now he knew different.

He raced up the path. And came to a grinding halt as his eyes found what he had stumbled over.

The dead fox Robert McCallum had killed lay strewn across the pathway, its sightless eyes staring into his soul. Something had torn into its belly leaving a trail of glistening viscera.

Dan recoiled, fighting the urge to throw up, battling with the fear he had known all of his life.

It was easy to forget about it in the city. But out here death lived and breathed.

Forcing his feet onwards, Dan skirted the mangled body, trying not to obsess about the way its tongue lolled out of its mouth like a fat worm.

He staggered back into the cottage. The door to Lucinda's room stood open.

In the pale moonlight from the window, diamond shadows lay on the wooden floor. Dan's eyes followed the pattern until they came to rest on the glass case. He swallowed.

Slowly, he crept across the room, never taking his eyes from what lay within. The birds and small mammals regarded him with their glassy stares, a mournful interpretation of what they had once been. Death captured and put on display.

But what he had come for was almost hidden in the depths of the moss and dry branches lining the bottom of the case. In the milky glow, the tiniest shimmer of blue against the darkness.

Dan raised the object in his hands above his head, curling his fingers around its shaft. He brought the axe down on the glass with all the strength he had left.

Dan had expected the old glass to break easily. He thought it would be brittle. But the case had held its secrets for a long time and it wasn't prepared to give them up easily.

Sweat, borne from exertion and fear, trickled down Dan's spine. His shirt stuck to the small of his back.

Again and again, he swung the axe, the impact as it hit the case vibrating through his fingers, racing up his arms.

'God damn you, you will break!' He screamed his frustration into the room, part of it at his own inadequacy and partly at Lucinda who hadn't passed on her own secrets. But then how could she? How could she tell a fourteen-year-old boy about the darkness that clung to this cottage? About the rot which lived in the skin of Barrington Hall.

Dan's muscles throbbed, the axe heavy in his hand as he hammered it into the corner of the glass. A fragment broke away, leaving a smooth dent. He wiped his sweating palms on his shirt and doubled his efforts, striking the spot once, twice, three times.

A hairline crack appeared on its surface.

Minutes ticked by, marked by the old clock on the mantle. Minutes in which he felt Faye being pulled away from him ever deeper.

Dan began to wonder if the case was moored by magic, and this thought scared him almost as much as the body of the fox lying strewn on the path. If he believed in magic, that meant he believed in the old ways, in everything people had warned him about.

The thought welled up, thick and oozing, like pus from a wound. He threw down the axe, grabbing hold of the back of the case with both hands.

Using every ounce of energy he could muster, Dan heaved. The glass slipped away under his fingertips. He wiped his hands on his shirt again, then remembered the work gloves he had thrust into his rucksack. He grabbed them from the kitchen.

The old leather on the gloves gave his fingers more purchase. Gritting his teeth, he tried again, and the case moved slightly. Slowly, slowly, it inched towards the edge of the stout wooden shelf it sat upon.

By the time the case rested on the edge, Dan's arms felt as though they were made of wet string. Every muscle in his upper body screamed in rebellion.

But it made him even more determined to get inside. Whoever had put that *thing* in the case had gone to a lot of trouble to make sure it never was disturbed.

With one last almighty heave, Dan yanked the case so that it hung over the edge of the shelf.

He raced into the kitchen and grabbed the coil of rope. As he crossed over the hallway, he heard the dry snap of aging wood. The timeworn shelf gave up its ghost, the weight finally too much.

Dan watched as the case crashed down. The thundering sound of splintered wood and breaking glass, the scent of old dust. The vibration travelled across the floor, shivering under his feet. A few feathers floated in the air, torn from the hapless stuffed grouse imprisoned within.

He prayed that the thing in the corner hadn't broken apart.

Dan strode across as the dust settled. The blackbird lay with broken wings. The dormouse had lost its tail. Old moss and dried bark from the ancient branches lay scattered all around. He bent down, carefully picking his way through the shards of broken glass and shattered wood.

For one awful moment he thought that it had disintegrated, but the edge of the knitting needle caught his eye and he followed it down to find what he was looking for.

The point had pierced the creature through its abdomen.

Dan closed his fingers around the needle, not wanting to touch the small, still body. His eyes took in the graceful sweep of dragonfly wings, the antennae folded neatly behind its head. Its abdomen swelled around the cruel plunge of the needle, and hinged forelegs sprang from its body, clasped together as if in prayer. But dear God, its face was far too human.

Revulsion crawled over his skin along with the absolute conviction that this creature had something to do with Barrington Hall. But he had to get it there first.

He stuffed a layer of moss into the bottom of the rucksack and laid the creature upon it, trying not to look at the vicious gleam of the needle.

Carefully, he slipped the rope and the gloves around it for added protection, then unfastened the belt on his jeans and slipped the handle of the axe through the leather, like some kind of medieval sharp shooter.

Grabbing his phone from the table by the front door was more like an act of habit than of necessity. Once he had fretted over taking a day off, at not being in the loop of his friends' social media activities, not wanting to be left out of meet ups and weekends away, not wanting to be the odd one out.

Dan saw now how insular he had become, how privilege

had turned him into a man whose grieving wife had been just something else to deal with. How he had buried his own guilt and remorse beneath the shackles of work. He hung his head in shame.

His eyes flicked to the black-and-white photo in the frame on the table. Lucinda stood with four other people, in a snapshot of captured time. She stood on a gravelled driveway, her gaze on something the viewer couldn't see. Dan studied her companions.

Jem Porter. Albert Jenkins. The woman who had been with him in the forest. Robert McCallum.

And behind them all, the front door to Barrington Hall.

He ran to the kitchen, scattering the pile of papers stacked by the sink. The ones he had been going through. His fingers flicked through them, his eyes scanning for the piece of paper with the legal print. Agitation churned in his blood. It was here. He knew it was here...

He found one sheet with a name printed in Lucinda's neat handwriting in the margin. But this wasn't what he was looking for.

And then it was in his fingers, his eyes running rapidly over the densely worded paragraphs. He saw, then, what he had signed. What he hadn't truly read.

Lucinda Latimer hadn't simply bequeathed him the cottage.

She had also bequeathed him Barrington Hall.

THIRTY-SIX

The gamekeeper had picked up his pace. Faye found herself running to keep up. She had lost all sense of direction.

The night pressed against her with phantom hands.

Once, Tilly ran back and pushed a wet nose into her palm, whining softly, but Robert whistled her to his side. There was an impatience about him that Faye hadn't seen before. A new fear lodged under her ribcage like a stone.

'Robert, please stop. I've got a stitch.'

It was only half a lie, as the sharp pain was forming in her side as the words left her lips.

The gamekeeper turned, his face lit by a shaft of moonlight piercing the bare branches of a long dead oak. He studied her for a moment, and then a smile broke on his face. Faye had the weirdest thought. For a moment, it looked like the crack on an eggshell.

Her stomach churned uneasily.

'Sorry, Mrs. Morgan, I forgot that you're not a country dweller. Not far now, then you'll see what all this has been about.'

'I want to go home.' Her voice trembled. A quiet plea in the dark. But she didn't want to go back to the cottage. It was no longer a safe place, if it ever had been.

'Soon.' Robert's curt reply came as he set off down the

track, his torch beam bouncing.

Through a gap in the trees, with the moon on its shoulder, came the brooding hulk of Barrington Hall. They had skirted the lake somehow, and were approaching the house from the other side. Faye caught the scent of stagnant water. Her nose wrinkled.

In an upstairs window was a tiny flickering glow from a candle.

'Here we go, watch your step now, it's slippery.' Robert stood before a small enclosure. Rusted railings, crowned with fleur-de-lis tips, surrounded a weather-beaten tomb. An angel with its wings outstretched to the heavens rose from the old stone, speckles of lichen covering its face.

Robert angled his torch in a slow circle.

The tomb sat on a slightly raised patch of ground, surrounded by an army of tall grasses. Faye reached out, let her fingers trail through their feathery tips.

'It wasn't uncommon for a family to be buried on their own ground. William Kidd had marked this space before the house was even done. Back then the lake surrounded it, made it a natural island. A perfect place for eternal rest.' He paused and hung his head. 'But after the first deaths and how they occurred, the people here were glad of it. They didn't want that curse in the village graveyard.'

Faye found herself hanging onto Robert's every word. A sudden breeze swept through the trees, and with it came the tiny peal of a bell.

Faye searched the darkness. 'What do you mean, how they occurred?'

'The whole family gone, all apart from one. In the space of a year. It rocked the village, took away all of the work whilst the lawyers went through the will. It was a harsh winter. A lot of the poorer families starved, those who relied on the forest work.'

Tilly whimpered, a thin, animal song of knowledge.

'Of course, it all passed down to William Kidd's only son. But he vanished without trace after being sent to some exclusive boarding school near London, a few months after this all started. Other people said he had run away, gone insane, because of what happened to his family.'

'But what has all this got to do with Dan, with me?' Faye asked.

'What that boy did'—Robert spat on the ground—'was unspeakable. He upset the balance of the forest, a balance that had held for centuries. But his actions turned the few that were left. Turned them to darkness and laid a curse upon this land. And now we all pay.'

His face had grown stern, deep frown lines etched across his brow. One hand clutched his crook, his fingers tight.

A wave of despair swept over Faye, numbing her fingertips. Robert's words had the awful ring of finality. She took one tentative step backwards. In her peripheral vision the tall grasses swayed, a whisper of green kissing stone. Against her ears the soft lap of the lake.

'I'm sorry, Faye, I really am, but my hands are tied. We have to make amends, look after what's left. Give the house what it wants.'

A sound came from Faye's throat, something that was half whimper, half shocked surprise at Robert's betrayal. He had lured her here.

Robert swung his torch beam out onto the ghost of a narrow track leading from the tomb. 'You went inside

Barrington Hall, and now it wants you back.'

Something that could have been regret settled on his face, and then was gone as his lips tightened.

Faye did the only thing she could, turning her face to the behemoth walls of grim stone.

She began to walk. The urge to flee raged in her veins but she forced her feet forwards.

As she drew closer, the walls of Barrington Hall seemed to loom a little taller. Milky moonlight washed over its slate roof.

The breeze stilled. The only sound her feet as they moved through the tangle of grass and weeds, and the crunch of old gravel. The watery beam from Robert's torch went out.

Her foot caught on the edge of a stone step, and she stumbled. Three steps, her memory told her, three steps that you raced up quite willingly only a few days ago…

Before her she could sense the solid wood of the front doors. In the terrifying silence, a creak fell into the darkness. Faye had forgotten how to breathe properly. She forced a gulp of air through her lips, through her chattering teeth. It was so very cold.

Her feet felt like lead weights as she mounted the steps.

Reaching out with one hand, she felt what she had known would be there. Nothing at all.

Because the doors of Barrington Hall had opened to welcome her in.

THIRTY-SEVEN

Dan was by the gate when he realised he hadn't closed the door of the cottage. The golden glow from the hallway spilled out into the night, but it didn't reach past the confines of the porch. The darkness had lapped away any light.

He thought about going back and closing it, but it really didn't matter. No one would be coming this way. He saw it now, as clearly as if someone had etched it into his thought pattern. As soon as he brought Faye here, something had been set in motion that he had no control over.

His jaw clenched as he went through the gate, letting it swing back on itself. The harsh click of metal against metal rang out into the darkness.

Over his shoulder was the rucksack with its disturbing and jumbled contents. Everything he thought he knew, all of his good sense and understanding, swam around in a sea of confusion, shadows from his past caught in the undercurrent, determined to drag him down into the bottomless depths.

Fear curdled in his stomach; he curled his fingers over the handle of the axe, trying to find some comfort in its solidity.

He tried to ignore the way the branches of the trees creaked above him as he entered the forest. The light from his torch, so bright in the cottage, was a pathetic pale line fighting its way through the dark.

Small twigs crunched under his feet as he made his way along the pathway. *Little bones break so easily.*

Someone had said that to him once. Or he had overheard it. He couldn't quite remember, but as he trudged alone in the darkness, it seemed important. But memory is a fickle beast, and only gives you crumbs when you are starving for a banquet.

The corpse of the lightning tree appeared in his torch beam, and now, in the dark, its broken, blackened branches were clawed fingers beckoning Dan closer. A sheen of sweat prickled his brow. He shook his head, angry at himself for letting his thoughts wander off into the shadows, away from what truly mattered. Faye.

She had tried her hardest to get him to talk about his childhood, because she knew something was deeply wrong here, something twisted and unnatural nestling amongst the tranquillity.

Dan's thoughts skipped, and he heard her voice. *I think there's a boy living in Barrington Hall.* She saw the ghost of Toby everywhere. And maybe that's what had drawn her in, the ghosts of what had lived here before.

The sketch she had done of Barrington Hall should have been the catalyst for him to gather her up and get the hell out of this place. Within a few sweeping charcoal strokes, she had managed to produce the suffocating presence of that house, the way it sat on the land like a black, distended scar, the oozing rot inside it daring anyone to pick at the scab.

Barrington Hall had touched his wife with its poison and held her in its thrall, just like it had done to him all those years ago.

He veered to the right, following the crooked path, his

whole world contained in the thin circle of light from his torch.

Something moved in the undergrowth. A slight rustle of old autumn leaves. Dan swallowed.

He moved his torch beam. A white bobtail disappeared in a quiver as a small rabbit ducked quickly for cover.

If his friends could see him now. Spooked beyond reason by a bunny. But he had only shown them the Dan who refused to give up on a sales lead, even when the trail went cold; the Dan who was always the first to buy a round of drinks on a night out; the Dan who could cope with anything life threw at him. Even the death of his son.

Remorse welled like a droplet of blood from a pinprick.

A sound travelled through the air and Dan paused, trying to locate it. But all was silent. He shrugged, convinced it was simply his mind playing tricks.

The pathway came to the crossroads, where the old woodcutter's shack stood forlorn, its corrugated tin roof the colour of old blood.

Stacks of logs still sat beyond its open entrance, and there, by the door, Dan could just make out the legs of an old table.

We played here. A memory surfaced, bright in the darkness. *We used it as a den sometimes. I told him this was where the bogeyman lived.*

The memory faded, its edges softening, even as Dan fought for more.

Something wet rolled down his cheek. He swiped at the tear with his hand.

His thoughts were a confused wash of hazy images, a nonsensical line of cracked snapshots fluttering like butterfly wings. His limbs grew heavy as the rucksack slipped down his arm.

Then a barbed pain jolted him into the present, chasing away his befuddlement. He clutched at the back of his arm, letting the rucksack fall to the ground.

The pointed end of the knitting needle gleamed through the canvas.

Dan wanted to unzip the bag, to check that the thing was still in one piece, but his fingers refused to obey. He hefted the rucksack onto his other shoulder.

The darkness grew thicker. Dan turned the torch towards his face. On the circle of glass rested the largest moth he had ever seen. It had two sets of papery wings, and as Dan watched in fascinated horror, it curled its slug-like abdomen towards him.

He dropped the torch as though it had scalded him.

The sound he had heard before came again, and this time his brain made the connection. It was buzzing.

Blindly, he wheeled around, his heartbeat thundering in his ears. A smell wafted out of the dark, something heavy and sweet and rotten.

He gagged, a flood of saliva in his mouth. He knew that smell.

It had come from the decaying deer they had found in the woods on that long-ago summer evening. Trapped in a deep manmade pit, its belly distended by gas, sightless eyes covered in flies. More swarmed from its gaping mouth, crawling over the lolling grey tongue.

He had been revolted but entranced, rushing off to snap a thin sapling, shaking off the quiet words that they shouldn't disturb it. That the forest claims what it wants.

He hadn't been alone. Dan could still see the pale, solemn

face and the wide-eyed fear. Fear for Dan's safety. The boy who had been such an integral part of his childhood here. The boy he had teased mercilessly for being a country mouse.

And the boy who had pulled him out of that pit when the sides collapsed, and he had tumbled head first down onto the deer, the force of his fall splitting the creature's bloated belly open, the stench of rot invading his nostrils, squirming maggots on his hands as he screamed and screamed and screamed.

The flies had been everywhere, incessantly buzzing. They had settled in his hair, on his skin, crawled into his open, shrieking mouth.

Dan's legs turned to jelly as the sound from his nightmare punched into the present.

They came upon him like locusts, the buzzing a high-pitched reverberation in his ears. He flailed at them, waving his arms around uselessly, the old fear exploding through his veins as they settled on his sweat-slicked skin.

One crawled into his nose. He panicked and tried to snort it out. Nausea rose in his throat and he doubled over, throwing up the contents of his supper, whisky tainted. Warm vomit splashed onto his face.

The flies crawled down the collar of his t-shirt, the itch of their legs and wings driving his mind to the edge of madness.

Dan fled blindly into the dark. Spindly branches whipped against his face. Flaying him for past transgressions. He wanted to scream. The need for it was a pressure he felt at the back of his brain, a desperation for release, flicking all his gauges to overdrive.

His foot snagged on a raised root and he stumbled, his head connecting with the side of a tree as he fell. His felt his skin grate on the rough bark, the pain leaving an eruption of colour behind his sightless eyes.

The force of his face hitting the ground drove a tooth through his lip. Blood welled in his mouth as he fought to stay conscious.

Dan managed to drag his knees underneath him. Then the cloud of flies descended again, relentless in their assault.

A piercing noise drilled into his skull as he collapsed onto his side; dizziness claimed his fight to stay upright.

The forest claims what it wants.

The echoes of the country boy's words. The boy he had left to die.

PART TWO

WITHIN
the walls

THIRTY-EIGHT

The doors of Barrington Hall stood open.

Faye hesitated just beyond the threshold, caught in the quagmire of terrible choices. She didn't want to return to Robert McCallum. She didn't want to return to the cottage in case she found her husband dead. A whimper built in her throat, wavering like a reed in a storm. Dried leaves skittered across the stone steps as a strong gust of wind buffeted her suddenly from behind.

The strange boy lived within these halls, and some part of her knew he was the only one who could help her.

She bit her lower lip and hovered on the threshold.

'I'm here.' Her whisper fanned out into the cavernous space, disappearing quickly, as though the house had eaten it.

Her fingers strayed across the peeling paint of the door, reluctant to leave it behind. To leave the wide, open space beyond it.

The lake was as black as pitch, apart from the glittering pathway of the moon. That same cold light shone through the doors of Barrington Hall. Showing her the way. For an instant, she thought about trying to make her way back to the village in the dark. But that would only be putting off the inevitable.

Everything that had happened since Toby's death had been building, layer upon layer. And now here, in this God-awful place, where the past had clawed its way into the present, everything had come to a head and burst, like a lanced boil.

Something on the hearth tiles caught her eye. A small, dark mound. Slowly, she edged across, the sound of her breath filling her ears. She touched it with the toe of her trainer and it flopped to one side.

A little cry of surprise left her lips and she jumped back, the noise startling her more than the discovery. A magpie, covered in soot with its neck broken, a vacant eye fixed in death. *One for sorrow.*

A floorboard creaked above her and Faye wheeled, her eyes searching through the gloom of the upstairs gallery.

The sound of a tiny, tinkling bell.

Faye crept to the foot of the sweeping staircase, finding shapes in the thick darkness beyond as her eyes adjusted to the lack of light.

She drew her phone from her pocket, fingers fumbling on the screen.

A gust of wind rattled the tall windows at either side of the doors. Then a squall of rain hit the glass in an angry lash. She took a deep breath, put one foot on the bottom step, her ears strained for any tiny sound as she sent her meagre light into the darkness.

Slowly, she crept up, one stair at a time, the dust of decades on the curved rail of the bannister gritty under her fingertips. Now she was on the small space where the stairway swept around on itself before disappearing into the gallery. The air here was sour, like spoiled milk.

Her torch light skimmed over the huge mirror at the top of the stairs. Its surface was silvered with age and dust. She averted her eyes as she crept past. Didn't want to see what it might reflect.

Faye angled her light into the deep gloom. An upstairs gallery, two corridors leading from it in an L shape. A carved chair sat against one wall, under a faded watercolour of the lake. A frayed carpet runner ran down the length of the corridor to her right, melting into the blackness.

Faye glanced down the staircase towards the open door. From this vantage point the great hall took on a different feel. Images of how it once must have been pulsed before her eyes. The black and white tiles gleamed like a polished chessboard. A fire crackled in the cast-iron hearth. A fine carriage waited outside of the doors, two chestnut horses with their coats burnished copper in the sun.

She covered her face with her hands. She wasn't sure what was freaking her out more. Being in this house or seeing things that weren't actually there.

Faye forced the panic down. Concentrated on the beating rhythm of the rain, and the sudden chill settling around her.

She crept along the hallway. Something disturbed the darkness. Something moving.

Faye sent the line of her torch into the blackness, imagining monsters and indescribable horrors. But what she found was a small rag doll, tattered and filthy.

It was hanging from the end of a rope.

✝

A strange disquiet washed over Faye as she stood in the near dark, the damp from the old house seeping through her skin. To see a child's innocent toy hanging from the end of a rope made her stomach roll. Her logic tried to make sense of how and why, and came up empty.

It was as if someone had been playing with it recently.

Goosebumps pricked her skin, a cold sweat on her brow. And then she heard it again. The tinkling of a bell.

'Who's there?' Her words trembled.

She turned towards the sound. Felt the shadows solidify.

Her breathing accelerated as a sharp jolt of adrenaline coursed through her veins.

At the top of the staircase stood the boy.

Faye calculated how long it would take her to push past him and race down the stairway and out into the night. But what good would that do?

In the dark of the forest she hadn't taken note of what he was wearing, but now, in the light from her phone she took in his strange clothing. He was dressed in filthy jeans, torn off below the knee, and an old-fashioned shirt with tattered lace at the cuffs. The long sleeves hung down over one hand. On his feet, canvas shoes, falling apart at the seams. He was also soaked to the skin, his hair plastered to his face, as though he had just come in from the rain.

'Who are you?' she asked, finally. She stood tall.

The boy looked her up and down, shielding his eyes from the glare. She lowered her phone a fraction.

'You don't belong here.'

'Don't I?' Faye blurted out. 'Robert McCallum seemed to think I did.'

The boy's eyes moved past her shoulder. She wheeled, her phone carving a line of light across the peeling walls.

The rope swung slowly side to side, like a forlorn swing in a playground.

The doll had gone.

She turned back to the boy, but the space at the top of the stairs was empty.

THIRTY-NINE

Frustration threaded itself through her fear-tinged surprise. She was tired of not understanding what was happening to her, tired of feeling like she was a dried-out shell of her former self.

She pressed her lips together, forced her shoulders down and inched across to the top of the staircase, sending her phone light into the darkness of the other corridor.

From above came the sound of doors creaking open, each noise echoing down through the floors, an amplified chorus of dread.

The house was opening its secrets. It wanted her to know.

She crept inside the first room on the left, turning in a slow circle and letting her torch play over the contents. A study, walls lined with bookcases from floor to ceiling, the spines swollen by damp. A large wooden desk with engraved edges stood in the centre of the room, an open book on its surface. *Like life has just been suspended here.*

Above the mouth of the empty fireplace was something shrouded with a dark cloth. Faye edged across the floor, the shadows around her long and thin, like grasping fingers. Standing on tip toe she pulled the edge of the cloth. A fall of dust coated her skin and she coughed, shielding her eyes till it settled.

Not a mirror but a family photograph. In shades of black and white, the family who had lived at Barrington Hall stared back at her. A man in a black, long-tailed coat stood behind a padded armchair, his hand resting on its curved back. A girl with her eyes downcast stood on the other side of the chair, dressed in a long black gown with a cameo pinned to her throat. By her feet knelt a small boy with a mop of pale hair. But it was the figure on the chair that caught Faye's attention.

A little girl, propped against a cushion, in a frilly white gown and dainty white shoes. But there was something odd about her eyes. Faye crept a little closer, her hand reaching to touch the frame.

Eyes had been crudely painted onto the child's closed eyelids. Faye's hand flew to cover her mouth.

The little girl on the chair was dead.

Faye knew the look on the family's faces. She had seen that look staring back at her from the mirror so many times. The numbness of grief.

She stared at the portrait again, this time studying the small boy. He was the only one who didn't wear that mask.

She thought about the doll on the rope and her eyes strayed to the door. There are no such things as ghosts she told herself, only what the human brain makes up from fear and loss and longing. Hadn't she wanted the boy in the forest to be Toby, even though her son was cold and still in the ground? Longing can make you want anything.

Faye stole across the floor, entering the gloom of the hallway again. A glimmer of bright blue at its end.

'Are you sure you want to see?' The boy stood before her, drifting from nowhere into her line of sight.

'I don't think I have any choice.' Her words were shaky,

her teeth chattering from the cold that drenched the darkened corridor.

'There's always choice.' His reply contained the weight of sadness. The weight of hindsight.

Faye pointed her phone towards the floor, the diffused light illuminating him from below. Her breath escaped in a thin white mist. 'Where did you come from?'

He turned his head, inclined it to one side so his face was hidden in the shadow of the door.

'I don't know.' His voice was soft in the darkness. 'I'm nobody important.' Such melancholy words, as though remembrance was a war he had fought and lost.

Faye leant against the wall. Cold seeped into her spine. The kind of cold she associated with old stone. She pressed the back of her head against it, suddenly bone tired.

Her hair snagged on something sharp, but as she tried to pull away the boy's arm came out of nowhere and she flinched. The back of her skull slammed into the wall, the impact clouding her vision for an instant. His hand came down behind her head, his other pulling her forwards.

Tears sprung to her eyes as pain juddered across her skull. She wheeled, her gaze fixed on the spot she had been leant against. It was undulating, a hank of her hair in its core.

Faye watched, struck dumb, as the hank slowly disappeared into the wall. There was a flurry of movement within as though something had pounced.

'What the hell…,' she began, but she didn't have any more words. The back of her head throbbed with a pulsating ache she could feel in her teeth.

The boy released his grip on her arm. 'They live in the walls,' he said. 'They live everywhere here.'

'What do?' She shivered, her eyes still locked to the wall.

'The ones like Corrigan.' His voice fell to a whisper. 'The dead ones.'

A high-pitched click sounded somewhere in the darkness and the boy turned his head towards it. Whatever lay in the bottom of the glass case in the cottage had once made that sound.

The terrifying, twisted reality of it burned at the back of her throat, his words an ice-cold fist around her heart.

'You're very brave,' he said, as he led her into the dark.

FORTY

From out of the damp-sodden darkness, Corrigan pounced. She hovered over them, the bright flash of blue from her belly illuminating every detail of her abominable form. Horror slid across the woman's face, her features contorting. Once upon a time that same expression had graced his own.

Corrigan was a nightmare of nature's violation. For one reason only she had evolved her species into its current form. To spark fear and revulsion.

In a blur of two translucent wings, she alighted on his shoulder. The woman screamed and flattened herself against the wall, then pulled away from it as though it had burnt her.

A slow, sly smile spread across Corrigan's all-too-human face as her antennae vibrated with pleasure.

'This won't do at all.' The tip of her proboscis extended. A droplet of slime quivered there.

It took him a moment to realise that the woman had actually understood too. She was rooted to the spot, the light clasped in her hands. Corrigan rarely lowered herself to human speech.

'You did well, my love.' Corrigan lapped at his cheek.

The woman shuddered, her eyes wild pools of terror.

'Perhaps it is time for you to remember? As a little gift for your obedience.' A coaxing, simpering tone that oozed inside his head like warm honey.

He gritted his teeth, didn't want to give her the satisfaction of knowing that the loss of his memory was the one thing that had made him feel like nothing at all.

This was how Corrigan worked, combining hope and horror in one simple swoop, daring you to lower your guard.

'What the fuck are you?' the woman managed to stutter. The smell of her fear was ripe in the dark.

Corrigan laughed, that shrill, sharp sound that echoed through the darkened forest nightly.

He felt the touch of a foreleg across his jaw, steeled himself for the sharp sting that followed. He knew, without looking, that Corrigan would be tasting that blood, letting it sit upon her tongue like nectar.

But her sting didn't just draw blood. It could gift him with a memory of her choosing.

The glittering molten steel of the lake, the full moon reflected on its tranquil surface. The wind whispers in the treetops. His sweat prickles across his skin.

'Let's swim,' says a voice and he turns to see the moon mirrored in a boy's eyes, eagerness in his smile. 'What can go wrong? There's no one here.'

But he can feel it then, the weight of a gaze he can't see, the feeling that what they are doing is far worse than just trespassing on someone's land.

'Don't you ever disrespect Barrington Hall, Milo, do you hear?' He remembers his grandfather's voice, his hand on Milo's shoulder, adding authority to his words.

A burst of blue in the dark, the pungent scent of late forest bluebells. And before Milo can form the warning words, the boy lifts the flowers into the air, waving them from side to side.

'See? They don't even ring a little bit.'

The boy tosses the flowers into the lake. They land with a small ripple, float away like blooms from a funeral pyre.

But Milo hears the tiny tinkle of a bell on the midnight breeze.

'There you are, Milo,' Corrigan crooned. 'Is it all coming back to you now?'

Milo sank to a crouch, his hands in his hair, the sound of his name pounding in his head. How he had longed to remember, and now he knew why she had made him forget.

'It really wasn't your fault at all, was it?' Corrigan shook herself and the flash of blue pulsed in the dark. 'You were always the one who respected the forest, who tried to protect it.'

'I don't want to know anymore,' Milo whispered. Because he knew the worst was yet to come.

Corrigan had returned his name but the memories that came with it were ponderous shadows in his brain, creeping ever closer. He was desperately afraid of what remembering more might do, and that dread clamped its jaws around his heart.

His legs trembled as he forced himself to stand. Corrigan spun into the air. Milo wanted the silence of Barrington Hall, the comfort of its curdled gloom, because this was his reality.

He wondered why Corrigan had chosen now to unfold that part of his memory. But the thundercloud of veracity hung over his thoughts, and he couldn't weather that storm.

Milo sprinted down the corridor, the woman's scream of anguish nipping at his heels. Running like a crazed animal with no sense of where his steps were leading. Running away to escape what he now knew was unavoidable.

The full truth of how he came to be here.

FORTY-ONE

Robert McCallum stood by the overgrown tomb, the moon an opal perched in the trees behind him. Tilly sat at his feet, whimpering softly.

'I know, girl, I know. But I didn't have a choice.'

The spaniel glanced up at him with liquid brown eyes.

What he had done stuck in his throat like a stone. Faye wasn't at fault. Unless marrying Danny Morgan could be called a crime.

He remembered Danny as a boy, hurtling through the woods with his friends, whooping and hollering and scaring all the wildlife in a half-mile radius. Danny had changed over the past few summers, becoming too bold, too impudent. The city was carving him into what it needed. Robert had no doubt all of that concrete and chaos had its own heart, just like the forest. And it, too, was hungry.

He'd tried to patrol the boundary of Barrington Hall more, had told Albert and Jem to spread the word in the village. The kids were not to go near the old house. It was unsafe structurally, they were told. Rotting floors just waiting to swallow small bodies whole.

But it wasn't the real reason, and the ones who had dwelt in the village for generations knew it.

Barrington Hall would only suffer a little disrespect. Push

it too far, and it would administer its own punishment, aided by the creature who ruled over its tainted carcass, her thirst for revenge burning in her dark veins.

Don't go inside, the children had been warned. But, of course, it was inevitable some would.

Robert had glimpsed Milo on many occasions, sometimes as he plunged headlong in the dark, desperately trying to evade his winged pursuers. Once, he had seen him by the lake, and that was an image that still haunted Robert's nightmares.

He left offerings on the stone steps the nights the rain fell. Trapped rabbits in the wood for the boy, because that's all he could do.

But it shouldn't have been Milo. Robert had seen what happened on that night.

And he had known, the moment Danny Morgan returned, that Barrington Hall would finally have its pound of flesh.

Slipping a crushed sleeping tablet into Danny's whisky had been easy enough. He knew the man was thinking of leaving, and that couldn't be allowed to happen. Not again.

In all his decades, Robert McCallum understood one thing more than anything else: Karma was a bitch with a very long memory.

What his forefathers had done ruled Robert's life. Joseph McCallum had taken the tortured creature from the hands of Elliot Kidd, following the orders he was given because he had no choice.

'Hide it,' Elliot had said, 'I will have need of it later.'

The young master of Barrington Hall might have been a child, but his heart was as devious as the devil's.

Joseph had gone to the cottage, had pleaded with the woman who many thought was a witch, to keep the creature safe.

He asked her to sedate it and she had, but when Joseph had discovered she had skewered its plump body with a knitting needle he had panicked. He feared the sleep was permanent, and if Corrigan ever found out she would unleash her hell upon his family.

Robert knew Lucinda Latimer had watched over the glass case in her family's cottage for years. Had tied countless knots in her balls of wool. Binding spells. He just didn't know if she was protecting the creature inside the case, or herself.

Lucinda's last wish had been for her ashes to be scattered in the lake. A genuine penance for any wrong that had been done.

The secret Robert would take to his grave was that his grandfather had been complicit in the destruction of Corrigan's mate.

How could he have explained this to Faye? She would have thought him crazy. But she would find her own madness soon enough.

The crisp trill of laughter spilled from the open door of Barrington Hall and Tilly cowered behind his legs.

Faye Morgan would never see daylight again.

FORTY-TWO

You watch as the woman stumbles into the darkness, her steps following the boy. Delight flickers in your eyes as you unfurl your proboscis, flick it into the shadows.

There it is. The distinct taste of unbridled fear.

For some time now you have become dissatisfied with the reactions you have drawn from Milo. You know each other too well, like lovers. *My love. Mi lo.* You flutter your wings quickly and the blue light paints them in kingfisher hues. How you have adored your game with him.

But it was time for Milo to learn the truth. What you had kept from him all of these years.

You wonder if the truth will finally break him and find that, despite everything, there is a small pang of tenderness there. He has been a worthy adversary.

There are plenty of things in Barrington Hall that will feed from his madness.

You can feel them stir within the walls, what is left of them writhing and desperate. Desperate to devour anything with breath.

You have tried to keep them quiet. Keep them at rest. Your hold on this place is dying.

But survival is an instinct that never dies and yours is vampire sharp. It was forged from the husks of your children, mouldering in the attic, and in the mate ripped from your side. Your kind join for life. Taking him had not only been an act of barbarous cruelty; it was the destruction of a whole species.

Allowing yourself to pine away was never an option.

Sometimes, as you doze in the warmth of a sunbeam, letting the golden light nourish your body, you think back to the days of before, when your kin worked alongside the people of the village. They left you gifts of sugared water, planted wildflowers on every patch of green. And you managed the balance of the forest, pollinating fruit and field, so that winter was not a season to starve. Until Elliot Kidd decided to leave his mark.

You chastise yourself for letting the monster's image ruffle your hold on control.

He ripped away your purity. Your belief in goodness. Sometimes you are not sure what you lament the most.

The drum of rain on the tiled roof brings you back to the present and you quiver, shake away the maudlin thoughts. Milo will be trapped here tonight, unable to use the run of the forest to ease his torment.

You can hear his soft steps on the servant's stairwell, winding his way to the small rooms with the tiny windows. As far away as he can get from what he fears the most.

It is perhaps too close to the attic, but this time it does not matter.

You flit down the hallway. The dampness of Barrington Hall clings to your wings; it weighs them down, pulls you in as it does to everything. Your dark magic has long since been devoured by the memories here. They have their own heartbeat now.

You fly along the labyrinthine corridors, each one part of

the maze you have created leading to Penrose stairwells on the upper levels, a never-ending sequence of steps climbing upwards, and to nowhere at all. Nowhere but madness.

Your victims always try. And try again. The human mind has such capacity for attempting the impossible.

Some had climbed and climbed and climbed, until exhaustion took their limbs and laid them hard upon the steps. And still they dragged their bodies onwards. You would watch and judge from your vantage point, study them as a biologist studies a bug. How the tables have turned in this place of death.

You keep a few, lock them in windowless rooms in the pitch darkness. Their cries ring out night after night. Some you visit, show your form, tease with the promise of release. Most cringe in the corner, steeped in their own waste, or bolt from the room, breaking bones in their stumbling haste to flee. You do not have the patience to mend them.

Not until Milo did you find one worthy of your time. He begins like all the rest, but quickly learns. The first to attempt to speak your language. The first to know the hunt was always going to end the same, but running anyway. You give him the boundary of the forest, and the tiny flame of hope burns in his chest that maybe he will reach the edge and break free. Deluded child.

Sometimes you even let him get so close. Because that is the key to keep him keen, the thought that maybe there is a way out of his nightmare.

He endures the exhaustion and the pain, his reactions lightning quick as he plunges through the forest darkness. Milo has learned how you think. But you always knew this would be his fatal mistake.

You come to a crossroads of corridors on the second

level. The sound of the woman's footsteps up ahead. The creak of a door not opened for years. You can taste her sweat on the damp air.

So, she is going to ground, like a startled rabbit. A good sign. The levelheadedness to hide rather than exhaust herself running in the dark. The woman is much older than Milo but she is strong, and she has come to Barrington Hall willingly, even though she knows that it is…different.

You imagine endless nights of discovery, of finding out exactly how far you can push her boundaries. Her son, or the thought of him, brought her here. You can bring him back, if the game demands it. But best to treat her kindly for a while. Or, at least, not drive her to an early suicide. Barrington Hall has seen more than its fair share of death.

Perhaps she can play with Milo for a while. Let them both scheme and whisper. Kindle that little flame of hope that has travelled with the boy for so long. But it won't be long before he knows who she is.

You will need to keep them undisturbed. Any outside influence will break the fragile bond.

Time to pay a visit to the man you know is watching from the overgrown tomb. The one who serves you to pay for the crimes of his kind.

Robert McCallum will play his part.

FORTY-THREE

Milo found himself in the narrow corridor of the upper floor where the roof sloped and the air was thick. His heart was a wild thing in his throat, a desperate bird fleeing from the net, his thoughts as scattered as fallen feathers.

He forced himself to stop; he stood in the cold dark with the sound of rain hammering against the roof. As much as he thought he played the game well, Corrigan had always held the missing pieces. *Milo.* He mouthed his own name and it felt foreign on his tongue.

He turned, narrowing his eyes, but the darkness held nothing. She had left him to stew in his own juices, knowing the memories she had given him were a double-edged sword.

His thoughts churned around in the sea of his mind, storm-tossed and as black as the ocean's depths. Little shreds of images floated on the water, coming together to make a…

His lips pulled back on his teeth in a grimace. He wasn't ready to know it all.

Milo slipped inside the first door on the left, the space little more than a large cupboard.

A sound echoed up through the bare floorboards. Running feet.

A heavy squall of rain hit the window and Milo cringed against the doorframe. His breath started to race and his chest tightened—the memories he had tried to hold back came flooding in.

The water is freezing cold. He strides into the lake, pushes his legs through the weight of it, his teeth chattering so much he half expects them to fall out and float away. A voice laughs and then a splash. The ice chill of water against his face. He gasps, his eyes widening, the moonlight oozing across the surface of the lake, the tattered shreds of the bluebells floating away…the pebbles on the lake floor shift under his feet and the water suddenly deepens to his neck now, his arms windmill, legs kicking to keep himself afloat.

'See, I told you it would be okay!' A triumphant yell from another shape in the water.

But Milo doesn't feel any joy. He turns towards Barrington Hall. The oppressive hulk of it broods in the dark. He wants to be anywhere else but here.

From amidst the inky black there comes a flicker of quivering light. He catches his breath, his eyes trying to pinpoint where it is. The spread of the glow grows larger.

It is coming from the great doors of Barrington Hall. The open doors.

'Race you to the jetty!' A yell and a splash as someone dove.

Milo wants to shout out, but his voice is dead in his throat.

The light begins to move, drawing slowly closer, and despite his fear, Milo is strangely enthralled.

He treads water gently, his fingertips open, floating slowly backwards. There is no sound from whoever is with him.

Shadows dance in the air, indistinct shapes advancing

with the light.

A bright flash of blue.

He knows he ought to scream. He knows he ought to fight his way to the opposite bank and flee into the woods.

'Did you hear the bell, Milo?' A voice drifts from behind the light, which Milo can now see is a single candle.

The words are honey and belladonna, sweetness and poison.

Milo has grown up knowing that if you ring a bluebell the fairies will carry you away. His grandfather tells him each and every spring as soon as the blue flowers burst from their stems.

'No more, please, no more,' he pleaded into the darkness, splayed his hands against the damp wall, using the solidity of it to slow his panic.

He heard a door creak open on another level. The slow rolling screech of small wheels turning in its wake.

Milo forced himself to move. Even though the veiled form of the little girl had never challenged him before, he remembered what it was like to see her for the first time.

It wasn't a sight you should see alone.

He crept out into the corridor again, listening, trying to decide which stairwell would lead him to her the quickest.

He knew where the woman was and why the wheels had stopped. Setting off at a run, he skidded to a halt at the end of the corridor. No, this wasn't the quickest way.

That was down the other stairs. The ones he had never been allowed to use because they were too close to the attic door.

Milo gritted his teeth. If Corrigan had changed the rules by giving him back his memories, let her see he wasn't afraid to break a few himself.

But the darkness seemed deeper as he ran, as thick as treacle, as cold as grave earth. The edge of the wall that sheltered the attic doorway flashed by to his left. The low gleam of yellowed once-white wood to his right, the steps leading down into the gloom.

Despite the terror in his chest, Milo risked a glance towards the door as he raced past. And came to a sudden halt.

The door to the attic stood open, a great gaping wound of a hole beyond it.

Whatever lay within was no longer a secret.

FORTY-FOUR

Faye closed the door and it shut with a soft click. Her hand flew to the cold metal knob again, easing it open just a fraction—her panicked mind had imagined it locking behind her.

The room was pitch black with an almost overpowering smell of mildewed cloth and decay.

She listened as her heartbeat hammered against her ears, trying to coax it into submission. Logic warred with what she had just seen.

The image of the winged…she paused. Corrigan. A name made it real. It had been there on the boy's shoulder, speaking a language she understood.

Milo. She whispered his name into the cold dark, seeing again the look in his eyes as the creature crooned, that hideous limb stroking his jaw.

Faye leant her forehead against the door and caught the sob in her throat. She had to get him away from here. Away from that terrible creature.

Maybe it only came out in the dark, like all the monsters in story books. And maybe she was delusional. Because as much as she wanted to believe this all had an explanation, it was all coming down to one in her mind. Fate.

She turned, scanning the darkness, vague shadows now

visible as her eyes adjusted.

The shape of something she thought was a bed stood against the opposite wall. A draught licked around her ankle, coming from her right. A fireplace?

Faye pulled out her phone. The screen was black. She pressed the power key. Nothing happened.

Jamming it back into her pocket, she felt her way across the room. The side of her foot found the hard edge of a hearth. Carefully, she reached out, running her hand along the mantle. Her fingers closed around a small, cold object. Tried to make sense of the shape. A tin soldier.

Again she tried, looking for something she might be able to defend herself with. Another metal object, a round base this time. And a curled handle. Candle sconce. A little glow of triumph filled her chest.

The stub of a used candle poked from its centre.

Her stomach sank. What good was a candle without a match?

But just as she was about to discount it, she knocked something from the mantle. Something that rattled. She crouched, patting the bare wooden floors over and over, the frenzied attempts of a blind woman.

She could hear her own rapid breathing in the cold silence. Her skin prickled with sweat. Her searching fingers found a rough edge, and she clutched the tiny box in between her palms. Carefully, she slid the lid open and fumbled for a match. *They'll be damp*, an inner voice laughed.

The first one fell from her trembling fingers and she swore. She picked up another, held this one so tight she feared she might snap it in two.

She drew the head against the striking surface. It didn't

catch.

'Come on, come on,' Faye whispered into the dark.

She tried again, willing the match to ignite with the passion of the devout.

It drew flame.

The room illuminated in a soft, golden glow as she touched it to the wick of the candle stub. A flicker as it stuttered. Her heart seemed to mirror the action. And then the joy of a small flame, keeping her company in the dark.

Slowly, she turned, the room coming to life before her eyes. A bare mattress on an iron bedstead with an old blanket in a heap at its base. In the space between the bed and the fireplace stood a rocking horse, the dappled paint on its surface flecked and peeling.

Faye crept towards it, holding her candle aloft like a sword. The eye of the rocking horse had been scratched away, leaving only a wild, half-blind look that had no place on a children's toy. Its ragged mane was thin and matted. Faye reached out, brushed her fingers across it.

A floorboard creaked behind her.

She spun, the small flame guttering in the sudden movement, but there was nothing there. Only the shadows her candle cast, dancing on the walls.

Certainty. That one thing, present in her life before Toby had been ripped from it, died another death. She had thought she would see her son grow and leave home. Return with his own family one day. But here in this house, where darkness was more than simply the absence of light, certainty had no place.

The sound of something rolling, something squeaking, came from the hallway.

It stopped outside of the door. Faye cupped her hand around the flame, trying to be invisible. Heat seared her palm.

Slow scratching against the old wooden door, like tiny claws.

A drop of hot wax dripped against her thumb and tears sprang to her eyes. Faye yelped, the sound eaten up by the darkness.

Something rattled the door knob. The moments that followed seemed to stretch into the night like a lost soul.

And then the door creaked slowly open.

She steeled herself for whatever monster might be there, torn between blowing out the flame and the desperate need to cling to its small light. Her breath left her lips in a trembling exhale.

But it wasn't a monster. It was Milo, his forefinger against his lips.

She went to him without a second thought, drawn to the presence of a boy adrift in this terrifying ocean of loneliness.

The door slowly closed behind them, but before it did, Faye glimpsed the rocking horse moving slowly back and forth.

Something had been in there with her.

She jammed her hand against her mouth, bit down on a knuckle to stem the cry.

Milo led her down the hallway, his feet soundless. The candle flickered against the walls, long shadows creeping alongside them.

She didn't know what level of the house they were on. After she fled from the creature she seemed to have climbed countless steps, but however hard she climbed, they all seemed to lead back to the same place, defying reason.

Her mouth ran dry as the chill deepened. As the belly of Barrington Hall swallowed them into its darkness. If Milo left her now Faye had the awful feeling she would never find her way back to the great hall.

Something brushed against her face and she recoiled, the flame dying to a tiny point of light.

Milo snatched the sconce from her hand, held it aloft so she could see the thick blanket of cobwebs hanging from the ceiling. She ran her hands through her hair, the silken threads wrapping themselves around her fingers as she tried to shake them off.

Milo was staring upwards, fitful shadows making the hollows of his face more pronounced. More corpse-like. His lips were drawn tight and so pale against his skin they looked as though his mouth had disappeared.

One hand held the sconce; his other, the hand he kept tucked inside the trailing sleeve of his shirt, brushed a floating strand of web from his cheek.

Faye gasped in horror at the sight of it.

The flesh on his fingers had been stripped to the bone.

FORTY-FIVE

Milo saw the shock dawn on the woman's face. He fought the urge to bury his withered hand inside his sleeve. But she had seen and there was no going back now.

Once you crossed a certain line, your fate was sealed. He knew that to his cost.

In truth, he had learned to manage with his thumb and what was left of his fingers. The nerve endings had been severed so there was no feeling in them, although sometimes he thought he could sense the ache in his knuckles, a ghost memory of phantom digits.

A flash of that night seared against his mind, against the scar that grew there, ugly and misshapen. The night he had fought back.

Rain blasted against the arched window at the end of the corridor, and the tiny flame guttered in his outstretched hand.

The game tonight would be played inside the belly of Barrington Hall and that was always the most dangerous place. He understood the forest, knew each season as it birthed. The places he could hide in summer when the leaves were full, the ditches he could leap into, covering himself with fallen leaves as autumn grew into winter.

But the house never seemed to be the same on any one night, as though it were perpetually changing, growing into itself like a cancer. He knew Corrigan's magic had a lot to do with it, but sometimes even she treated Barrington Hall with a healthy dose of respect.

The open attic gnawed against his thoughts. He'd finally had a chance to see what was inside, but his conscience had led him to someone who needed his help.

In the flickering shadow of the candle, the woman's throat rippled, her wide eyes begging for an explanation.

But here was not the place.

He let his tensed shoulders fall, leading her onwards, unsure of what would greet them when they came to the end.

It was an empty landing, save for a covered mirror above an old blanket chest. The arched window was a black hooded eye, the night beyond angry, the wind throwing itself petulantly around the house eaves. Tiles lifted and rattled in its fury.

The tiny light of the candle caught the edge of a silver key that sat inside the lock of the chest. Milo knew what was inside but he wasn't about to tell.

To their right, another hallway, leading to what were once guest bedrooms. To their left, a staircase leading upwards.

Milo chose, using what he knew of Corrigan's logic.

The woman folded herself inside his shadow as they crept up the narrow stairs, and Milo's senses tuned into the slightest change in the air. Because this was where he felt it the most, the instant before anything happened. Barrington Hall exhaled its thinking in each damp, corrupted breath.

It was colder on this level, a draught blowing across the floor from a broken window. The corridor was narrower, the walls almost too close for comfort as Milo led the way.

He pushed open the first door on his right. The woman

hesitated on the threshold and he wondered how the room looked to her eyes, the space illuminated by the flickering, nearly burnt-out candle.

She came in and he closed the door. The latch clicked sharply, the noise fanning out into the darkness.

The nursery was a long, thin room at the back of the house with a sloping roof and small windows overlooking the stable yard and the carriage house. Behind those were the woods, the tall trees sheltering this side from the harsh winds that swept across the valley.

The woman licked her lips. A nervous gesture. Her gaze flitted across the room. To the lace-shrouded crib with its moth-eaten canopy. To the wooden doll's house on the floor under the window, two peg dolls perched against its wall. To the three small beds huddled together in the shadows. To the rocking chair with a shawl bundled on its seat.

Milo left her to wander, creeping to the window, watching the raindrops as they slid down the glass.

'It's impossible.' The disbelief in her whisper made him wheel.

A hiss came from his lips and her head jerked up, but she was already clutching what she'd found in the crib.

A tattered rag doll dangled from her fingers.

'Put it down!' His warning came too late.

The nursery door flew open, crashing back against the wall.

A flicker of far away lightning illuminated the threshold for the briefest of seconds. The figure of a small girl stood there, dressed in her funeral gown, a dark veil covering her face.

Milo heard the woman take a deep breath, and he waited

for her scream. Goosebumps crawled across his skin as the temperature plummeted.

Another dazzling burst bathed the room in the sharpest contrast of black and white.

The doorway was empty, absolute blackness beyond.

'She took it,' said the woman. Her fingers were empty, stretched wide.

Milo's gaze flicked back to the door. In all the time he had been here, the small girl had never done more than push her doll's carriage along the hallways. Looking for something that was never going to be there again.

'What happened here, Milo?' Her face was as pale as milk, her pupils dilated in fear.

'Death,' he whispered. 'So much death.'

The candle flared once. Then went out.

FORTY-SIX

Faye stared into the sudden plunge of darkness. The smoke from the candle wick filtered into her nostrils.

The doll in the crib had been the same doll hanging from the end of the rope. She wanted to scream but her throat had closed, strangling any sound.

Milo grabbed her hand and pulled her across the room to where the three beds stood.

A shaft of weak moonlight pierced the rain-sodden clouds, thinning the gloom. They raced towards it. Faye stumbled, her mind still caught up in the tangles of what she'd seen.

He let go of her hand and dived over the last bed. Faye threw herself onto the mattress, the iron bedstead creaking at the sudden assault.

She glanced over her shoulder, and a draught of stale air hit her face. Then the boy was back, his presence almost as insubstantial as the shadows themselves.

'Crawl,' he hissed in her ear, dragging her across the bed onto the floor.

Dust tickled her nose. The musty scent of a space that hadn't been aired for years. She was reminded of the cottage. *Dan.* Her lower lip trembled.

'Move!' Milo's urgent whisper.

So she did, crawling into something she couldn't see, concentrating on the slow forward motion of hand and knee, hand and knee.

A jagged splinter pierced the soft flesh at the base of her thumb and she winced.

The click of a small latch sounded.

Faye raised her head sharply. The back of her skull cracked against something solid, and pain arrowed down her spine. She collapsed onto her elbows, her breath rasping in her ears.

'Just a little further.' Milo urged her onwards, and she felt the slight pressure of his hand on her ankle.

She gritted her teeth and crawled a few more feet into the absolute darkness.

'Stop. You can sit up here. There's room.'

Faye gingerly pulled her knees forward and eased herself to a sitting position. Her head pounded, a wave of nausea rolling up from her gut.

'I'm sorry if I scared you.' Milo's voice was soft in the dark. 'I had to be quick because we were trespassing in Mae Mae's space and she didn't like it.'

'Mae Mae?'

'The little girl who used to live here. The one in the photograph.'

Faye clutched her head in her hands. 'Where are we?'

For a few seconds there was no answer.

'It's where they put the rat poison. To keep them from the nursery.'

Faye shivered. She wasn't scared of rats. But in an enclosed space…she blew out a small breath and clamped her thoughts.

'You dropped this.' A flare of cold against her hand.

She closed her fingers over the familiar shape of her phone and pressed the home key, remembering how annoyed she would get when her favourite apps wouldn't load. And now all she wanted was a little light. Something she had taken for granted every day of her life.

The screen flickered. Her eyes flew to the battery level. Ten percent.

But in the faint glow, she saw where they were—a closed-in pocket of the attic, the rafters only inches above her head. Milo crouched beside her, one knee raised, his head cocked to the side. Listening.

She let the screen die, reluctantly, stuffing it into her back pocket.

'The little girl,' she began, not wanting to say her name. Her lips felt as dry as crushed bones.

'Her name was Mary but everyone called her Mae Mae,' Milo's voice was gentle, as though he was coaxing Faye to say it. 'The room you were in when I found you was hers.'

'But I thought...the nursery?'

'The children all used to sleep there before. Then William Kidd took his youngest daughter and locked her away. To protect her.'

A shiver ran down Faye's spine. 'From that creature? Corrigan?' Another name she could barely say.

'No, not from Corrigan. Not then. From Mae Mae's brother. He started all of this.' Milo paused. The air tightened between them.

Then laughter rolled softly from the dark. And the sound wrapped itself around Faye's heart like an iron fist.

She felt the air move as Milo spun, heard his hands

scrabbling around on the floor.

Her fingers fumbled as she reached for her phone. The faintest illumination from the screen.

Milo had braced himself against a slanted beam, his foot stamping down on a space between two flooring timbers. There was a splintering of old wood. Rising ancient dust. His jaw was set tight. But she didn't miss the way his gaze flicked towards the direction of the laugh.

He was afraid.

Faye's protective instinct raised itself from the bed of grief it had been sleeping upon. She kicked out, the heels of her trainers stronger than the flimsy footwear Milo wore.

'The door, Milo!' She pointed to where they had crawled through.

'It won't open.' Absolute certainty hung on his words. 'Corrigan will see to that.'

With a surge of dust the floor between the timbers gave way. Faye covered her mouth and nose with her hand but she could feel the grime settling on her skin. It made her eyes sting.

Milo swung his legs over, dangling them through the hole. He beckoned for her to join him.

And then his eyes widened as they stared over her shoulder.

Something grasped her upper arm, something cold and repellent. Milo's fingers found hers and she was wrenched forwards, the repulsive grip on her arm torn away.

Dust filled her mouth as momentum and Milo's falling weight dragged her headfirst through the hole, and they tumbled into a pit of darkness.

FORTY-SEVEN

As Milo grabbed for the woman's hand and pitched them both into plummeting darkness, he prayed he had been right in his calculation of what lay below. If he was wrong he could kill them both, or, at the very least, break a limb.

Their dive seemed to last for far too long, as though someone had removed all the floors beneath and they were being vomited straight to hell.

The harsh rip of cloth as they plunged through the rotting bed canopy, then a moment of spine-jangling connection as they hit the mattress below. The coil springs creaked in protest at the sudden load but the bed held firm. The scent of damp and dust arose, and for a few seconds they both lay there motionless.

Plaster fragments drifted down from the hole they had dropped from, and Milo half expected to see whatever was up there peering through it. He had only caught the slightest glimpse of a face, but it had been enough for him to risk the fall.

He scrambled from the bed and took hold of the woman's hand again. She was shaking.

'Come on, we have to keep going.'

This time she pulled her hand free of his grip. Her chin tilted stubbornly upwards, but he saw the slight quiver on her lower lip. 'Why can't we just bolt for the door?'

Milo bit the lining of his cheek. 'Because she'll follow us outside, into the woods. And you'll be an easy target. It's too wet and muddy out there.' He didn't mention the fact that he was terrified of the rain.

'And I'm not an easy target in this place?' She waved a hand in the air.

'There are more places to hide here.'

He was finding it extremely difficult to explain just how Corrigan thought. That if you played the game and made the hunt enjoyable, she would reward you with time left alone. At least that's what happened in Barrington Hall. Outside, in the night forest, all bets were off.

It was so much simpler on his own. But he was desperate to keep the connection with another living person. And he felt like she needed him too. Right now, that had to be enough for both of them.

'What's your name?' he asked.

She opened her mouth to speak, her dark brows drawing together as though the question was absurd.

'Faye.'

Milo nodded. Now he knew her name, she was his responsibility. Someone had told him that once.

He glanced up to the hole, his ears tuned into the tiniest of sounds. But whatever had been there was gone. Unless it was sitting in the dark, watching.

He swallowed the itch of dust lining his throat. The whisper of a plan floated across his mind. A plan that terrified him.

This time she was the one who reached for his good hand, her chilled fingers interlocking with his. He led her through the bedroom doorway and along a narrow corridor leading to a wider landing. They were still at the back of the house, away from what a general visitor would have seen. Whoever had slept in that room would have been close enough to the nursery to hear the children scream.

Milo pulled open another door, set deep into a wall, Faye's sweating palm against his.

He needed to tell her a little of what he wanted to do. Actually, that wasn't true. He didn't *want* to do any of it. But it was the only thing he could think that might give him some sway over Corrigan. Might give them a chance to escape.

He tamped down the heady rush brewing in the pit of his stomach at that thought.

Closing the door quietly behind them, he led the way down the narrow, wooden staircase, the one the servants had used. He knew the feel of the steps well, but let the fingers of his good hand trail along the wall at one side just in case. Faye followed in the dark, her open-mouthed breathing the only sound.

The stairway ended in a small square space. To the left was the butler's pantry and the housekeeper's office. To the right, the kitchen. Milo pushed open the second door. The room was barely larger than a cupboard. Stacks of old leather-bound ledgers mouldered on a corner shelf. Most of the floor space was occupied by a rectangular desk.

He reached across it, closed his hand over the battered oil lamp. In a drawer, wrapped in a wax cloth, was the precious match box. His nimble fingers plucked one out, striking it quickly. A blaze of sudden light. He lit the wick of the lamp, letting it flare before turning down the flame.

Faye moved towards it, captivated.

On the desk was a fine layer of sand he had found in a sack in the scullery.

He pressed a finger against his lips, to tell her this must be a silent explanation. Because in Barrington Hall something always seemed to be listening. He drew the outline of the house, like a child might do, tracing *BH* beside it. Pointing to the attic level with his forefinger, he shook his head, then drew Corrigan's likeness. Faye's throat rippled.

He wrote a word. *No.* Then pointed to himself.

The small flame from the lamp was reflected in her eyes as she nodded. Slowly, he raised his withered hand. Made chewing motions with his mouth.

She recoiled, her hand flying to her lips, her eyes wide with the dawning horror.

In the soft glow he studied the result of his misbehaviour. How he had paid dearly the last time he tried to see inside the attic.

She reached out and let her hand rest on his shoulder, her eyes shining with unshed tears. But he wasn't looking for pity; he only needed her to understand the lengths Corrigan would go to.

The one thing he had taken from that night, as he laid there in blinding agony whilst dozens of tiny mandibles gnawed away his flesh, was that whatever dwelt in the attic was the key to Corrigan's weakness.

And now the door was open.

FORTY-EIGHT

Faye let her hand slip from Milo's shoulder. He didn't want to be touched. And really, could she blame him?

She had only wanted him to know that his disfigurement didn't matter to her. Her cheeks burned. How old was he? Thirteen? Fourteen? *Toby's age.* But sometimes the strange boy in front of her, with the glow of the oil lamp painting his pale skin with honey, looked a lot older.

Faye took a deep breath, brought her thoughts back to the present. His fingers moved quickly in the sand. He was pointing to the attic again. And then to her. To himself. One more word. *Yes.*

Her jaw slackened. Right after telling her Corrigan had destroyed his hand for going to the attic, he was asking that they do exactly that.

Faye shook her head, holding up her hands.

His teeth clenched, the tendons on his neck straining. He swept his hand across the sand, then wrote with one finger, savagely. *I'll go alone then. I need to see.*

It was too difficult to ask for a further explanation but Faye guessed it didn't really matter. He had made up his mind.

She thought about letting him go alone, using his absence to try and find her way to the door, to bolt like a terrified hare into the woods, taking her chance in the dark. But she couldn't leave him here. Although appearing back at the cottage with Milo in tow, looking like some feral Peter Pan would be a challenge. Dan would insist they call the police, that Milo must have relatives somewhere.

If Dan is okay. She wouldn't let her thoughts dwell on any other alternative.

The sensible part of her knew she couldn't simply slide Milo into the empty, screaming place that Toby had left. Her mind swam, showing her an out-of-body image of herself and Milo standing in the tiny room, unable to speak in case something that shouldn't exist heard them. And what about the little girl and the doll, and whatever had grabbed her in the attic pocket by the nursery....Had Milo seen what it was before he yanked her through the floor?

She needed a real conversation with him, one where she could ask all her questions without worrying what might be watching in the dark.

But despite the fucked-up situation she was in, energy burned within her veins, an energy she hadn't felt since before Toby died.

She had a purpose.

Milo's head jerked up. He leapt across to the desk on soundless feet, blowing out the wick. The flash of his eyes glanced over her shoulder as the light died. She held her breath and turned slowly, the hair in the nape of her neck rising.

Out of the corner of her eye, that spark of blue.

It drew closer, the colour ebbing and flowing as though it ran through the beating of a heart. She heard Milo sweep a hand across the sand, obliterating his words. The air seemed to drain from the small space in the room. Faye could hear, quite clearly, the hum of wings cutting through the darkness.

But there was something else. An echo of that hum. Milo's chilled fingers curled around her arm. A warning.

Her breath left her mouth in an unsteady stream.

The door flew open.

Corrigan hovered in the doorway, the space around her lit by an ethereal glow, one long foreleg stroking her plump belly. From behind, the sound of rapid clicking pierced through the hum.

'Hiding away in the dark, Milo? You know that isn't how this works. Time to run.'

A cold wave of disassociation washed over Faye.

A phrase settled. Something she'd heard in an audio book just a few days ago, watching the blur of the countryside flashing past the car window. *Reality bites.*

'One,' Corrigan began.

Milo sprang to life, pushing her out into the corridor. She wanted to resist, because Corrigan was far too near, but Milo was strong. Determined.

'Two.' The hum grew louder. A series of high-pitched clicks, all running together in a reverberating stream that sounded too close to laughter.

Somewhere far ahead a small red light flared.

'Three.'

Corrigan stopped in mid-flight, suspended in the dark, the flash of blue suddenly as bright as moonlight. Faye saw where the sounds were coming from.

From out of the dark arose a swarm of winged creatures. And with them came the bitter scent of green Faye had grown accustomed to. The air around her was filled with them, their attention fixed upon their queen.

Milo grabbed her hand and fled down the hallway,

towards the dim red light. There was no time to ask questions. No time to even glance behind. But she knew they were close.

Time stilled, concentrated into a wild ball of shadows and panic. It tore its claws across her skin. She put her trust into Milo's leadership, hanging her hopes on his slim shoulders.

Countless times he paused, scanning the darkness before leading her on. She lost all sense of location, the bowels of Barrington Hall a never-ending trail of doorways and corridors. Finally, just as she thought that she couldn't run any further, they emerged onto the landing where the old chest sat by the arched window. The pale glow of the moon washed over the floor. Her muscles burned with exertion and she doubled over, her hands on her thighs.

Milo's eyes swept over her. 'Go hide in one of the rooms,' he whispered. 'I'll find you later.' Then he disappeared into the blackness like a wraith.

But she didn't want to hide in any of the rooms, because of what else might be there. Her eyes fell on the old chest, a fragile hope in her heart that it might be empty. She knelt and eased up the lid. The old hinge creaked and she grimaced. She plunged her hand inside, found a blanket at the bottom, covering something hard and uneven.

'Taking your time, Corrigan. Lost your touch?' Milo's voice taunted from the far darkness, leading them away from her.

There was a drone of wings in the distance and a single click as an outrider searched for clues.

Faye climbed into the chest. Something cracked under her feet like a dry twig. She curled herself onto her side, pulling the lid closed as quietly as she could. In the instant before the shroud of complete darkness, her hand closed over a round object. Her exploring fingers found two deep holes.

Faye bit down hard on her tongue, fought the urge to scream.

Beneath the blanket, and beneath her body, was a skeleton.

FORTY-NINE

Milo flew like a shadow in the dark. It was so much easier without Faye. Part of him regretted asking her name. Letting her become important.

He pressed himself against a wall, felt those within shrink away. No sound from Corrigan or her kin. And that was always a bad thing.

What if they'd gone after Faye?

But if they were otherwise occupied it gave him a chance to get close to the attic. The part of him that regretted asking her name smiled darkly.

Creeping as softly as thistledown, Milo skimmed towards the side of the house where the servant's staircase stood. That put another wall between him and Corrigan. Even though he knew walls were no barrier to her magic, it was also the quickest way to the upper levels of Barrington Hall. Sometimes he thought he saw wavering images of long-ago people, their faces drawn and exhausted, carrying their single candle towards their humble chambers.

Milo slipped through the door.

It was silent. Too silent.

His gaze flicked to an outside window before the door closed behind him. The rain had quietened its fury, and was now just a constant drip drip against the old glass. He could almost smell the wet earth, hear the slither of creatures rising to its surface.

There was a different quality to the air on the staircase. The dampness was still present, but curled against it, like an extra layer of skin, was an energy Milo didn't know. He inched his way up, step by step, that strange vitality making his teeth ache. He stopped for a moment, taking his bearings in the dark. If Corrigan wasn't spinning her magic, he was on the level above the great hall, the place where he had first watched Faye enter.

An instinct, honed from years of living in his nightmare world, took hold, pressed its claws across his throat.

Something was outside. Something that was going to come in.

But another diversion could work out in his favour, and despite wanting desperately to see what was there, he continued up the winding stairs. Two more levels before the servant's quarters. Before the long, narrow corridor with the sloping roof that always seemed to want to crush all the air from his lungs.

A thundering crash from below echoed through the walls.

No one had ever entered Barrington Hall with the challenge that sound conjured.

Milo hesitated, then retraced his steps. He opened the door a crack. A draught licked around his ankles.

Torn between two choices, he wavered.

'Faye! Are you here?' a voice shouted from the great hall, its resonance dancing in the dark. A man's voice.

Milo hissed between his teeth and eased himself through the door, letting it close softly behind him. He crept along the tattered carpet runner, his muscles coiled for fight or flight.

A gust of wind burst through the open double doors. A few loose threads trembled like reeds in the lake.

They wrap themselves around his ankles, drag him down into the midnight water. He remembers holding his breath, sinking, desperately trying to detach them. Waiting for someone to pull him up, hope a tiny winged bird fluttering in his heart...

Milo drove the memories back into the recesses of his mind. They settled into place, formed another piece in his puzzle.

The top of the grand staircase loomed out of the dark. A strong beam of light scanned across the gallery, backwards and forwards in a sweeping arc. It caught the gilt edge of the mirror, sparks of gold shimmering in the gloom.

Milo shrank against the wall, then crouched as the edge of the beam slid over his head. He pressed his face into his knees.

Another gust of wind from outside brought with it the scent of the lake. Dried leaves rustled across the marble floor. He heard the sound of feet on the staircase.

Milo inhaled the ripened tang of fear. He crawled forwards, as silent as death, watching the light flick across the gallery landing.

'Faye?' This time the voice was softer, not as sure as it had been, the bravery seeping away as Barrington Hall latched its fangs.

Halfway to the top of the stairs, at the place Faye had paused, was a man. His wet hair was plastered to his head, his shirt stuck like a second skin. Dried blood coated the side of his face, an angry gash marking his temple.

They had tried to stop him and still he had come.

The man swallowed. Tension corded his neck. His eyes swept over the mirror; his fingers white-knuckled on the torch. Something gleamed at his waist.

Milo focussed his vision. His breath skittered in his chest. 'Faye, are you here?'

Milo's fingers slid around the vertical wooden spindles on the gallery, their curves and twists digging into his palm. He clutched them so tightly he thought they might snap.

The man's face was now in shadow as he crept tentatively up the stairs. Then he tilted his head, his eyes scanning across the space where Milo crouched.

Something unleashed itself from a cage inside Milo's gut. A sudden and heated rage, travelling at lightning speed along his limbs.

Slowly, meaningfully, he stood, his gaze fixed on the visitor.

The man's intake of breath was part shock, part horror. His lips moved but no sound came out.

Milo's fingers curled into a fist on his good hand. His phantom fingers ached. 'What makes you think you deserve her?' His eyes darkened. 'Don't you owe me something?'

The man took one step backwards, his heel slipping on the edge of a stair. He stumbled, his face contorted in terror. But before Milo slipped into the darkness, his own thoughts tumbling down around him like rocks in a landslide, he had a realisation: all things turned in a circle, and now the beginning was the end.

The boy who had left him to die on that night had returned as a man, to claim what he loved.

But Milo had no intention of giving her up.

FIFTY

Faye waited in the claustrophobic dark. The pronged edges of old bones dug into her skin, and her sore hip screamed its agony. But she dared not move.

Her heart rammed against her rib cage, and as tears clouded her non-existent vision, she tried to work out what she could do next. Milo had led them away from her, but she knew he would pay for his rebellion. His bravery in the face of a horror that up until a few days ago she couldn't imagine, made her throat constrict. Tears slipped down her cheeks in the dark.

Clutched in her hand was a small oval shape. She clung onto it like a talisman.

Her eyes blindly darted to a sudden clatter against the floor in the hallway. Slowly, she traced her fingertips to the top of the chest, finding the empty keyhole. That was what had made the sound. The key falling to the floor.

Terror gripped her, squeezing every ounce of logic she possessed and crumbling it away to dust. What if something had locked her in here? What if that's what had happened to the skeleton beneath her?

Her breath stalled in her lungs and panic rose like a fanned flame. The walls of the chest closed in around her. Faye's hands flew to the lid, and for one long, awful moment it refused to move. Warm urine soaked the insides of her thighs.

Then joy swept in as the lid creaked open. She grabbed the side of the chest, the old bones splintering under her feet as she flung herself out onto the floor.

All was silent. Her outstretched hand lay in a patch of diffused moonlight.

Faye crawled into its pale comfort, twisting her hands together on her lap.

Had they caught Milo? Were they now punishing him for her weakness at not being able to run and meld into the shadows?

She saw him in the tiny room with the flickering light of the oil lamp playing against his skin. She saw him at the edge of the forest, the glimpse of his waif-like form parting the shroud of grief she constantly carried. And she knew what she had to do. Her eyes lifted. Her jaw set tight.

Faye walked into the darkness, passing doors strewn with cobwebs that hadn't seen a human face in decades.

The intimacy of sound pressed against her skin. She thought about Dan, whether he had woken and found her gone yet, the other awful possibility curdling in the pit of her stomach. She thought about how much she had changed in a few short days. How everything superfluous had been stripped away, leaving the throbbing nerve of the only thing that mattered. Survival.

Ducking under a sloping lintel, she picked her way through chunks of crumbled masonry. Some of the floorboards sagged under her feet and Faye had to edge forwards one footstep at a time. They led her to another landing. Narrow steps wound their way upwards, the staircase a dilapidated line of broken spindles, sticking up like rotted teeth.

Part of the roof had collapsed here at some point, tearing through what had been on the right side of the stairs, leaving a gaping hole that looked as deep as a bottomless well. A brave shaft of moonlight pierced the gloom.

Faye tested the bottom step with her foot and it gave slightly, the mushy wood underneath riddled with damp and woodworm.

She exhaled softly through her mouth. Using the wall as her guide, she eased onto the step, inching her way to the next, her fingers dragging damp ribbons of wallpaper like a gingerbread trail. Then she remembered what lived in the walls and tore her fingers away. To her right, the yawning blackness, and she had no doubt that it went right through to the ground. If she stumbled, the rotten rails wouldn't catch her. She would die.

After Toby had gone, there were long days and even longer nights where she wished for the soft blanket of death, for nothingness to claim her so she didn't have to breathe, didn't have to exist in a world without him. All completely normal, people told her. People who had not gone through it and didn't have a fucking clue how much she hurt, how much she was flaying the skin from her soul daily at not being home when he left.

But now she had a chance. A chance to help a boy who wasn't her son, who didn't appear to be anyone's son. That last thought notched against her heart like the point of a dagger.

A few stray leaves floated from the hole in the roof, dancing their way down into the nothingness below. Faye didn't even know if the stairs led to the attic, but she was climbing and that had to be one step closer.

Somewhere in the depths of the house, a loud crash

rooted her to the spot, her clenched fists pressed to her mouth. Her eyes wheeled towards the sound. The echo took a long time to fully diminish, as though Barrington Hall was repeating it over and over, chewing it before it swallowed.

She began to climb again, and as she did the air grew colder, the kind of cold that seeped through your skin and seized your bones.

In the shadows just beyond the top of the stairs, something moved.

Faye mouthed Milo's name. An invocation. A deep-seated hope.

Two more steps and she could see something hunched under the sloping roof. Her eyes widened as the scent of disturbed earth rolled out of the dark. An oily green floral. Something intoxicating.

She knew what it was, even as the gasp lay heavy on her tongue.

The scent of the posy she had picked in the woods. The one she had laid on the grave.

Her whispered words floated back to her. *You're not forgotten.*

Bones creaked as the shape shifted, uncurling itself like a moth emerging from a cocoon. A small hand clutched the wilted blooms.

A low laugh.

'Toby couldn't come out to play. So I came instead.'

FIFTY-ONE

Dan stared at the space where Milo had stood. His jumbled thoughts galloped through his head at a hundred miles an hour.

It was impossible. Absolutely fucking impossible.

Milo looked exactly as he had on the last night they were together.

An image sharpened itself, separating from the fog of his memory, cutting its way into his mind like a shard of glass.

They are both in the lake. Dan swims across to the old jetty, drawn by a bright flash of blue skimming across the water. He can see it resting under the sunken boards, shining like a dazzling jewel. But when he reaches out it isn't there. He turns and sees Milo floundering in the water. The ripples from his struggle fan towards Dan but he can't move, his attention drawn by the flickering glow of a candle at the edge of the lake.

His heart shoots into his mouth. They have been discovered and Aunt Lucinda is going to wipe the floor with him.

Even then he is looking after his own skin…

A sound spun out of the darkness above and wrenched him from the past.

The taste of blood clung to the back of his tongue and the gash on his temple throbbed in time with his heartbeat. His whole head ached like someone had hit it with a plank of wood, and that wasn't far from the truth.

What had attacked him had been no ordinary swarm, he realised that now. The pointers had been there ever since his car passed the sign for the village a million days ago.

The deer. The beetles. The dead flies in the bath. All warnings that something knew he was home and they were planning a visit.

But somehow Faye had got herself caught up in the barbed wire of his past, chasing the ghost of the son they had both lost. And the boy she had seen, the boy Dan had dismissed as a fragment of her troubled mind, was Milo.

Guilt and grief had torn them both apart. Torn them from each other. Because they both knew if Dan had offered Toby a lift, had left the laptop for just ten minutes, their son would still be with them.

Dan's gaze travelled along the upstairs gallery as he swept his torch beam across it. A forlorn space, filled with ghosts and silence. *Impossible.* He muttered the word over and over, in the vain hope if he said it enough he would start to believe it.

An ear-splitting crash came from behind and he wheeled, his heart leaping into his throat. The great doors of Barrington Hall had slammed closed.

This place. A house that had haunted him since childhood. It was time to lay it to rest, whatever the consequences.

He ran his fingers down the strap of his rucksack. Then, with his shoulders squared, he ran up the last of the stairs. At the end of the corridor came the familiar flash of blue. His lips tightened, his fingers instinctively doing the same against the barrel of his torch.

'Faye!' he called again, hating the sound of her name in this place of regret. He had promised he would look after her. And he had spent a glorious few minutes watching as she fell asleep. How her lashes had fluttered, her fingers curling softly on the pillow. He had moved a ringlet from her brow with his fingertips. Then he had fallen asleep and woken to find her gone.

Dan followed the rise and fall of the blue light, letting it lead him further and further into the darkness. He kept his torch beam on the ground, making sure there was nothing to stumble over. If he cracked his skull again he'd be no good to anyone.

The image of Milo, staring at him from the shadows, haunted his every step.

He tried to get his bearings but the corridor had twisted back and forth on itself like a serpent.

Impossible. The word was starting to lose its energy, like the dimming of a bulb before it dies.

Dan turned left and the bright flash of blue vanished. He was standing in a small space, a closed door ahead of him. The one on the right had been boarded up quickly. The metal nail heads glinted in his torch light. What was inside?

He had the sudden feeling that something was watching him from the dark. Assessing his weaknesses.

Dan gave himself a mental slap.

The door in front of him slowly creaked open and he rose to the balls of his feet, ready to flee.

'I'm sorry, I'm sorry, I'm sorry.' A girl's whisper from within.

Dan took a few steps forwards, holding his torch high above his head, spreading the beam as much as he could.

It was a small bedroom. A narrow bed with its head against the opposite wall. He swept his torch to where the window should have been but there was nothing but a blank space. Nothing else in the room.

'Hello?' he called out. 'Don't be scared; I won't hurt you.' The thought of a child here alone caught at his throat.

He went in, looking behind the door first because that's where all the bogeymen lived.

Slowly, he stole across the bare wooden floor, the boards creaking under his weight. The bed was covered in a dirty patchwork quilt. Feathers spilled from the pillow, as though something had torn it apart.

Dan thought he could see a shape under the quilt.

His hand shook as he peeled away the corner. The torch beam flickered as though it were a candle flame, and for an instant there was utter darkness. Something trailed across his cheek, something that felt like spider thread but heavier. Like fingers.

He jolted back as the torch flared to life. A shadow drifted from the bed, but there was nothing solid to make that shadow. Dan's breath hitched in his chest.

'I'm sorry.' The soft voice came again.

In the far reaches of his puddle of light stood a figure. Long hair trailed down over her shoulders. Her hand reached out towards the door, fingers outstretched.

Dan tried to focus but she was ebbing and flowing like seaweed caught in a drift, her form not substantial enough to solidify. Her head tilted slightly as he moved but he couldn't see her face for the curtain of hair.

'Who are you?' he whispered, and the dark laughed at his words.

A disorientation took hold of Dan and he swayed, his balance ripped away. He fell to his knees, hitting the floor in a bone-crunching jolt.

He raised his face, fully expecting her to be gone, for all of this to be the result of a blunt blow to the skull. But she was still there, her hand slowly falling to her side.

'Who are you?' Dan tried again, his question rising to a demand.

Now she turned towards him. Dan glanced away, a crazy notion taking hold that looking at her face would turn him to stone.

'I'm damned,' she whispered, and Dan had to strain to catch her words. He forced himself to meet her gaze. 'We're all damned.'

A girl made of shadow and sorrow. It rolled from her like a midnight mist.

Her lips were pale and blue, her hair curling down across a once-white nightgown. But it was her eyes that tore all the breath from Dan's chest. Because they weren't eyes at all, just the black, empty holes of a skull.

FIFTY-TWO

Milo retreated into the darkness. Revenge flowed through his veins, burning its way along them like a red-hot wire.

The boy who had left him to die was inside Barrington Hall. It didn't matter that Milo had escaped death by the merest of fractions. Danny Morgan had turned his back on him when it mattered the most. But there was something else hovering on the edges of his consciousness. The final piece in the puzzle he couldn't grasp.

He paused for a moment, clenching his hand into a fist by his side. Confusion trampled through his turbulent thoughts.

Then the scream tore down through the empty floors, chilling his blood.

Quiet for so long in fear of her life, something had broken the terror from Faye's throat. Something that was more terrible than dying.

He sprinted around the corner, mentally working out which way was the quickest to reach her. Right now he wasn't even sure if he'd find her alive. That thought twisted against his nerves. If she died, his life would be as before. But if she lived, part of him wanted to keep her here, as payment for all the years and all the suffering Danny Morgan had put him through.

Milo knew it wasn't fair, that it would make him no better than Corrigan and her unconditional need to avenge her kin, but as he raced onwards, speeding down hallways that led to dead ends, looking for stairways reaching up and finding only those that led down, the idea fizzed in his blood.

There was no sign of Corrigan or her outriders, but he knew she was there, folding the darkness around him, putting obstacles in his way. Milo clicked a few choice sounds with his tongue against the roof of his mouth. He had no idea if she understood, but his frustration was clear in his tone. Frustration edged with Fuck You.

Just when he thought he must be running around in circles, something in the air shifted. The gloom lightened, a harsh energy dissipating as though for a moment sunlight had touched the mist laying over Barrington Hall.

Either Corrigan had grown tired of her game. Or something else had piqued her attention.

Danny Morgan.

Corrigan did not play nicely with those who dared to step over her threshold, and Danny was an old score to settle.

From out of the shadows a staircase finally loomed. Milo leapt towards it, his good hand glancing against the dust-covered banister. His feet touched the mouldy carpeted treads and he raced upwards, his steps as light as thistle down. He strained his ears to every creak of bone from Barrington Hall, but the scream had been the last sound he had heard. And that didn't bode well.

He reached the upper landing and looked over the half-rotted rail. Around and around swung the steps, like the coils in a seashell. There was nothing but blackness at the bottom of this ocean, a dark that was almost liquid.

Milo picked his way over a mound of fallen plaster and a decayed wooden beam, the smell of ruin clinging to his skin. The doorway he needed to go through was barred by the debris. He didn't know why that surprised him.

A flurry of dust drifted down from above and a small bat shot out of a hole at the edge of an ornamental ceiling rose. A decorative oil lamp hung from its centre. Milo ducked his head, but the bat avoided him with ease.

He was certain the floor above led to the servant's level. Unless Corrigan had dealt another dose of disarray.

Carefully, he clambered on top of the debris, the uneven jumble of plaster and brick and dust beneath him. Far below, the dizzying drop to hell.

He reached out, his fingers grazing the bottom of the lamp. The hole was there, tantalisingly close. Would the debris hold his weight if he jumped? Enough for his hand to grasp the side of the hole? Milo was small and light, as small and light as he had been on that night by the lake. Corrigan's magic had seen that he never grew up. That this house became his own twisted playground.

If he wanted Faye for himself he would need to find her before Danny did. And something told him that she would be trying to get into the attic, just like he had shown her on his sand drawing. Striving to help him.

His phantom fingers itched, and he rubbed his withered hand against his shirt.

Blowing a single breath through his lips, he sprung like a grasshopper. The rubble collapsed under his feet as his fingers grazed across the ceiling. A drawn-out moment of hanging in thin air, completely weightless, as that long-ago night thrust itself from the swamp of his memory.

'You choose, Danny, who do I take?'

His fingers closed around the metal scrollwork on the lamp and the fitting swung perilously. The glass shade cracked under the sudden impact and Milo winced. He braced his shoulder, then thrust his mangled hand upwards like a spear. It broke through the hole the bat had come from, but there was nothing firm to grasp onto.

A rain of plaster fell from the ceiling as the light fitting dropped inch by inch, tearing away from its anchor. Hanging by a thin chain, it bore the whole of Milo's weight.

Desperately, he searched with his withered hand, looking for something to hook his wrist around.

The fitting broke away in a sudden shower of plaster. His heart shot into his throat and Milo steeled himself for death. For plunging into the black abyss below.

All he could see was a curtain of dust as it stole his breath away.

But through the cloud came the low groan of timber. A beam crashed down, one end spearing into the middle of the rubble. Milo saw it in his peripheral vision as he fell. Using every ounce of his strength and focus, he threw his weight towards it, an anchor in the certain death that awaited him. But it was inches too far that might as well have been miles.

The beam settled, trying to find its own mainstay in the muddle of collapse. There was the slightest of movements in his direction. His foot grazed along one edge and a whimper left his lips.

A jolt as his shoelace snagged against something, enough to halt his descent. He twisted towards it, his hand scrabbling over rubble that was only ever moving downwards. The beam rolled slowly towards the wall, and the adrenaline spark of relief shot through his veins. He let its momentum pull him away from the death drop, so grateful when it came to a shuddering halt against the wall that tears sprang to his eyes. Milo reached down and unhooked his lace from the nail head that had saved his life.

The other end of the beam lay jammed against the ceiling, the slope almost as good as any ladder.

Milo didn't stop to think—he pulled himself up onto its edge, splinters of torn wood under his palms as he clambered up towards the hole. Just as his hand found the rough edge of the floor above, the bottom of the beam shifted.

Milo felt himself toppling, and he tried desperately to stop that shift, but he weighed barely anything at all.

The beam end skittered through the rubble, its long edge coming to rest against the rotted rail of the balustrade.

Milo looked down. His stomach flipped over. But still he clung to the wood. A rock in the ocean of his final seconds.

From up above came the sound of a child's voice. A sweet voice but the words were madness.

'Follow, follow, eyes a-hollow,
Chase me down the stair
Little teeth go swallow, swallow
Find me if you dare.'

A splintering of wood as the rail gave way.

I don't want to die, Milo thought.

He'd had that thought before.

FIFTY-THREE

Dan had bolted from the room like a greyhound from a gate, his senses spun together in a heaving mass of disbelief and stomach churning terror. *There is no fucking way I just saw what I did*, his reasoning insisted.

But he could still feel the whisper of the words from the girl. They breathed against his ear, as though she was still there.

His head throbbed and blooms of dark flowers drifted in and out of his line of vision. Concussion. He should be queuing in A&E, not wandering around in the dark in a house that was rotting outwards from its core. But he knew deep inside that the moment he'd heard Albert's voice on the other end of the phone, the inevitability of this moment had been sealed.

Dan staggered down the corridor, his fingers trailing across the wall. If he backtracked it would lead him to the great hall. *And the door*, a little voice whispered. *Run away, she doesn't love you anymore.*

A strangled sob built in his throat and he stopped, doubling over, his palms flat on his thighs.

Milo's face swam across his mind. Not the hard, calculating face he had seen only a short time ago, but the face of the boy he had thought of as a brother, as pale as bleached bone, as he thrashed in the cold, midnight lake.

From out of the depths of the lake comes something he has no name for. Something made of nightmare itself. A bright blue flash as it spins into the air, translucent wings glittering with water droplets.

He watches, struck motionless, as it flies nearer. Its hinged forelegs are silhouetted against the face of the moon, its plump, round body covered in hair. And, oh God, please no, its face, so human, those liquid eyes tearing into his soul.

A sound drifts across the water, a clicking like old bones, that somehow changes to syllables he can understand.

'You choose, Danny. Who do I take?'

He remembers hiding his eyes with his hands, pondweed slimed between his fingers.

'You rang my bell. You came into my house. You knew what it meant and still you came.'

No, no, no, he shouts, his scream echoing over the surface of the lake, ripples of sound spreading out, swallowed by the woodland.

'I left him,' Dan whispered into the darkness. The weight of the memory he had shelved, shoving it away with all of his other childhood thoughts into a cupboard called No Regrets had finally risen.

Barrington Hall sighed.

Guilt fell upon him like a ravenous wolf, and it took all of his resolve not to collapse in a heap by the wall like the pitiful creature he was. He had chosen to save his own skin, leaving Milo to whatever living nightmare this was. He had let his son walk out of the house. Out of his life. He had brought his wife to this place, despite the fragility of her mind.

His own sanity seemed to be slipping away, falling between the cracks of the rotted floorboards. There were no such things as ghosts. No such things as boys who looked the same as they did thirty years ago. No such things as creatures that talked in a human tongue.

But yet...

He straightened, his skin covered in a fine sweat, his hand trembling as it clutched the handle of his rucksack.

Just let me get to the great hall, he thought, *I can breathe there.*

Dan hauled his unwilling body forward, turning right at the end of the hallway that led to the landing where he had seen Milo.

He stopped, his eyes widening, looking for something that wasn't there. There was no antique mirror on the wall, no vast, galleried entrance hall. No door to safety. He was at the bottom of a set of narrow stairs, winding their way up.

Barrington Hall wasn't going to let him leave.

He forced his legs to climb because there was no other option. His torch beam pierced the brutal blackness. Sweat dripped into his eyes and his tongue felt like a dead weight in his mouth. But at the back of his mind the image of Faye burned.

Just as he reached the point where the pain in his muscles screamed for rest, a doorway loomed out of the darkness. He ran the light over its edges. Arched in shape and narrow, timeworn paint bubbling from its surface like blistered skin.

His fingers closed over the small, round handle. He was half expecting it to be locked, but the door gave under a gentle nudge, opening out into a thin corridor beyond.

Dan went through. A sound rolled down towards him. A cracking like fractured ice.

'Faye?' His voice so quiet in the claustrophobic dark.

Something drifted across his face and he flailed, the torch beam bouncing erratically in the confined space. He rubbed his fingers over his eyes and mouth, aware again of the throbbing ache as he skimmed the edge of his wound.

Only spider webs, he told himself, but they felt different. Stronger.

He could taste something on his tongue. Pressing his lips together there was a slight grittiness, something old in the quality of the air. Something that had been cracked open.

The sound intensified and Dan's steps quickened, along with his heart rate.

A puff of dust from the floor in front of him, a hole where it had caved in, the wooden boards looking as if they had been chewed open.

Dan fell to his hands and knees, setting his torch on its side so the light skimmed over the hole. He crawled slowly, testing the strength of the floor with the heels of his hands, the sound of skittering rubble from somewhere below. Another cloud of dust.

Inches away now, he could see the top of a wooden beam, the ragged edges pale in the darkness.

Then it started to slip away, swallowed by what was beyond.

One more inch. Dan stared down into the chasm below.

The shifting wooden beam. The boy clinging to its surface like it was a prayer. The decayed railing slowly breaking apart.

Dan flattened himself against the floor, distributing his weight evenly, just as the boy below had once told him to do if he was ever caught on thin ice.

He reached down, clawing for something to hold on to,

something to stop the beam from crashing through the rail and sending Milo to his death.

There was nothing but air between his fingers.

Dan stretched a few more inches, the splintered edge of one of the floorboards shredding the skin on his shoulder. A scrap of material against his fingertips. The tiniest hope.

With a grunt, he lowered his other shoulder through the hole. His fingers wrapped around a thin wrist and he yanked himself backwards. The beam toppled into the dark chasm below.

For one brief moment he thought Milo had gone with it, because the boy was so light. And then a hand gripped his own wrist, and Dan pulled the boy up through the rotted floor.

FIFTY-FOUR

The echo of Faye's scream faded into the darkness. Her mind cartwheeled over and over, her limbs desperate to flee but reduced to things without bone.

The shape became solid, cutting through the gloom like a knife.

Her brain juddered to a halt, trying to take in what stood before her.

A young boy with matted hair, shreds of clothing hanging from a gaunt frame. His feet were bare. His skin dusted with soil.

Faye forced her gaze up towards his face, a face that was twisting unnaturally to one side, watching her with an intensity of a bird about to devour a worm. The scent of wet earth crawled into her nostrils. Then a laugh that made the hairs stand up in the nape of her neck.

The wilted flowers lay in his hand. *I did this.* The impossibility of it stuck to the inside of her throat, as thick as clogged mucus.

'Forgotten,' he hissed.

Malevolence coated his words, and Faye took a halting step backwards. Something this small shouldn't be so terrifying. He reminded her of the time she once cornered a cat that yowled every night outside her bedroom window. She had stomped downstairs, clapping her hands together, fully expecting it to flee. But it had stood its ground, then advanced with a hiss, its fangs gleaming in the dark.

This child looked very much as if it would have fangs.

'Have you come to play with me?' Now the voice was innocent, the pendulum swinging away from malice.

'Would you like that?' Faye tried to keep her voice level. Soothing.

Behind the child the attic door stood slightly open, a soft glow coming from within.

The small face scowled for a moment.

'That's what she said.' The pale lips pouted. 'That thing.' *Corrigan.*

'I was only doing what I had to.' The child tilted his chin slightly upwards. 'And then she locked me in the dark. Just like Papa did.' His lower lip trembled.

Faye could feel the build-up of energy in the air, a low thrumming like a volcano waiting to blow.

'Why did Papa do that?' she asked.

'Because I was bad. Because I destroyed things.' The child reached out one thin arm. 'Would you like to see?'

Faye hesitated for a moment. Milo had said he needed to see what was in the attic. It was a few yards away, enticing her with its warm, golden light.

She nodded and forced her legs to climb the last few steps.

'After you.' The child swept a small bow, the elegance completely at odds with the madness. Because that's what it was, she realised, a mind unhinged from its moorings.

She crept forwards, the open door before her and the child behind. He was chattering softly to himself, a nonsensical stream of sound. She wanted to turn tail and run, but then she thought of Milo and everything he had endured and found a shred of courage.

The yellow light poured through the gap of the open door. Faye had to duck her head to climb through. The rafters here sloped acutely and there wasn't room for her to stand upright.

The source of the glow was a fat church candle pooling wax onto a milking stool. The light bounced from something just out of sight between the rafters.

She could feel the child in the doorway, his hungry eyes watching her every move.

'Go on,' he whispered. 'See what I did.'

This last fragment held a ring of triumph.

Faye picked her way across the uneven attic floor, her breath rasping in her throat, hyper aware that there was nowhere to run to.

The edge of the rafter blocking her view slid past.

Her eyes flicked around the attic space. Slowly, she crouched and picked up the candle, holding it out in front of her, bathing the rafters in light. A small cry left her lips. Here were the withered remains of countless birds, small skulls bereft of feathers. Here, a pipistrelle bat, its skin leathered by age.

All were pinned there by their open wings.

She turned, hesitantly. A glass jar glittered at her back, but something made her stop before she looked what was inside. She raised the candle again and her breath stalled.

On the rafters above the glass jar were dozens of creatures. Creatures that looked like Corrigan, desiccated, stripped of their wings. Faye's fingers trembled as she lowered her light.

It glittered from the surface of the jar. The reflection of

the flame guttered as Faye let out a juddering exhale. The glass jar was full. Full of translucent wings, of all shapes and sizes. Hundreds of them.

Her eyes flew to the shape in the doorway. 'What did you do?'

A small laugh drifted through the shadows. 'I grew bored of them after a while. When their light went out they were no fun anymore.'

Faye glanced down at the jar, full of the remains of death.

'So I decided to eat them instead.'

Suddenly, Faye understood Corrigan's reasoning. Why she had taken Milo. Why she revelled in pursuit and torment. She was avenging what this child had done. Torturing the species who had murdered her own.

Revenge. It was all about revenge.

Faye backed away, needing to get out of this awful place. But as she neared the door, as she prepared to push the child out of the way, he slammed it in her face.

The sound of a key turning in a lock sealed her fate.

FIFTY-FIVE

The feel of those fingers around Milo's wrist brought back a crash of memories. As Danny pulled him through the hole in the floor, Milo was catapulted into that shadowy glade. The ones where the birds never sung. The one where the insects never flitted.

Danny's face, his eyes shining, that grin on his lips that speaks of mischief and dare. Milo's stomach churns like a storm-tossed sea.

A year separates them in age. Danny goes to an esteemed grammar school in his city, where a new world beckons. Milo is home schooled by a retired teacher after constant bullying at the local comprehensive school eats away the tiny fragments of courage he arrives with.

It is the beginning of the summer holidays, that endless space of time in a child's life when the days are long and filled with freedom. But Milo sees the change in Danny, the way he carries himself is different. More self-assured. A little more arrogant.

Danny wheels around in the centre of the glade, his face tipped up to the thick, leafy canopies. He lets out a loud whoop that echoes through the trees, bouncing its way through the forest. It is a challenge.

'Don't,' Milo says, a shiver racing over his skin.

'Why?' That grin, edged with something Milo thinks might be pity. 'There's no one here but us. Isn't it time you stopped believing in everything your grandfather tells you?'

A jagged splinter of wood grated against Milo's leg and tumbled him into the present. He was on his feet in seconds, his eyes flicking up and down the hallway, half prepared to take flight.

There was a look of horror on Danny's face, a look that was seared against Milo's mind, and he had to fight to stop another memory from bubbling to the surface. Now was not the time for the past to rise. He knew where Danny's eyes were. The withered stump of his hand.

'Jesus, what happened?'

He met Danny's gaze. The smell of congealed blood and the salt tang of sweat clung to the man. A wound on his head glistened. Things had been feasting, leaving their poison to fester.

It was no more than Danny deserved.

They stood, facing each other down, both of them caught in the tethers of the past. Danny's throat rippled as he swallowed, a vertical line deepening between his eyes.

'Milo, please.' An outstretched hand, the hand that had plucked Milo from death's jaws. 'Have you seen Faye? She's my wife. I brought her here because our son died.' Danny's lower lip trembled. 'I wanted to reconnect, to take her away from it all. But I'd forgotten what happened here, what happened to you...' Danny's voice trailed off.

Milo knew he shouldn't care. Because if karma existed it had got a hold of Danny Morgan and shook him in its teeth until he bled.

But Faye didn't deserve any of it.

And there was something else lurking behind his thoughts. The fact that Corrigan had gone to ground since Danny appeared.

'I heard her scream. That's why I was trying to get up here.' The man's lips pressed together so tightly they almost disappeared. 'But this place...' Milo paused, his eyes darting into the shadows. 'It warps things. Walls. Floors. Minds.' He had to stop and bite back the bitterness flooding onto his tongue. 'I think she was trying to get into the attic, but there's only one way in there from here.'

'Where is it?' A grim determination had replaced the openness and the pleading.

'Through that wall.' Milo pointed into the darkness behind him.

Danny disappeared into the gloom for a few moments and returned carrying an old canvas rucksack. He set it on the floor, next to his torch, then pulled an axe from his belt. Danny hefted it from one hand to the next, feeling its weight.

'Remember this, Milo? Lucinda kept it in the outhouse.'

Milo did remember, the old woman's face stern as she told them never to touch it.

'I think she knew that one day I'd need it.' Danny voiced the thoughts that were in Milo's head. Aunt Lucinda, who sat in that room tying knots in balls of wool. The woman who visited his grandfather, both of them talking in hushed tones as Milo sat at the top of the stairs, his pyjama-clad knees pressed into his chest.

Danny angled the torch so its beam shone against the wall. He edged around the hole carefully, the axe held against his chest. The old boards creaked under his weight.

Milo drifted after him, pointing out the exact place in the

wall where he knew the attic was. He had heard the whispers in the night so many times, whispers in the walls calling him to this place where he wasn't allowed.

He felt that somehow this tiny space under the roof spoke of a weakness in Corrigan's shield. The only weakness he had ever found.

Crouching down, Milo traced the uneven wall, feeling for the hollow where the plaster dipped.

He pointed with his good hand, his other tucked up inside his shirt.

Danny motioned for him to stand back.

A small sound rolled down towards them but Danny had already swung the axe over his shoulder. A rain of old paint and plaster as he brought the blade crashing down against the wall.

Danny swore under his breath and moved his feet wider apart, swinging the axe again from a different angle. A jagged crack appeared in the plaster, like a lightning bolt.

With every blow, Milo expected Corrigan to descend with her army, screaming her fury at their audacity. He flicked the plaster shreds from his hair. And heard the sound again.

Small, eager footsteps.

The energy changed in the air surrounding them.

Danny was oblivious to anything but the task in hand, sweat rolling down his face as he swung again and again.

'Follow, follow, eyes a hollow.' The whisper sang through the dark and Milo stiffened, grabbing Danny's arm mid-flight. He could feel the bunch of muscle underneath. Muscle he would never have.

'What?' Irritation and impatience. Some things never changed.

'Chase me down the stair.' The words rolled to meet them like a ball across the floor.

The torch beam rose, an indistinct shape behind it. A moan left Danny's lips.

'Little teeth go swallow, swallow.'

A doll-like grin from a small face, the lips stretched unnaturally wide. Clutched tightly against its chest was the rucksack Danny had brought.

'No!' A roar from the man at his side that made the air vibrate in the narrow hallway.

The child smirked. But there was nothing in its eyes. It opened its mouth and Milo knew the words that tumbled out, squirming like worms in the dark. He had seen them scrawled on the walls of the boarded-up room.

'Find me if you dare.'

FIFTY-SIX

As the sound of his fury echoed after the disappearing child, Dan fought the wave of helplessness settling around him. It was this fucked-up place, he was sure of it. Not since that last summer had he felt so insignificant, so swept along by the waves of something unnatural. Something hell-bent on destruction.

The axe lay heavy in his sweating hands.

'I need to get that rucksack back.' He turned to Milo in the settling dark. The boy who shouldn't be.

'That's what it wants,' the boy replied. 'The thrill of the chase. Like everything else in this house.'

Dan didn't understand. And it appeared Milo didn't appreciate the urgency.

'Damn it, Milo.' He fought to keep his voice from sounding too harsh. 'There's something in the bag, something that belongs here, I'm sure of it.'

'Nothing decent belongs here.' Milo spat the words out, each one more bitter than the last.

Dan wanted to ask how on earth Milo could look the same after thirty years, but right now that didn't seem like the most important thing. He looked back at the attic wall, trying to formulate a plan. It was going to take a long time to break through. Time they didn't have.

Despite the crushing need in his chest to reach Faye, Dan understood getting the bag back meant more. He was relying on instinct, that trait he had buried under the weight of adulthood, carving his way in a world that lived off greed and a sense of its own importance.

What he was doing right now seemed like the most genuine thing he had done in years.

Dan's eyes became accustomed to the gloom as he pushed the handle of the axe inside his belt, bringing his thumb to his mouth to tease out a splinter with his teeth.

Milo watched in silence, his gaze flitting to the attic wall. Then his face suddenly stiffened. 'Maybe it doesn't matter anymore about getting inside the attic.' The boy chewed the edge of his bottom lip. 'Can't you feel it? The way things are tearing apart?'

Dan couldn't feel anything but his heartbeat galloping in his chest, along with the blinding urgency to do *something*. He stepped around the jagged black hole. 'I'm going after him,' he said, 'are you coming?'

Dan really hoped the answer to that question was a yes. He had no desire to wander around Barrington Hall by himself. He glanced at his watch. The digital display said 3:15 a.m. The same time it had said as he stood before the double doors.

Milo took one last look back at the wall then joined him as they picked their way through the dark.

'In here.' Milo stopped at a door and led them into a small room at the right hand side of the hallway.

Dan glanced around the empty space, frustration burning through his veins. They were wasting time. Time Faye might not have.

Milo crossed to the window. 'What's in the bag that's so important?'

'Do you remember the glass case in Lucinda's room?'

Milo turned, moonlight streaming onto his face. He tugged on the lobe of one ear. What he had always done when he couldn't make up his mind.

'Vaguely. It was a long time ago.' Milo's brow creased.

The boy hooked his fingers under the metal stay. It sprung open with a sharp rattle.

Dan stared into the darkness. A darkness that always seemed to be listening. He crept across to Milo, a strange déjà vu washing over him. For a moment Dan was fourteen again.

He cupped his hand around his mouth, leaning in close. The scent of damp rose from Milo's clothes.

'There was something hidden in the moss. I brought it here.' He paused, the next words fizzing on his tongue. 'I think this is where it belongs.'

Milo's grey eyes widened.

'It's dead,' Dan mouthed. He wondered about the sanity of his decision, whether it would only condemn them further.

Milo turned back to the window. The old frame groaned as he swung it out into the night.

'What are you doing?' Dan hissed as Milo hopped onto the sill, sliding out into the darkness in one fluid move.

The boy didn't answer, just extended a hand down to Dan. He grasped it, and for a moment it wasn't Milo's hand but Toby's. Toby would want him to help Milo. His son had always been altruistic. A jagged pain crushed his chest.

Dan shook the thoughts away and clambered onto the sill in an ungainly manner, easing himself through the small window.

Milo stood on a thin ledge with a dizzying drop below him. The moon shone down on the rooftop, painting it in a silver wash. Stone finials book-ended the ledge, covered in moss and age.

Dan's head started to swim as his feet touched the ledge. There was precious little to hold onto here. He glanced across at Milo, who was studying the outside of the house, concentration etched onto his brow. Droplets of moisture glistened on his face.

'I can tell where things are from here,' Milo whispered. 'Corrigan can't fold the exterior like she can the inside.'

'Corrigan?' The name felt like a maggot on Dan's tongue.

'The flash of blue, Danny. The thing we both saw and you refused to acknowledge.'

Milo brushed the hair out of his eyes with his withered hand.

The edges of Dan's reality melted away, leaving a shimmering pool of black water. His mind's eye cast down and saw Corrigan's face reflected in its depths, her translucent wings crimson-tipped.

Vomit rose in his throat as he pressed himself back against the security of the roof.

'Something's changed in there. A rift that hasn't been there before. I don't know what's caused it. It might be you or Faye.' Dan's heart lurched at the mention of his wife's name. 'It might be what you brought into the house. Or the child we saw. He's long dead but something's brought him back here.'

Dan blew out a breath at this last comment. It hung there in the night air, a small white cloud of his own making.

'Whatever it is, it's made Corrigan go to ground.' Milo glanced across, moonlight in his bedraggled hair, at one with the decay surrounding him. 'I think she's planning something awful.'

FIFTY-SEVEN

You sit on the uppermost stone finial on the roof, a weather-beaten fleur-de-lis, your wings folded against your body. Your antennae twitch against the night. Below, the moon-silvered tiles glisten like the surface of the lake beyond.

All is quiet. All is calm.

Clustered around are all that remains of your kin. Your sisters wait for your decision.

You can sense their frenetic energy, their need to hunt and punish. Especially now there are two fresh humans under this cursed roof.

You watch as Milo leads Danny Morgan out onto the narrow ledge, watch as the boy studies the house from the outside. He has learned well. A touch of pride swells, but you bite it in two and swallow it down.

Something has changed since Danny has arrived. Barrington Hall seems too eager for his bones.

Your own darkness has rebelled and now it seems it has its own agenda.

The house has opened the door to the attic, the door you keep closed. Because this is your own private space, where you go to mourn your lost children. Where you feed the flames of your revenge.

You think about the jar on the shelf, the sorry remains of

your family now exposed.

Elliot Kidd has come home and Barrington Hall has welcomed its young master into its folds. You should have torn him to pieces like he did to your children, not left him buried alive to ruminate over his sins. A thin line of drool escapes as your lower jaw slides from side to side

What to do now? A game of bait and chase, to pit them all against each other? You know this is what your kin crave. But there is something else, something that sours the usual unbridled joy of the hunt.

You know the moment Milo's eyes find you in the dark, the weight of his gaze tangible. Of course, he has seen your wings shining in the moonlight, has even possibly honed in on the faint blur of blue you have dimmed. The boy is becoming too clever for his own good.

You gave him back his memories, expecting him to crumble, but he has risen from his own ashes. Your eyes stray to the pewter glass of the lake where it all began.

Yes, it is time. You have Danny and Faye now, with all of the delicious possibilities. Matching them against each other to see which one survives will be a fresh and exciting challenge. Unless Elliot gets to one of them first.

You know Barrington Hall will not let you imprison him again. For some reason, it wants the monster to roam its halls once more. You also know that Faye freed him. You felt him break through the soil, your spell broken by the woman who opened up a wound in Barrington Hall almost as if she tore it apart with her fingers. The old is leaking out, bubbling up through the cracks. You can taste it on the air.

You spin into the night, a few choice clicks falling on the ones who wait, telling them to be still. Be ready.

As silent as snowfall you fly down across a lower ridge of roof, jutting out over what were once the servant's quarters, a loose tile your easy entry place.

It has been a long time since you ventured into the attic. You have no desire to see the glass coffin of your murdered children tonight. Elliot Kidd did more than take their lives; he stripped your whole species of its goodness.

Along the dusty roof space and out through a gap in the floor, into the narrow hallway that leads to the attic. The walls seem closer now than before, the ceiling a little lower. You gather the ever-present thrum of dark magic within your breast and pull it around yourself.

A fall of pale plaster dust on the floor catches your eye. Danny has been here, trying to break in. Trying to make amends for his past. You flit up to the ceiling again, find the tiny hole you gnawed all of those years ago. You squeeze through. Shake the dust from your wings. It still smells of death here.

A faint glow from beyond—the candle your magic lit each night so your children were not alone in the dark. You inch your way forwards, hover for a few seconds, try not to look at the shine on the glass jar.

And here is Faye, sitting on the floor, her arms around her hunched-up knees, the candle flickering at her feet.

A feeling descends upon you, a feeling of—you muse, search for the right word.

Inevitability.

It has crept upon you like a thief in the night, coating your throat with its shadow. Too many years of the same routine. Too many years of carrying your sorrow like a shield and your wrath like a spear.

'Hello, Faye.' You breathe your words into the stillness and the woman snaps her head up, her eyes wide with fear. 'What have you got yourself into?' You force a laugh. 'Playing with things you don't understand.'

Faye scrambles to her feet. The sloping rafters almost touch her hair.

'I know why you feel the need to punish.' Her voice is ragged. She points at the glass jar. 'That boy. This is his doing.'

Your anger erupts in a few choice sounds.

'I'm sorry. He was wrong. So very wrong. But it has nothing to do with me. Or Milo.'

These last two words tremble and your wings quiver. So the woman has connected with the boy. All the better for what is to come.

But being here, you feel like you are slowly suffocating. The shine from the jar glitters like falling tears.

'You have no idea of how they suffered. How he made my babies scream.'

A flash of pain shoots across Faye's pale face. She hugs her arms around her body and raises her head to meet your gaze. 'I know what it's like to lose a child,' she whispers.

You drop onto a rafter. You want to think the woman is lying, but you know that she isn't. For a few brief seconds, there is the faintest understanding between you both. A fragile and tremulous thread.

Then you force your eyes away, find the tiny withered husk spinning from a thread of cotton. The last one of your children.

'I don't want you in here,' you say, the words like bile on your tongue. 'I'm going to open the door and let you go free. Not because we have anything in common, but because

I want you to see what I'm going to do. Why things have to go full circle.'

A glimmer of hope lights up Faye's eyes, and you almost feel sympathy for the woman. Almost, but not quite.

But you know, without a shadow of a doubt, that what you intend to do to Milo, will tear Faye apart.

FIFTY-EIGHT

Faye bolted from the attic.

Corrigan's words trailed behind her. But it wasn't just the words, it was the way the creature had said them. There was too much hate, too much sorrow.

A splinter of wood raked across her cheek, the sting joining the adrenaline tingle in her limbs. But then she was through, the darkness beyond punctured by arrows of moonlight.

Down the rotting staircase she flew, with no regard for its danger. She was a bird in flight with only one thing on her mind: putting as much distance between herself and Corrigan as possible. Her mind reeled with the insanity of it—how she had held a conversation, and how, for a moment, they had even had some kind of empathy.

At the bottom of the stairs she risked a glance back up into the darkness.

Faye curled her hand around a blighted newel post and tried to take stock of her options. She was exhausted, her nerves frayed to the point of collapse.

And she was, for the first time in many years, completely alone.

There was no Toby. There was no Dan in the next room. And now there was no Milo. In that moment, her heart untethered, Faye realised how much she had come to rely on other people. Even if she drove them away.

She pushed her fingers into the mouldering wood and felt it crumble. Just like her reality. And she had to bite back a laugh as it crawled into her throat. A life-defining moment in a place riddled with decay.

From somewhere in the pit of darkness came the sound of laughter, echoing up as though it came from the bottom of a well. A child's peal of joy, but the tone of it was too high. Too wrong. The boy from the attic. *The boy from the grave.*

Faye took a couple of deep breaths then set off into the dark, her eyesight attuned to it now, the gloom a landscape of shifting shadows. As long as she managed to descend, she was on the right track.

Her old life seemed as far away as the floating fragments of a dream, this nightmare of blackness now her whole world. She passed door after door, sure she could hear whispers following her through the walls. Each glimpsed turn bringing hope that quickly plummeted like a dead bird as she rounded the corner. And there was a creaking now that hadn't been there before, a sound that made her think of rickety bones.

She could die here and no one would find her. Barrington Hall would make sure of that.

At last she came to an area which opened up onto a galleried landing, the sense of space making her head spin. A faint chink of light showed under a door and from inside came the homely rattle of china against china.

Slowly, Faye edged towards it, powerless to resist its draw. The door swung open and the light from within rushed out to greet her.

She stood, transfixed, as the scene unfolded.

A family sat in front of a blazing log fire. She could smell the scent of pine logs burning. A man dressed in black was seated in a wing-back chair, the gleam of a pocket watch catching the firelight. At his shoulder, a young girl holding a sheet of music in one hand. A cameo nestled on the lace throat of her dress.

Faye's fingers strayed to the front pocket of her jeans, found the oval shape she'd taken from the chest. *Sweet Jesus, the skeleton...*

She forced her focus back to the room.

A maid poured tea from a silver teapot into delicate china cups set on a side table. Steam arose from its spout, disappearing into the backdrop of flames. In front of the fire sat two children, playing with a set of tin soldiers. A little girl had a doll resting on her knee, its raggedy hair dressed in red ribbons like her own.

The doll from the nursery. Faye's hand flew to her mouth.

The other child had its back to her, and she couldn't see if it was a boy or a girl, only a shock of golden hair. And even though the family was talking and laughing Faye couldn't hear their voices.

The only sound was the chink of the china. They showed no knowledge of her presence.

Faye found herself drawn to the opulence of the room with its heavy, swagged velvet curtains and elegant damask walls. The richness of colour after the constant gloom was a feast for her eyes, shades of gold and teal and rose and lavender. A round table, topped with polished green marble, stood in the middle of an Indian rug. And on this table sat a globe of the world set into a mahogany stand. As she watched, the globe started to spin slowly.

Faye found herself being drawn inside the room as though it was trying to inhale her. Her vision darkened at the edges, the middle tunnelling as she fought the magnetic pull. Her foot stumbled over the threshold and she grabbed a hold of the door jamb. Her eyes flicked to the family group. Now the child with its back to her was turning. A meaningful movement, slow and measured.

Faye found herself staring into the face of the boy from the attic. A furtive smile broke on his lips as he met her gaze.

This version of him she had seen in the photograph on the study wall. In the photograph with the dead child.

The one who still pushed her doll carriage through Barrington Hall.

Ghosts.

The word punched her in the gut, and even as the knowledge of it cracked her wide open, as it wormed its way into all of her sense and logic, Faye's mind screamed in dissent.

The certain knowledge of what had happened here sat on her shoulder like a black raven. All of this family dead. All of this family still here.

The little boy with the angel face was a murderer of creatures that shouldn't exist.

But he had and they did.

Faye knew she was either one step across the line to crazy, or finally beginning to understand.

FIFTY-NINE

Milo stole along the narrow ledge, making his way to where the roof line dropped at the start of another wing.

Corrigan had made sure the upper levels near the attic were virtually impassable. He had an awful sense of foreboding that she was keeping Faye separated for a reason.

He could hear Danny's rapid breathing, smell the fear oozing from his pores. What he had said about the rucksack's contents twisted like a thorn into Milo's side.

Milo wondered just when they had fallen into a vague sense of companionship again. What had happened to his need for revenge? He reached the end of the ledge and dangled his legs over the side. His toes touched the roof tiles and he swung himself down with his good hand, his feet never making a sound.

'Fuck it, Milo,' Danny hissed, and Milo glanced up into a face ghostly pale against the black sky. Doubt shone in the man's eyes, and for a moment Milo wanted to disappear and leave him to his fate, like Danny had done to him all of those summers ago.

Milo sighed. 'Just keep your hands on the tiles up there. They're pretty solid. You've got longer legs than me; the drop will be easy.'

Danny's lower lip curled into his mouth, the muscles

bunching under his t-shirt as the man very slowly crept to the end of the ledge. His knuckles were bone-white as they clung onto the ridges in the tiles. Danny dangled one leg towards where Milo stood, his foot searching for a safe place.

An exhalation of relief as he found what he was looking for and a tumble of soft moss as he dropped. But Milo hadn't reckoned on Danny's weight.

'Easy as pie.' The man grinned, but the moment those words left his lips, his foot started sliding towards the gutter. The movement made him jerk sideways, his arms wheeling as he tried to keep his balance.

The gutter groaned as his weight hit its edge and there was a loud snap as the bracket gave way.

Milo reached out, his hand grabbing a fistful of t-shirt, and in that moment he was holding Danny's life in his hands. One simple push and the man would plummet to his death.

It was probably what he deserved. What Corrigan wanted.

Choice. The word that had decided his fate in the lake.

Milo stared into Danny's eyes and knew his old friend was thinking exactly the same.

He clenched his fingers and the tendons tightened in his wiry arms. Then he dragged Danny towards him. The man fell onto his knees, his hands scrabbling on the slate tiles, tufts of moss rolling down to the gutter.

'Thank you.' The whisper came with a tremble.

Milo didn't reply. He was warring with the emotions churning around in his gut. How many years had he prayed a moment like this would come his way? And he had wimped out, just like he had done on so many other occasions.

A small peal of laughter floated across the ridge of the

roof. It punctured the silence like an arrow.

Milo crept over the tiles as stealthy as an alley cat. As he reached the apex, the scent of water wafted towards him and his stomach flipped over.

The laughter came again, along with the sing-song line Milo had grown to hate.

Follow, follow, eyes a-hollow.

Crouched on the east wing of Barrington Hall like a gargoyle made flesh was Elliot Kidd.

The boy was baiting them, just like he had baited the creatures from the forest. A bright spear of loathing burned through Milo's veins. It softened his defences, honing his attention towards the child who was the cause of his misery.

Out of the darkness the swarm descended.

They landed on his shoulders, along his spine, fastened themselves around his limbs. Milo knew what they were about to do. He tried to shake them off but he needed his good hand to cling onto the roof and they were quick. So very quick. Spinning their threads around him. The threads that looked as delicate as mist.

As he flailed he was dimly aware of Danny scrabbling across the tiles, of the horror in the man's eyes. Milo had seen that look before.

And then Corrigan alighted on Milo's shoulder, that coaxing, lilting voice against his ear. 'My love. You were such a sweet delight.'

Past tense. Terror lodged itself inside Milo's throat and he twisted his body sideways, the steel strands of web already fastening his feet and knees together. He slid, his good hand desperately fighting for grip, but there were threads around his fingers. He could feel the pressure against his chest now as around and around they flew, trussing him up, their wingbeats a constant hum in his ears.

He was just a fly, wrapped up in their gossamer shackles, waiting to be devoured.

Milo remembered the pain as his flesh was stripped from his fingers and tears sprung to his eyes.

His frantic mind decided they blamed him for Elliot's return. And now he was going to pay the price.

A weight struck him and sent him sprawling, and then there were hands tearing at the threads. Milo wanted to scream that it wasn't any use, but his mouth was sealed now and only his eyes could talk.

Corrigan laughed softly as she hovered above, watching his hopeless struggle. The bright blue throb of her belly pulsed against the midnight sky.

But Milo continued to fight, because he knew this time it was for his life.

They were on Danny now, and even though the man was much stronger they had his hands bound. A few dropped onto his face, their long, curled tongues probing his mouth and nose. The scream that bubbled up from Danny's throat curdled Milo's blood.

All of his hope melted into the night along with that scream.

Corrigan clicked her demands and Milo felt himself lifted into the darkness, a simple cargo. He thought about how long it would take to die. About Faye all alone in the belly of Barrington Hall. Milo thought it had all been about revenge but it was only ever about replacement.

The time he had spent here was simply a postponement of that night in the lake.

Corrigan had dragged him out to use for her own amusement, but learning how she thought had been his worst mistake.

She only ever wanted him to be terrified.

SIXTY

Faye stared as the scene in front of her wrinkled at the edges like burnt paper. The fireplace distorted, as though she was looking at it through thick glass, then a smell, sweet and high and rotten, rolled over her. She gagged and turned away, holding her breath.

When she looked back, the room was in shadow. The furniture huddled in the dark. The globe was covered in a thick blanket of dust. Something had chewed along the edge of the Indian rug.

Faye tried to grasp what she had just seen. She looked at her dirty hand as it rested on the door jamb, felt the solidity of the wood under her fingertips. This was now.

Something tickled her neck and she raised her other hand, finding the trailing end of a cobweb. Instinctively, she flicked it away. Then she heard the crisp rupture as the thread broke away from its anchor, and she had just enough time to glance up, just enough time to see the swollen cradle of web split apart.

They fell like soft rain, tiny legs unfolding as they burrowed into her hair. Against her scalp, down the back of her t-shirt. She lowered her head, frantically shaking her curls, her fingers trying to pluck them out, even though she was repulsed by the thought of touching them. Faye knew then, in a burst of clarity, how Dan felt about flies. His fear of things with wings came from this house. From Corrigan.

A torrent of chaotic thought as she tore at her hair. It didn't matter that these were tiny, helpless creatures. It only mattered that they were crawling on her skin, and that in her haste, she was crushing them. The soft squelch as they burst under her fingers like rotten berries.

Small cries of horror bubbled in her throat.

Now in full panic mode, she ran down the corridor half blinded by fear. She tore off her t-shirt, throwing it on the ground and reaching around her body, trying to skim them from her back. But they were still in her hair.

Faye fell to her hands and knees. The chill of the house settled against her bare skin hungrily. The house was trying to drive her into madness.

'I'm not done yet,' she muttered through gritted teeth.

But maybe talking to Barrington Hall was the first sign of her descent.

Something disturbed the air in front of her.

Very slowly, Faye lifted her head. The small girl stood only inches away, made of tattered shadow with a melancholy Faye could almost taste.

The girl reached out a thin hand and placed it on Faye's head. It was like a winter breeze had gained form. Cold sweat trickled down Faye's spine. She wanted to pull away, but the little girl raised a finger to her lips, and Faye was strangely quietened.

Clenching her jaw she tried not to squirm as the spiderlings crawled out of her hair and made their way along the pale, shredded-lace sleeve. She tried not to wince as they burrowed through the holes of the lace, but the small girl seemed not to mind at all.

You're dead, Faye thought, and it wasn't fear that gripped her heart this time, simply a mother's ache for a child taken before its time.

'How do I get out of here?' The words came from Faye's lips in a whisper, as though she didn't want the house to hear.

The little girl shook her head slowly, her dark veil lifting from her face. Faye didn't want to see what lay beneath, but she couldn't look away. A dainty chin and pale rosebud lips. And two dark holes where her eyes had been.

Faye thought about the forlorn tomb. Barrington Hall wasn't prepared to let anyone who lived here rest peacefully. Barrington Hall didn't let anything go.

The hopelessness of her plight sucked all the air from her lungs and a great sob came with it as she lowered her head. When she looked up, the little girl was gone.

Faye picked her t-shirt from the floor and shook it, trying not to think about the squashed spider pulp. She turned it inside out and pulled it on, the soft cotton almost painful against her skin, which felt as if layers had been ripped away. Maybe that's what happened when you were touched by the dead.

But underneath the sting a weariness had settled on her bones. She forced herself to stand and tried to find her bearings in the gloom.

A slow creak came out of that gloom. She felt the horror of it in her blood.

Faye crept towards it, drawn by a need she couldn't control.

A burst of joy flooded through her as she recognised the mirror on the grand staircase, refracted moonlight playing on its surface from the tall windows by the doors.

A reflected rope hung in the mirror. A rope that was slowly moving.

The scene unfolded in the mirror before Faye's eyes, and part of her embraced the safety of this vision. It didn't seem as real if it wasn't right in front of her.

And she knew what she would find as the corridor walls fell away, as Barrington Hall unfolded yet another secret.

The rope was attached to the chandelier, but it was no longer dull and cobweb-ridden. Now, it was bright and gleaming, a beautiful piece of craftsmanship hanging over the black and white chequered floor of the great hall. The remains of a fire burned in the hearth, the scent of wood smoke in the air.

Faye crept to the galleried balcony rail, polished mahogany under her fingertips. The rope swung before her.

She forced herself to look down, to what hung at the end of it. A man, his head tilted to one side. Vacant eyes, riddled with broken capillaries, stared into space. His dark tongue protruded from his mouth, giving his expression a hideous leer. It was the man from the family scene. The one with the pocket watch. William Kidd. The name she had seen on the library computer.

And here it was, a snapshot torn from time. The man who had lost all that he lived for, offering his last breaths to the house that had devoured them all.

A wave of dizziness took her as the sound from the rope creaked against her ears. Faye fell forwards, desperately clawing at the balcony rail.

Barrington Hall was only showing her own inescapable demise.

SIXTY-ONE

Dan watched helplessly as Milo's body was lifted into the air. He could still feel the touch of the creatures on his skin. The violation of their tongues. He shuddered, his body reacting to the exploding grenade of his neurosis. The green and bitter taste of them filled his mouth and he wanted to retch.

They were all his childhood nightmares come back to haunt him. Nothing could be worse than this. Or so he'd thought. But that was before Toby's death. Before Faye's disappearance. Before finding Milo alive.

Now, it was all down to him. Because if he couldn't find the rucksack with the creature inside they all might die. The forgotten inmate of the glass case was his only bargaining chip. And he didn't even know why.

As Milo disappeared into the throat of the night, Dan knew if he had to choose only one to save, that person would be Faye. He would fail Milo yet again and that awful fact was like a dagger slicing through his ribs, looking for a soft and juicy organ to rip apart.

His wrists were still bound by the creatures' webs and no amount of twisting would loosen them. A child's giggle filtered through the darkness. Dan flicked his eyes over the roof, no longer afraid of falling. There were worse things.

He scrambled across, crab–like, to where he had carefully

dropped from only minutes before. The roof line edge was rough and weather worn. Dan began to saw the threads binding his wrists against a broken tile.

It was painstakingly slow, but with each torn thread Dan found a new determination. Each movement shaved the skin from his wrist bones but he didn't stop. Inside his head there was a time bomb ticking, and the fuse was short.

The night breeze brought the scent of the lake over the apex of the roof, as if it wanted to remind him of his failings. But the guilt was doing a good enough job of that already. All of these years when he'd hidden behind his fear of winged things, his fear of death. It was all masking what he'd really done: left his boyhood friend to die. Chosen him over his own sorry skin.

He saw it now in his mind's eye as his skin bled and the threads came away, little by little.

'It's your choice. Who dies?'

He clings to the wooden jetty, his mouth filled with the words he doesn't want to say. Milo goes under again as his strength fails, but Danny can see the water churning as he fights for the surface.

It's all his fault. He's the one who threw stones against Milo's window and persuaded him to come out in the dark. Who tossed the bluebells so carelessly, despite the wide-eyed terror of the boy standing next to him. Showing off. Scorning everything Lucinda had ever told him.

A cry bubbles up out of his mouth and the creature hovering above smiles. That is the final straw. The human gesture on the face of something so terrifying.

'Let me live. Let me live!' The cry grows into a scream, the relief and horror of it spinning his thoughts into a tornado

cloud of darkness.

And then, somehow, he had blocked it out, his memory of that summer as hazy as a dawn mist over the sea. He only remembered Lucinda's tight-lipped farewell and his parents' disapproval at his early return.

There were visits to medical professionals. Hushed rooms and soft lighting. His parents constantly exchanging frustrated glances. Their son was just another appointment to squeeze in. The doctors analysed him from over polished desks, blank notepads in front of them. Works of art on the walls, beautifully sympathetic in tone, seemed to study him too.

Extreme shock. That was the final diagnosis. Brought on by the time he'd spent in the water and an unexplained sting at the side of his neck. A sting they biopsied and found traces of water hemlock and an unidentified poison.

Shock that had erased his memory of how he got to be in the water and the time afterwards. Someone had pulled him out. Coughing and spluttering, his fingertips pale and wrinkled. They had laid his trembling body on the jetty and he had looked up at the night sky, at the tiny twinkling stars, witnesses to his sin, and had felt a small piece of himself break away and slip back into the lake.

Dan fought the shroud around his memories, trying to find a moment in which Milo was mentioned. But it seemed as if Milo's life had been erased from the earth. Dan's parents had never sent him back here, and he had never asked why. He'd locked his past inside a little room labelled childhood, wiping away any edges that dared to ooze under the door.

He swallowed the sour taste of his recollections. And the awful realisation dawned that he had been running away from the monsters, but the monster had been in him all along.

The last of the threads snapped, the spun silk fragments floating away into the night air. Dan scrabbled across the tiles to a window standing out from the pitch of the roof. With no qualms at all he kicked hard against the old glass.

He wondered what they were doing to Milo.

But it was no time for such thoughts. Dan booted the old woodworm-riddled frame and it crumbled under his assault. He had no idea where in the house the room led to, but as he squeezed his body through the small gap he imagined that Barrington Hall watched, smiling darkly at his struggle.

It was some kind of storage room, empty shelves against one wall. The door was missing, the hinges jutting out from the frame.

Darkness leered from the corridor beyond. Dan stared into it, his teeth clenched.

A flash of light strobed suddenly across the gloom. It stopped for a second, then came again.

Dan staggered across the floor, desperate to find its source. The smell of rotting wood and damp curled inside his nostrils. He was fixated on the pendulum swing of the light, sure that it would be snuffed out like a candle if he tore his eyes away.

The light came from behind a sagging doorframe. Dan picked his way across and ducked under the lintel. The beam pulsated erratically, coming from the bottom of a tightly wound set of stairs. A child's laughter filtered up from the darkness.

Dan's jaw tightened. He remembered the name printed on the paper back at the cottage. *Elliot*. Lucinda had known that their paths would cross.

The boy had his torch and was turning it on and off. But

if he had the torch he might still have the rucksack.

Dan stumbled down the narrow stairs. One hand trailed against the wall as he hung on to each sweep of the glorious light. He couldn't make his steps soundless, and he was tormented by the possibility the boy would hear him and career away to hide. Everything seemed like a game to him.

The thought dropped like a penny into a pool. An idea rippled from it.

'Elliot,' Dan called into the suffocating darkness.

Silence answered, along with the cessation of the light.

Dan tried again. 'Would you like to play with me?'

Dan edged his way further down into the well of darkness. He had no way of knowing where Elliot was or whether his offer had tempted the boy.

He faltered as his feet found an area of flat space. A shuffle from up ahead.

'I've got a gift for you. Something with pretty lights.'

Slowly, he reached into his back pocket and slid out his phone, swiping his thumb across it. The screen flared to life and he squinted against the sudden brightness. It lit up the stairwell like a firework and Dan could see the hallway beyond, the gloom bleached out to grey. Elliot was crouched about six feet away, stuffing the torch into the rucksack at his feet.

The child's eyes were wide behind the thick tangle of his hair.

'Look what it does.' Dan flicked through a few screens, finding something that he hoped the boy would understand. He held it out in his hand.

Elliot stood and took a tentative step forward. 'I never win at that game.' A stubborn pout formed. 'And Lottie says only bad men put their faith in cards.'

Dan pressed his lips together. So much for solitaire.

He wondered if he could simply rush at the child and snatch the bag from him, but he had seen how quickly Elliot disappeared into the darkness before. Like a shadow born from this house.

Flicking through the screens again, he found another game. A crazy ping–pong kind of app with brightly coloured shapes you had to feed into tunnels. This time Elliot's mouth fell open and he reached out.

Dan waited until the boy edged closer, then brought the phone to his chest. 'Let's trade: this game for the return of my bag.'

Elliot's eyes narrowed to dark slits. 'How do I know you will keep your word? Papa always said honesty is a virtue. That's why he was so cross when he found out what I'd done.'

For a few moments the small boy in front of him was simply a confused child, and Dan felt the stirrings of sympathy. But then he remembered Milo.

'Your Papa was right. Honesty is a good thing.' Dan's mind tried desperately to find another foothold.

From out of the darkness, from somewhere far below, came a scream.

Faye's scream.

Adrenaline speared through Dan's veins. His heartrate launched into overdrive. His mouth ran dry. The sound rang from the walls, filled with fear and something else. Desperation.

'Give me the bag, Elliot. Now.' Dan had no more time to bargain.

'Can I have that, too?' Elliot pointed towards Dan's belt.

Towards the axe he had almost forgotten was there.

Dan pulled it free from the leather and hefted it in his hand. Did he have it in him to kill a child who should have been dead decades ago?

He bent down and placed it on the floor together with his phone, still flickering insanely with the coloured shapes.

Part of him was waiting for another scream. Somehow only one seemed much worse.

He took a step back, giving the boy space, trying to coax him forwards. And at last, Elliot did shuffle closer. Dan's rucksack dangled from one thin hand.

Words formed on Elliot's lips, silent words, as though he were talking to people Dan couldn't see. The hair rose in the nape of Dan's neck.

He knelt on the floor and held out his hand, his eyes level with the boy's face. He paused as the child reached down, that small, white neck close enough to snap. How would it feel to hear the crunch of that spine under his foot? Little bones, as fragile as a bird's.

It was impossible not to think of Toby's bones as he rolled over the bonnet of that car and smashed into the ground.

Dan bit his lower lip hard, watching the boy first pick up the axe, and then the phone. Elliot was close enough to grab, close enough to shake the life from.

Dan made himself concentrate on the rucksack, the way the phone highlighted the rough weave of its fabric. Very slowly, he reached out. His hand brushed against the cool metal of the zip. He curled his fingers around the old suede-covered handle, hoping that what he had brought here was still inside.

Elliot's eyes were fixed on the phone screen. Dan could

see the coloured lights reflected in them.

As Dan rose to his feet, the boy snapped his head up. All traces of the child had gone, leaving only an evil Dan could taste on the back of his tongue.

The gleam of the axe head shone in the boy's hand.

Dan fumbled his way into the bag, his hand closing over the stout barrel of the torch. His fingers found the thick button at the bottom. The one Lucinda used when foxes would stray too close to her garden. The one he had completely forgotten about.

As Elliot raised his hand and swung the blade, Dan pointed the torch beam directly at the boy's face.

It blurred his features into a mass of white light, the usual pale golden beam eaten alive by its hungry sibling. Dan had never seen a torch quite like it. Lucinda always said it had been made to scare away the darkness, and now Dan knew why.

He hoisted the rucksack onto his shoulder and turned, fleeing down the stairs, taking them three at a time, the light a blinding arc dissolving the night in front of him.

Dan was breathless by the time he reached the doorway. He catapulted himself through it, and then through another, finding himself on the galleried landing above the great hall.

The double doors stood open. Dan could see through them to the lake beyond, the moon shivering on its sable surface.

Movement by its shore.

But that wasn't what drew his attention. It was his wife on her knees in the doorway, her hands clasped to the sides of her face, Robert McCallum blocking her way out.

SIXTY-TWO

As he was lifted into the air, Milo knew instinctively where the creatures were taking him. The thought burned through him like wildfire. It scorched every nerve ending, churning his mind into a relentless wheel of panic.

They were taking him to the place he feared the most. The lake.

The scent of it crawled into his nostrils. Cruel. Black. Bottomless. It was pointless to try to fight against his bonds, but he did it anyway. A last-ditch attempt to save himself.

Corrigan's flash of blue hovered above, a kingfisher star against a midnight sky.

As they lowered him down to the lakeside, Milo heard Faye's scream cut through the darkness. She would be alone there, inside Barrington Hall, its tongue licking away her reality, whilst Corrigan twisted her mind.

He was back by the lake and Danny was close. And this time Milo knew he would die.

His spine hit the hard earth with a jolt as the creatures dropped their spun ropes, then alighted on his body. He could hear their jaws working as they chewed through their own bonds, their wings fluttering against his skin. But his wrists remained bound.

He thought about running, trying to make it into the

forest, but they were much faster and this time it wasn't a game.

As his legs were freed, Milo shuffled around onto his knees, his wrists tied in front of him. A coldness like he'd never felt before oozed over his skin. He was trembling, his heart a cornered beast drumming out his own death knell.

He twisted around and found Corrigan inches away from his face. Her dark eyes held his, the glint of moonlight suspended in her wings.

'Don't.' Milo forced a word out of a throat that had lost all moisture. Then he clicked his tongue against the roof of his mouth, pleading in her language. *Please.*

'My love,' she crooned, settling on his shoulder. Milo turned his head, desperately looking for any signs of regret. He thought about begging, about telling her that he would behave now, that he would run every night and make their chase into a hunt worthy of their time, but he stopped just short.

It wouldn't matter.

Instead, he found a crumb of courage. 'Let Faye go. She doesn't deserve this.'

Corrigan laughed softly. 'And take Danny in her place? Now wouldn't that be the perfect conclusion. Making him suffer what you have. Would you like that, Milo?' She stroked a feeler across his jaw.

Milo thought for only a few seconds. 'No,' he replied, even though some buried part of him screamed the exact opposite. 'It has to end. You can't keep making people suffer because of what Elliot did.'

Corrigan spat, the spurt of moisture hitting the side of Milo's neck.

'I do it because someone has to understand what

happened. It can't disappear into history.' There was such bitterness in her voice. And such sadness too. 'Goodbye, Milo, sweet child. Return to whence you came.'

Milo's eyes widened in shock, her sting a burning flare against his cheek. A final, poisonous kiss.

A cloud of creatures settled onto his wrists. Milo managed to stagger to his feet, trying to resist as they raised his hands above his head. The water spread like a dark ocean behind him.

Milo fought with every ounce of his strength, but numbness had seized his limbs. His legs went from underneath him as the poison took hold, as the creatures' momentum dragged him onto his back. Dragged him towards the hungry lap of the lake.

The sound of the water seeped against his bones.

He gasped as the first chill licked against his skin and bled into his clothes. His shoulders screamed in pain as they hauled him further from the shore line. His feet scrabbled frenziedly against the bottom of the lake, small pebbles finding their way inside his tattered shoes.

And then the moment his feet found nothing but water. He cried out, and his desperation echoed into the merciless night.

The jetty was a black shadow in the distance, water-bloated boards sagging under their own rot, but still unwilling to give themselves over to the lake.

On and on, they pulled him. He couldn't feel his arms anymore, only a strange sensation like his nerves were shredding away, one by one.

Moonlight stroked the surface of the water, rippling away in his wake like a dream long forgotten.

In the centre of the lake the creatures released him. His arms fell with a loud splash. He glanced up and saw them disappearing into the night, their task completed.

They had left him in the deepest part. Milo kicked against the drag of the water, tried to move his bound wrists in an oar-like motion. But every movement was a huge effort as the poison in his veins sapped away his strength. He felt his eyelids flicker. His chin touched the water. Milo jerked his head up, gasping and spluttering, panic trampling through his veins.

He wondered how long it took to die.

A tiny flash of blue hovered over the rippling water. Corrigan was watching him drown, just like she had on that summer night long ago. Until Danny had condemned him to the life that he'd had.

As the water forced itself into his nostrils, sending a scream of pain into his skull, Milo so desperately wanted to keep it.

SIXTY-THREE

Faye watched the horror unfold in front of her. She had seen Milo's struggle through the tall windows of the great hall, the awful image of William Kidd's death collapsing in on itself like a house of cards, until all that was left was the gloom and the chill and the feeling her world was again tipping on its axis.

She ran down the staircase with no heed for her own safety. Her foot slipped in her haste and she tumbled down the last few steps and landed in a heap at the bottom.

Up on her feet in an instant, Faye galloped for the doors, a sick sureness in the pit of her stomach that they would be locked against her.

Just as her outstretched hand was within a few feet of the peeling paint, the doors swung open and she stumbled to her knees. A blast of fresh air hit her full in the face.

A shadow fell over the stone steps. Robert McCallum.

An onslaught of emotion surged in her chest. This was the man Dan had trusted. The man who had fed her into the belly of Barrington Hall.

He watched her, seemingly oblivious to Milo's struggle in the water.

Faye dragged words from her throat as she forced herself to stand. 'You have to help him, Robert. They're trying to drown him. He's only a boy...' This last word trembled on her lips.

'You don't understand,' Robert replied. 'You city folk, coming here with your arrogance and grand ideas. You've no idea how any of this works.'

Faye tried to dodge past him but his hand shot out and grabbed her forearm. Milo's battle to stay alive pummelled against her heart. She remembered how he'd shied away from the rain against the window, how he had withdrawn within himself like a snail into a shell.

'Leave her alone!'

Dan's voice thundered from behind her. She glanced back. He was stood at the bottom of the stairs in a shaft of moonlight. His eyes were dark circles on his face, his lips set so tight they were almost invisible. He was alive and he had come after her.

A swell of warmth burst inside her chest, a glow that was at odds with the cold fear twisting against her heart.

'Milo…,' she began, but Dan held up his hand, his gaze meeting hers.

'I know,' he whispered. 'I know it all.'

Robert was twice the size of her husband, but right now with the look on Dan's face, she wouldn't bet against him. A rucksack hung over his arm, and as he walked across the hall, he unzipped the top and delved deep inside it.

'Tell me, what did you mean when you told me never to get rid of the glass case? How did it matter to you?' Dan's voice was too soft. The anger boiled underneath it like a riptide.

Robert yanked Faye towards him. He snaked his arm across her chest, pinning her to his body. The stench of sour sweat rose from his skin.

'Don't play with things you don't understand.' Robert's

words matched Dan's softness. 'Lucinda knew what she had there. Knew she had to keep it hidden.'

Dan had lived in the cottage, completely unaware of the secrets it held. She had slept under its roof as it drip-fed its horrors into her veins. She twisted against Robert's grip, wincing as it tightened.

And all the while came the sound of thrashing water from the lake. Her heart turned over.

Dan was in the doorway now, the gloom licking at his heels. He withdrew his hand from the bag. Speared upon a knitting needle, like a chunk of meat, was the creature from the glass case. The glint of its wings shone through a veil of tangled moss strands.

A vibration rumbled through her back, Robert's anger a tangible thing. 'For God's sake, don't let her see it.'

'You knew.' Dan shook his head sadly. An ugly wound on his temple glistened in the moonlight. 'All of this time and you knew? Let me believe you were my friend.'

'Don't talk to me about the betrayal of a friendship, Danny.' A growl sounded in Robert's throat. He wrenched Faye's head back until her throat was exposed, her face towards the watching midnight sky. 'Put it away, or I swear I'll break her neck.'

A sharp pain shot down Faye's spine. She knew full well the gamekeeper had ample expertise in this department.

Desperation and hopelessness snared her in their jaws, as hot tears pricked the back of her eyes. Then a small movement caught her attention. A glimpse of something pale against the inky blackness, moving along the roofline of Barrington Hall.

Something glinted, caught in the moonlight like a shard of mirror glass.

Jammed up against Robert's chest, with her neck at a painfully acute angle, she heard Dan's feet advancing.

Robert jerked to the side as Dan hit him full force in the knees, rugby-tackling the giant of a man to the ground. The gamekeeper's grip loosened and Faye twisted free, driving her elbow into his ribs. She scrambled away, watching in horror as Robert flipped Dan onto his back, those large hands curled around his throat.

'I warned you, Danny. I told you never to come back. That night on the jetty when I found you half drowned. But you didn't listen. You've made things worse, regurgitating all the pain.'

Dan flailed against the gamekeeper's bulk but it was like beating against a rock face. If she didn't do something, Dan would die before her eyes.

The air stirred above and Faye glanced up. Her breath seized in her chest.

Like a lead weight the axe plummeted, its heavy blade like the tip of an arrow. Its target, the two men battling on the ground.

She tried to move, to warn them both, but she was rooted to the spot.

From out on the water, Milo screamed.

The axe found its mark with a sickening crunch, cleaving Robert McCallum's skull almost in two with its impact. Warm brain matter spattered across her face.

Robert's ruptured arteries spurted in a crimson fountain. His crushed skull gleamed amidst globules of pinkish-grey bobbing up and down in an ocean of red. An eyeball plopped onto Dan's blood-sodden chest. Then Robert McCallum toppled to the side; a mountain of a man, felled.

For a moment, Faye couldn't look away. But then she had to, because Dan was on his side, gasping for breath, his face almost grey. He crawled across to the rucksack and somehow found his feet.

He reached out towards her.

She took his hand and clasped it to her chest as her faltering breath inhaled the scent of death. She could taste it on the back of her tongue. Pungent and raw and horrifying.

'Run, get as far away from here as you can. I'm going to try and stall what they're doing.'

She met her husband's gaze, tried not to look at the fresh blood dripping down his face.

'No.' Her reply was firm as she shook her head. 'We can't leave Milo.'

'I left him, Faye. Thirty years ago…' His voice tailed off, haunted shadows in his eyes.

Milo. The name Dan had muttered in his sleep.

The boy Corrigan had kept in her twisted Neverland.

Faye drew in a shaky breath and threw her arms around Dan's neck. She pressed her lips to his in a swift kiss that was both apology and restoration. His chilled hands clasped her face, his forehead resting against hers as though he wanted to hold this moment forever.

She pulled away, but not before she saw the love in his eyes. The promise of a new beginning burned there too.

But her feet were already moving towards the lake, towards the boy she refused to abandon.

SIXTY-FOUR

Faye's kiss burned against Dan's lips as he sped after her. He ran towards the things that had haunted his unconscious mind for decades. He ran towards the lake, where his childhood friend was fighting for his life. Again.

The world had turned full circle.

He tried not to think about the moment the axe blade had struck Robert McCallum. Or the gamekeeper's warm blood drying on his face. The sound of his skull breaking open, as easily as an egg shell, would never leave him. Dan didn't have time to process this death. Or his reactions to it. Other things needed his focus now.

Out on the silvered darkness of the lake, Milo was level with the old jetty. The place where Dan had condemned him.

He had to keep Corrigan's attention. Somehow persuade her Milo's life was worth what he had to offer.

Dan's hopes lay in the husk of a creature long dead. The odds didn't seem that great. All he could pray for was that Corrigan would want this one back.

'Stop!' Dan mustered all the authority he could and powered it through his demand. 'I have something for you.'

The creatures were a living curtain by the side of the lake, and above them all hovered Corrigan, that awful light pulsing within her. A surge of vomit exploded into his mouth and he spat it on the ground, the caustic sting coating his throat.

He could charge through them and break them apart, but even as this thought settled, he knew it wouldn't help Milo, and it would only anger Corrigan more.

She turned those soulless eyes upon him.

Dan stopped. He squared his shoulders. Watched as she flew towards him.

This time he wasn't running away.

He risked a glance across and saw the pale form of his wife almost at the jetty.

But he couldn't see Milo in the dark water. An ache bloomed in the centre of his chest.

'Choice.' That one word from Corrigan wormed its way under Dan's skin. 'I wonder if you would make the same decision now.'

He wouldn't indulge her with a reply, but inside his heart screamed its fury over what she'd done.

A chorus of high-pitched clicking erupted from the water's edge. They were mocking him.

Dan unzipped the bag, never taking his eyes from her hovering form.

Slowly, he withdrew the needle. A wingtip touched his wrist and he shuddered.

The effect on Corrigan was instantaneous. A single shriek split the night, a primal sound that made the marrow in his bones turn to ice.

The creatures around her stilled as one, as though that shriek had frozen them in time.

'I didn't kill it,' he began, the sin of others on his lips, 'it was in the cottage all along.'

Out on the lake a stiff breeze arose. The surface quivered

as though it was waking.

Dan had the sudden feeling everything was looking at him. The water. The trees. The sky. He was somehow part of it all and somehow deeply disconnected, as if all of his life had been a shadow until this moment.

'Take it out.' Corrigan's malice-ridden voice spiked through him. It took a moment for Dan to realise that she meant the needle.

He would have to touch the creature, feel the brittle remains against his palm. If it fell to pieces in his hands he would lose the little bit of sanity he had left. But some part of him knew he couldn't give it back to her with what had killed it still attached.

Dan glanced across to the jetty. He could see Faye on her knees, her arm outstretched to the water.

Summoning every ounce of courage that he had, Dan cupped his hand around the creature on the needle. He bit the inside of his cheek as the wings settled on his palm, as those long feelers lay across his fingers. Taking a firmer hold of the needle, he twisted, and started to pull it from the creature's body.

What was in his hand felt like nothing at all, yet how could something so unsubstantial have the power to sap every decent thought from his mind?

Corrigan's tongue unfurled and Dan's hand began to tremble. The needle came away stubbornly, unwilling to give up its attachment to the thing it had been a part of for so long. He was almost glad he couldn't see the damage it had inflicted. But he could envisage it. And maybe that was worse.

He was buying time. The modern world shrunk away, eaten by its own self-importance, and all that remained was this moment of brutal clarity.

The needle came away, and Dan was left with the dead creature in his hand. His childhood panic rose out of his gut, and this time he quashed its flare. The only thing that mattered was getting Milo and Faye to safety.

'Let Milo go,' he forced his voice through gritted teeth, 'or I will crush what's left of this before your eyes.'

An ultimatum. Or a bluff. It was up to Corrigan to decide.

A loud splash came from the lake. Dan's head jerked up, just in time to see the water part as Faye dived in. Euphoria fought with his fear.

A noise came from Corrigan that sounded like the breaking of a great branch from a tree. The ground around her shook and the creatures took flight, their speed too swift for his brain to comprehend.

He glanced down at his curled hand.

A shudder of something soft and yet as tattered as rust. Dan opened his fingers and stared. The body in his hand was moving, the wings flicking backwards and forwards as if it was emerging from a chrysalis.

It was beauty and horror combined, and Dan's mind cartwheeled in disbelief.

It quivered on his blood-caked palm, its legs unfolding one by one.

Then Dan saw the impossible. A faint pulse of blue.

The thing that had been in Lucinda Latimer's glass case for over a hundred years was alive.

SIXTY-FIVE

Faye sped across to the jetty. With the moon streaming down onto the lake, the frail structure looked like a wooden skeleton rising from its depths.

She didn't dare glance back towards Dan.

Her feet hit the rotted slats and the jetty moved underneath her like a boat at sea. Milo was about twenty feet away, but his efforts were weakening and his cries had ceased. All she could see was his pale face, the moonlight blurring all of his features.

Every instinct in her body wanted to surge forwards but she made herself go down on all fours, spreading her weight on the splintered boards. Bits of brain matter were glued to the fine hair on her arms.

Painfully slowly, she advanced, one slat at a time. In the middle of the jetty some of the boards had already given in to time and damp, and she had to crawl over the space where they had been. The black water sloshed underneath her, Milo's struggle waking the sleeping lake.

Dan's voice drifted over from the lakeside and still she didn't look.

The end of the jetty became more shape than shadow and Faye quickened her pace, the wood groaning beneath her. The pilings that held it in place had all but rotted from their moorings and the end swayed with the water's movement.

Milo had gone under again. The rippling water stilled.

She waited. But this time the boy didn't surface.

Her heart plummeted into her stomach and she reached down with one hand, her fingers breaking the ice-cold surface.

She stood, the jetty snaking underneath her feet, and dived into the lake.

The shock of the water forced the air from her lungs. Gasping, she searched frantically for any sign of Milo. Taking a couple of deep breaths, she dove, the light from the moon barely visible beneath the lake surface. She hunted desperately for any movement but there was nothing in the water but her own fear and panic.

Small bubbles of air escaped from her nostrils. Everything felt numb, and even as she struck out again, she suddenly understood the peace people talk about before drowning. That giving in to an element much stronger than flesh and bone.

Faye fought against its pull and broke through into the pitiless night air. Into the nightmare her life had become.

Nothing moved and she wanted to tip back her head and howl at the unfairness of it all. Then, at the periphery of her vision, in the pitch black by the jetty, she thought she saw a pale shape.

Her focus snapped into place. She swam, front crawl, her quickest stroke, cutting through the dark water, her teeth clenched against the relentless bite of the cold.

Her outstretched hand found one of the pilings and her fingers curled around it.

'Milo.' She called his name and the darkness underneath the jetty seemed to swallow it whole.

Faye ducked underneath the boards, where the

pondweed grew thick and bitter green. It slimed around her legs and a sliver of fear stroked her reasoning. This was where she had gone under.

Milo was there at the other side of the jetty. His hands swept back and forth through the water, small ripples spilling like music from his fingers. A dizzy relief flooded through her. Somehow he had managed to free himself from his bonds.

He turned to look at her and Faye's words froze on her tongue. His eyes swam with the colour of the lake, dark grey, troubled, and filled with a tortured understanding.

She reached out one trembling hand, and Milo smiled, although it did nothing to permeate the sorrow. His hand stretched out to her and their fingers brushed.

'I didn't know,' he whispered. 'All this time and I didn't know.'

Faye's brow furrowed.

Then something touched the back of her legs. Something soft and snow cold. A shape floated up from the dark water, and she watched it rise. She watched it rise and her heart shattered.

Pale and slender, hair floating like the weeds it had been a part of for so long. The body surfaced, its face breaking through. A thin hand brushed languidly against her arm.

She wanted to scream. And yet she wanted to hold onto it, to drag it out of its watery prison and make it breathe again.

Milo's lips formed her name, but he was already fading.

One more moment where he clung onto their connection. Where Faye could see the bank of the lake through the translucency of his face.

Then he was gone. And all Faye had was the body of the boy who had died in this lake thirty years ago. The body of a boy whose tragic song was finally concluded.

Ghosts. Milo had lived amongst them, never knowing he was one of their kind. Corrigan had known all along Milo could never leave. She had watched him drown on that summer night, and then had resurrected his form so that she could play her game of bait and dare. So she could make him suffer again. The cruelty of it seared itself against Faye's heart and a sob rose from her chest, falling into the dark water.

In front of her eyes the flesh on Milo's bones was beginning to soften and break away. His face collapsed, lips dissolving against strong white teeth. Flesh and strands of hair brushed up against her as the lake consumed what had always belonged to it.

Corrigan's spell was broken.

SIXTY-SIX

Dan watched, horrified and fascinated, as Corrigan flew like an arrow towards what he'd set free.

The creatures danced in the night air, whirling together like butterflies, their wingbeats a blur against the darkness. Dan had the feeling he was a witness to something almost sacred, something that belonged to the very fabric of the forest.

His eyes found Faye in the water by the jetty but he couldn't see Milo. Rage burned under his skin, along with a suffocating hopelessness. He had been too late to save his childhood friend, just as he had been too inattentive to save his son.

He wondered how he was supposed to explain Robert McCallum's death. And he wondered why he assumed that he'd get out of this alive.

A chorus of clicks and chirps came from the creatures. They soared together, a protective guard of honour for one of their kind, returned. A strange energy thrummed through the darkness. It raised all the hair on Dan's skin. It was old and wild and dangerous. And also, addictively beautiful.

Milo's grandfather had known. Lucinda Latimer had known. And Albert Jenkins, Lydia Koster and Jem Porter still knew.

Hindsight was a thing that crept up behind you and sank

its fangs into your neck.

Dan remembered how he had mocked and insulted this mystical place. Shame speared through his chest.

He glanced across, sure he would see Faye on the jetty.

But she was still in the water. Fear prickled across his scalp. He was acutely aware of how cold he was. And how cold that water would be.

The creature he had saved spun higher into the air. For one moment it was silhouetted against the pale face of the moon.

A low chortle of laughter came with the wind. Dan turned, the brooding façade of Barrington Hall a backdrop for the small figure standing before it. The boy raised his hands level with his chin. His tongue protruded from his mouth in concentration.

Dan didn't get a chance to shout a warning. Something hurtled through the dark. He felt the air move as it whistled past his head.

And then the sickening wet splat as it found its target.

The creature he had saved fell to the ground, its new life cut short by the catapult Dan had put inside the rucksack. Because he thought he might need it.

Elliot whooped with joy, thrusting his fists into the air. He twirled in triumph.

Dan didn't wait for Corrigan's wrath to unfold. He bolted towards the jetty with one thought on his mind. He had to get Faye out of the water.

The memory of her kiss, the hope of it, and their future, torched through his veins.

His feet found the first weathered boards, the weight of his body turning them to matchwood. He stumbled. His head cracked against a wooden strut. The taste of copper on his tongue. A shooting pain erupted from behind his left eye and his head suddenly felt too heavy for his neck to support. Dark flowers bloomed at the edges of his vision as he fell.

The icy shock of the water numbed his limbs in a matter of seconds. Pondweed tangled around him, and the more he struggled the more it seemed to hold him fast. He couldn't see Barrington Hall from where he was, but he had an awful feeling it was still watching him, still judging his every move.

Dan took a deep breath and lowered himself under the water. His head hurt like hell, the ringing in his ears muffled by the pressure as he frantically tore his legs free of the weeds. Something was in front of him, about six feet away. He kicked towards it, fighting the sudden wave of nausea rising in his throat. It was too close to Faye.

Sometimes, when sight discerns what is in front of it, it refuses to acknowledge fact.

Dan saw the reason Faye couldn't climb out of the water, why she was just floating under the surface.

Something was attached to her ankle, anchoring her to the lake.

The skeleton's fingers had entwined themselves around her foot, its form hunched over, knees drawn tight against its chest.

The foetal position. As in the womb. As in death.

How Milo had always slept.

EPILOGUE

The man who lived by himself in the old cottage in the woods kept himself to himself. On the rare occurrences when he visited the village, people crossed over the street to avoid him, as though whatever he was carrying inside was some kind of virulent virus they could catch.

He walked with a limp, the right side of his face disfigured by the after effects of a small stroke.

Some thought he had left a high-powered job in the city, but as the years passed by, those who knew departed from the village, although some of them never really left. Their bones lay still in the churchyard.

Some said he was slightly crazy, that something had happened that warped his mind and tore out his heart.

The children were warned never to approach him if they met him in the woods, for his eyes had a wildness to them, and he became the thing they feared from an early age. It wasn't as if he had ever done anything to hurt any of them, but when a man spends his time filling hanging lanterns with sugar water, you can never be sure if, or when, he would snap wide open.

Some said they had seen him leaving small parcels at twilight on the stone steps of Barrington Hall, or that he had been spotted sleeping by the lake in all weathers.

What he was waiting for, nobody knew.

Some secrets go with us to the grave.

✝

Some people think darkness comes in only one shade. Black is black, an absence of light. But these people live in a city or a town, surrounded by bricks and concrete, tucked up safe in their beds with the soft glow of streetlights keeping their dark at bay.

It's an anaesthetised blackness. A drowsy, de-clawed state, gelded by modern society. It's the twenty-first century. The digital, shiny age of man—look how clever we are, sending out our space probes to other planets, whilst systematically destroying our own.

We harvest our fear carefully. Always knowing we can switch on a light if the latest download crosses the line between sanitised scares and a dread that threatens to seep into our bones.

Terror is a drug as long as we hold the needle.

We don't believe in anything we can't see or understand. If something we dislike comes too close, our standard reaction is to kill it.

We scoff at ancient lore, at the things our forefathers feared.

But there is a truth to everything, whether we like it or not. And the old ways are only sleeping, just waiting for their time to rise.

DID YOU ENJOY THIS BOOK?

You can make a big difference. When it comes to getting attention for my books, reviews are the most powerful tools. Much as I'd like to take out full page advertisements or put posters on buses, I don't have the financial muscle of a big publisher.

But I do have something those publishers would love to get their hands on. **A committed and loyal group of readers.** Honest reviews of my books help bring them to the attention of other readers and helps me to continue to create stories for you to fall in love with. If you've enjoyed reading this book I would be very grateful if you could leave a review (it can be as short as you like).

ACKNOWLEDGEMENTS

A book starts with the writer, but there are so many other people who nurture it through its growth from seed to flower. Following a much-loved series has been a daunting task, and this book bears many scars but I hope it is stronger for them. Without my support crew, I'm quite sure I would have lost the last of my sanity. My grateful thanks again to my wonderful editor, Kate Angelella, who teaches and inspires me. My beta readers who received an early draft of this and waded through with comments and suggestions – G.R. Thomas, Lydia Koster, Becky Wright, Josh Radwell, Lisa Niblock, and to Sarina Langer for that all important first critique. To Andrew Brown of Design for Writers for my haunting cover creation. To Platform House Publishing for beautiful interior design. You are all absolute stars.

Thank you to my friends and loyal supporters on Twitter and the #bookstagram community on Instagram, for showing me the human side of social media. Writing is a solitary craft but I am never alone with your constant loyalty and encouragement. And to those who discover my books through other sources— welcome, and my warmest thanks.

ABOUT THE AUTHOR

Beverley Lee is the bestselling author of the Gabriel Davenport series (*The Making of Gabriel Davenport*, *A Shining in the Shadows* and *The Purity of Crimson*).

In thrall to the written word from an early age, especially the darker side of fiction, she believes that the very best story is the one you have to tell. Supporting fellow authors is also her passion and she is actively involved in social media and writers' groups.

You can visit her online at beverleylee.com (where you'll find a free dark and twisted short story download) or on Instagram (@theconstantvoice) and Twitter (@constantvoice).

Made in the USA
Middletown, DE
29 October 2020